promise of the valley

a westward dreams novel

Books by Jane Peart

Brides of Montclair Series

1 | *Valiant Bride*

2 | *Ransomed Bride*

3 | *Fortune's Bride*

4 | *Folly's Bride*

5 | *Yankee Bride/Rebel Bride*

6 | *Gallant Bride*

7 | *Shadow Bride*

8 | *Destiny's Bride*

9 | *Jubilee Bride*

10 | *Mirror Bride*

11 | *Hero's Bride*

12 | *Senator's Bride*

13 | *Daring Bride*

14 | *Courageous Bride*

Westward Dreams Series

1 | *Runaway Heart*

2 | *Promise of the Valley*

3 | *Where Tomorrow Waits*

4 | *A Distant Dawn*

5 | *Undaunted Spirit*

The American Quilt Series

1 | *The Pattern*

2 | *The Pledge*

3 | *The Promise*

promise of the valley

a westward dreams novel

BOOK 2

Jane Peart

ZONDERVAN®

ZONDERVAN.com/
AUTHORTRACKER
follow your favorite authors

ZONDERVAN®

Promise of the Valley

Copyright © 1995 by Jane Peart

Value Edition 978-0-310-28800-8

Requests for information should be addressed to:
Zondervan, *Grand Rapids, Michigan* 49530

Library of Congress Cataloging-in-Publication Data

Peart, Jane.
      Promise of the valley / Jane Peart.
         p. cm. — (Westward dreams series)
      ISBN 0-310-41281-1 (softcover)
      1. California—History—1850—Fiction. 2. Women pioneers—California—Napa
River Valley—Fiction. 3. Napa River Valley (Calif.)—History—Fiction. I. Title. II. Series:
Peart, Jane. Westward dreams series.
PS3566.E238R76 1995
813'.54—dc20
                                             94-44198
                                                 CIP

Printed in the United States of America

08 09 10 11 12 13 14 15 16 • 21 20 19 18 17 16 15 14 13 12 11 10 9 8 7 6 5 4 3 2 1

To Lloyd,
with gratitude
for his generous help and patience

Prologue

VIRGINIA

SEPTEMBER 1870

Adelaide Pride looked up at the blackened structure—all that remained of her beloved grandparents' home, Oakleigh. Between two charred chimneys the roof lay open to the sky. Gutted. Torched by the Yankee invaders. All that was left of the once beautiful house were the burned, crumbling rafters, the sagging floors, and the scorched walls.

Her hands clenched in helpless fury. Why had it been necessary to destroy it? After the battle of Seven Pines, the Union Army had used it for temporary headquarters. Why had they felt it necessary to burn down the place when they left? Just another case of the wanton destruction that generated so much of the blind hatred throughout the South since the war's end.

From behind her came the soft voice of her aunt Susan waiting in the small one-horse buggy. "Addie, dear, better come along now. It'll be getting dark soon, and it's a long drive back to town."

"Yes, Auntie, I'm coming," Addie called. Still she could

not seem to move. Memories of the past held her prisoner. Oakleigh was her grandparents' home. There, as a child, she had in summer played on the velvety lawn under the sweeping boughs of the giant trees that surrounded it while the adults carried on leisurely conversations on the shady verandah. Images floated back to her hauntingly. Days of gracious hospitality, gaiety, laughter; lazy summer evenings of soft dusk and flitting fireflies.

Was it really possible that all that was gone? Was it all lost as surely as the cause for which so many of her cousins, her friends, her beaux, had fought?

"Adelaide, we must go," Aunt Susan's pleading reminder came again. "Honey, the livery stable closes at six, remember? We have to get the horse and rig back before then."

Addie sighed. She needed no reminder that they no longer could afford to keep horses themselves and had to rent them to drive out this afternoon. With sad reluctance she turned from the skeleton of the house and climbed into the buggy beside her aunt.

The older woman placed a sympathetic hand on Addie's arm. "I know, darlin', what you're feeling. There's no use standing around mournin'. It won't bring anything back— or anyone. The main thing is that *we* survived, and we have to go on."

"But it's all such a waste, Auntie! So much and so many lost. Like Ran." They were silent a minute, thinking of Randolph Payton, the man Addie had expected to marry, who was killed in the battle of Antietam. Addie also thought of her parents, both of whom had died by the end of the war.

Aunt Susan patted Addie's hand. "But *you're* young, Addie. You've still got your whole life ahead of you. Don't let what's happened embitter you. Too many have gone that route." Addie knew her aunt meant her own husband, Uncle Myles, whose unrelenting anger at the South's defeat had transformed him into a twisted, emotionally crippled man—old before age sixty.

"I don't intend to, Aunt Susan. After today, I'm not going to look back." Addie drew on her driving gloves, picked up the reins, and clicked them. The horse moved forward. "That's why I've decided to take that position with Mrs. Amberly," she said resolutely, looking straight ahead.

Her aunt gave a little gasp. "Surely *not!* Not with that— that *Yankee* woman!"

"What choice do I really have, Auntie? Yankees are the only ones with any money these days. The salary she's offered is more than I could hope to make at any job here. And I need a way to support myself."

"But to go all the way out to California!"

Addie lifted her chin determinedly. "What else can I do?"

Her aunt shook her head silently, pressing her lips together. For the next few minutes, as they rode along, the only sound was the soft clop-clop of the horse's hooves on the dusty country road. She knew Addie was right. Her niece had been left without family, fiancé, or fortune. What else was there for an impoverished Southern gentlewoman to do? At twenty-five, in the South, Adelaide was considered hopelessly on the brink of spinsterhood. Particularly now that so few eligible men of her age and class had returned from the war. Marriage seemed a remote possibility. What alternative did she have but to take the offered position as companion to an elderly widow?

The job offer had come through a distant cousin of Susan's. One of his "new" Yankee friends had asked him if he knew of a refined young lady to be the paid companion of his great-aunt Sophia Amberly at a famous soda hot springs health resort in the Napa Valley of California.

Susan had refused to have anything to do with Cousin Matthew since he began doing business with their despised conquerors. Many affluent Northerners had swarmed into

Richmond since the surrender, buying homes and property the natives could no longer afford. Matthew, however, had assured the man he had the "perfect answer" to his elderly relative's search for a "young, healthy, intelligent, ladylike" employee. The salary offered was one Adelaide felt she could not turn down.

Susan glanced over at her niece's cameo-like profile. Before the war, everything would have been so different for a young lady of Adelaide's beauty and breeding. She had certainly inherited both parents' good looks, if nothing else. She had her Carrington mother's high-arched nose; winged eyebrows; dark, lustrous, and silky hair; marvelous eyes the color of cream sherry. Of course, her erect carriage and the elegant set of her head were all definitely Pride.

Pride! Her name could not have been more appropriate, thought Susan, although some called it stiff-necked stubbornness. But maybe that's what would carry Addie through whatever lay ahead of her now. Surely, she'd need all the strong will and strength of character she could muster as she set out on her new uncertain future.

The next few weeks were busy ones, full of preparations for Addie's long journey. Hours were spent stirring dye into pots of boiling water to renew or freshen faded dresses, turning hems, changing buttons, adding braid or bows, to get Addie's wardrobe ready to pack. She and Aunt Susan stayed so busy, in fact, that there was little time to dwell on the parting they both knew lay ahead.

A few days before she was to leave for California, Addie went out to the cemetery. The September day was warm Indian summer lingered. She opened the wrought-iron gate and entered the enclosure, then walked toward the Pride family plot.

At the foot of the two headstones engraved with the names Spencer and Lovinia Pride, she place the mixed bouquet of late-blooming fall flowers from Aunt Susan's garden: asters, cosmos, Queen Anne's lace. Standing there for a few moments, Addie was lost in affectionate remembrance of her parents: her tall, strong-featured father, with his kind eyes and humorous mouth; her gentle mother, known endearingly to all as "Lovey." They had given Addie a wonderful heritage, and she was only beginning to appreciate it. All the values they had lived, she silently promised to try to practice in whatever lay before her.

After a few moments of reflection, Addie moved on through the graveyard, pausing here and there to read inscriptions on the markers. Many names she recognized. Boys she had grown up with who had gone off as soldiers and never returned.

A cloud passed over the sun, suddenly darkening the afternoon as though mourning these who had died too soon, without living out their lives, finding love, having families.

Then she reached the grave she was looking for and placed her smaller bouquet on the granite stone marked "Randolph Curtis Payton, Lieutenant Confederate Army, 1840–1861." A smile touched her lips as she thought of Ran, his bravado, his laughter, his light-hearted optimism when he had told her good-bye on that long-ago day he had ridden off to join Lee's army. He had been twenty, she sixteen. A hundred years ago!

Her arms, now empty of flowers, fell to her sides. She had come to say her farewells, now it was time to go. In six weeks' time, she would be far away from all she had ever known. Slowly she turned and walked out of the cemetery, closing the scrolled gates behind her.

Her hardest good-byes were still to come. To leave her aging aunt and uncle, who had taken her in after her parents' deaths, would be the most difficult of all.

Mixed with her natural sadness at the parting, however,

Addie felt a faint stirring of excitement. After all, was this not going to be the great adventure of her life? Although Addie had always been considered imaginative, something blocked all but the faintest vision about California. The future seemed hidden by a dim curtain of uncertainty.

Oct. 10th, 1870

Well, here I am, off on my journey—"the greatest adventure of my life," as dear Emily described it. Emily Walker, who has been my best friend for as long as I can remember, gave me this leather-bound journal as a going-away present. She told me it was to be filled with all the wonderful and exciting things that are going to happen to me on this trip and in my new life in California. Emily has always been an incurable optimist. Even when Evan, her husband, a strapping six-footer, came home a helpless cripple after losing his leg at Gettysburg, Emily never gave way. Dear gallant Emily. We were to be bridesmaids at each other's weddings. I was hers, but she never got the chance to be mine. Ran died the first year of the war.

I do wonder with what I'll fill these blank pages.

Cousin Matthew, full of self-importance, came out to Avondale with his fine new carriage to drive me to Richmond and escort me to the train station. When he arrived, Aunt Susan treated him coolly. She has stated over and over that she cannot abide to be around him since he's "taken up with those carpetbaggers—even though he *is* kin." But I cannot afford that luxury. After all, he arranged for me to take this position with Mrs. Amberly, which will provide me with money enough to send back to Aunt Susan and Uncle Myles. It will be enormously helpful to them. It is more than I could earn any other way—especially here in the South, crushed and defeated and with a surplus supply of impoverished gentlewomen with few or no "marketable" skills. With the salary she is paying me, I can also accumulate a little nest egg for the future. A future as a spinster, in all probability!

Aunt Susan was teary but brave as we said good-bye.

12

When I gave her a last hug, I could feel her tiny birdlike bones under the thin shawl, and I almost said I wasn't going. But I knew I must. I climbed into Matthew's shiny buggy, with its new-smelling leather seat, and I nearly fell out waving to Aunt Susan as she stood at the gate.

When we got to Richmond, Cousin Matthew saw to my trunk and assorted baggage. As we waited on the train platform, he shifted from one foot to the other, hemming and hawing and trying to make conversation—feeling uncomfortable, but doing his "familial duty." Aunt Susan lamented that before the war, no lady would travel unless accompanied by a male relative or a maid. Since I have no maid, Cousin Matthew was my only option. Finally, when the whistle blew, he handed me a box of bonbons and pressed two twenty-dollar gold pieces into the hand I extended to bid him good-bye. Then he hurried off, obviously mighty relieved to have me safely on board and settled in my seat. Could he possibly feel guilty that he is sending his cousin off into the unknown?

Aunt Susan packed me a hamper, fearing I had to go three thousand miles without any food, and she also gave me plenty of instructions and advice. My very outfit is the result of her strongest admonition about journeying alone. She insisted that I wear black, declaring, "For a lady traveling alone, wearing mourning is the best protection to avoid unwelcome attention from undesirable fellow travelers." I agreed, not only to put the dear lady at ease, but also because it could not be more appropriate. I *am* in mourning. I have lost everything I once held dear in life: parents, home, inheritance, the man I was to marry.

But so has everyone else I know. Certainly Aunt Susan and Uncle Myles lost everything—property, servants, a splendid home where she entertained lavishly many notables, including President Jefferson Davis himself. Emily and Evan too are nearly destitute. Yet I look on these two couples with some envy. They may have lost everything material, but they still have each other. The love and devotion between them is so tender, so beautiful to behold, that

I find myself bereft. There's a longing within me for something to fill that void in my heart.

When I opened this book, I saw the inscription Emily had written: "Journeys end in lovers meeting." Didn't I say Emily was an optimist? She is also a romantic. But could she be a prophet as well? Only time will tell. On to California.

PART 1

CALISTOGA, CALIFORNIA

NOVEMBER 1870

Chapter 1

*C*alistoga! Next stop, Calistoga!" the conductor's voice rang out as he wove his way down the aisle of the passenger coach.

"Thank goodness, at last!" Addie murmured with heartfelt relief. Although the last few hours of winding through the beautiful Redwood-covered hillsides on either side of the railroad tracks had been lovely, she was glad to reach her final destination at last—after all these weeks of traveling.

Her cross-country trip had been an adventure to say the least. In 1870, westward-bound trains boasted none of the amenities of eastern trains, which now had dining and Pullman cars. The western railway companies made no effort to make travel easy or comfortable for passengers. Clean hotels were nonexistent. In their place were rustic buildings with cots, hardly a proper resting place for a genteel person. Meal stops were mostly at towns consisting of a shack, dignified as a "depot," a saloon, and a water tank. Food was beyond description. What meals were available were often inedible. They were usually served by a saloon keeper or bartender, for there never seemed to be a scarcity of "spirits" for those who would rather drink than eat the awful fare provided. The menu rarely varied: greasy meat fried to a crisp, canned beans, biscuits called "sinkers," rancid butter, bitter coffee. One either had to develop a sense of the ridiculous or a cast-iron stomach along the way. The last straw was that the "rest and refreshment" stops were limited to twenty minutes, just long enough for the train crew to take on water. This gave the harried passenger a choice of bolting what food he or she could eat or taking a few minutes of fresh air and exercise before reboarding and enduring another long, grueling ride in the cramped quarters of the coach.

Addie enjoyed the scenery, however, which was so different from anything she had ever seen. Still, after a while, the hundreds of miles of wild prairies and endless deserts became monotonous, and she longed for the sight of civilization.

When the train finally pulled into Sacramento, Addie, like most of the passengers, took the ferry to San Francisco. There, Addie decided to splurge. Using one of the gold pieces Cousin Matthew had pressed on her, she went to a fine hotel where she obtained a comfortable room, luxuriated in a warm bath, washed her hair, and had dinner sent to her on a tray. She didn't even feel guilty about it.

The next morning, after the first restful night's sleep she had had in weeks, she sought information about getting to Calistoga. She was told that the steamer left San Francisco twice a day. She had a choice of two departure times, morning or afternoon, to make the sixty-eight mile trip to the Napa Valley. Taking the 2:00 P.M. steamer would break up her trip so that she could spend the night in Vallejo; then, the next morning, she could board the train of the newly established California Pacific line, thus enjoying the scenic trip through the Redwood-covered expanse in daylight. Having read and heard so much about the giant trees, Addie decided that this is what she would do.

She spent the morning walking around the city, being

sure to keep within sight of the impressive hotel where she had stayed the night before. San Francisco amazed her with its many fine buildings. It was a city bustling with commerce. The streets were crowded with different kinds of vehicles, from large delivery wagons to polished coaches pulled by matched horses and driven by drivers in flashy livery. Elegant shops of every description lined the hilly streets, their display windows filled with all manner of expensive wares, millinery, fabrics of silks and satins, jewelry, fur-trimmed manteaus, beaded purses. Florist stalls stood on every corner and offered a profusion of flowers, some of which were long out of season back east: gladioli, phlox, chrysanthemums. The sidewalks were crowded with all sorts of people, from stylishly attired men in frock coats and top hats, and women in the very latest Paris creations, to roughly dressed workmen hurrying to their jobs. Construction seemed ongoing, buildings seemed to go up before your eyes, and the sound of hammers banging was constant in the misty, sea-scented air.

Addie window-shopped until it was time to take a hack to the dock to board the steamer. Living as she had for all these years in the small Virginia town, and deprived of seeing such luxurious abundance of merchandise, she felt quite dazzled by it all.

Therefore, she found the leisurely river trip relaxing by comparison. The steamer moved languidly over the placid sun-dappled water. Standing on deck, Addie was awed by the variety of fall colors in the trees that lined the bank. Now, in early November, they still retained abundant foliage in glorious array of polished cinnamon, old-gold, flashes of brilliant scarlet against the sage green of the pines. The river trip passed all too quickly for her, and the afternoon had grown chilly by the time they reached Vallejo.

Upon disembarking from the steamer, the passengers

19

were herded to the only hotel available and served dinner—if the food could be described as such. Later, Addie was shown to a small, dingy room with a narrow iron bed, covered with doubtfully clean blankets, into which she could not bring herself to crawl—even though she was bone tired. There was a little stove whose fire only smoldered instead of burning, and then she could not budge the window to clear the room of smoke.

If Addie had not been blessed by a sense of humor, she might have been totally undone by the situation. It seemed so ludicrous that she found herself having a fit of giggles as she tried a dozen different positions on top of the lumpy mattress. She awakened before dawn and went outside to walk to the train shed. There, alone in the misted morning, she breathed deeply the pine-scented air, as fresh and intoxicating as wine, and heard birdsong high in the majestic trees, and felt she had an idea of California at last.

The whole trip had been an education. She became accustomed to the casual camaraderie of travel, the heart-warming generosity of fellow passengers, and the willingness of strangers to share and help. Although the usual protocol required in polite society was often ignored or dismissed while traveling, there was an unexpected pleasure in mingling with others who were also enjoying the excitement and adventure of crossing the wide, varied country of America.

She felt the train begin to slow, and the chug and the grinding of metal wheels on steel rails began to lessen. They slowly passed orchards, vineyards, and farmhouses. People on the streets stopped to watch and sometimes waved as the train rolled down the tracks toward the yellow frame building with a sign that read "Calistoga."

As the train pulled to a stop, Addie adjusted her black-dotted face-veil on her black *faille* bonnet, securing it more firmly with a jet hat pin, then checked it critically in her small hand mirror before slipping the mirror back into her purse. She pulled on black kid gloves, picked up her valise, and started making her way down to the door of her coach.

A well-dressed man just ahead of her in the aisle looked over his shoulder and cast an admiring glance in her direction. Then breasting his hat, he stepped politely aside to let her go first, his eyes following her slim figure.

At the car's exit door, Addie halted for a moment and drew a long breath. Here she was, for better or worse. Then she took the conductor's hand, with which he helped her down the steps onto the wooden platform.

Calistoga, California—where she would spend the next year of her life.

Chapter 2

The town of Calistoga lay nestled in the Napa Valley, rimmed in rolling oak-studded hills, surrounded by acres of vineyards under the blue-purple shadow of Mount Helena.

As Addie stepped from the train onto the wooden platform, the first thing she was aware of was how warm it was. It had been cool in San Francisco yesterday, with wisps of swirling gray fog obscuring the tops of the buildings and with a chilly wind off the bay. Here it might as well be midsummer. She ran her forefinger under the edge of her high-necked basque and took a small hankie from the sleeve of her jacket and dabbed her damp upper lip.

The last communication she had received from the nephew of her employer-to-be was that someone from Silver Springs Resort would meet her train when she got to Calistoga. Addie looked around hopefully.

As she did, her gaze met that of a man standing a few feet away. For a moment, their eyes locked. Could he be the person sent from Silver Springs? Almost immediately, she decided no. He looked more like a cowboy from pictures she'd seen of the West. He was tall, over six feet, lean, broad shouldered, long limbed, wearing a faded blue cotton shirt, buff-colored breeches, and knee-high, worn leather boots. His brown felt hat had a dented crown, and its wide brim looked as if it had often been exposed to wind and rain. When he removed it, as if in greeting, it revealed a deeply tanned, strong-featured face, with deep-set light-gray eyes and a cautious expression. He took a tentative step toward her, as if he thought he knew her, yet wasn't sure.

Addie wondered if she should acknowledge him. Perhaps he *was* a hotel employee here to meet her. As their gaze held, Addie had an uncanny sense of recognition. But that was impossible. How could she possible know him? And yet . . .

As he continued to stare at her, suddenly she felt dizzy, almost faint. It must be the glare of sunlight, the unaccustomed heat, the long train ride over the winding hills, the sleepless night in the dreadful Vallejo hotel, the lack of food—all were combining to make her feel disoriented.

Just as he seemed about to approach and she started to speak, she heard her name spoken. "Miss Pride? Miss Adelaide Pride?"

Quickly she turned away from the man whose gaze had captured hers to see an elegantly dressed gentleman striding toward her, smiling broadly.

Reaching her, he swooped off his hat and announced, "Brook Stanton, your host at Silver Springs Resort, at your service. Mrs. Amberly told me she had received a message that you were expected today, but since she was scheduled for one of her health treatments, I volunteered to welcome you to Calistoga."

A little taken aback by this exuberance, Addie murmured an appropriate "thank you" while she took in his appearance. He was strikingly handsome with a smooth olive complexion, flashing smile, dark curly hair cut close to his head and slightly silvered at the temples, and he sported a flourishing mustache. In contrast, his eyes were a surpris-

23

ingly vivid blue. He was dressed like a dandy, in a biscuit-colored broadcloth coat, brocaded vest, ruffled linen shirt, and highly polished black boots.

A sudden flash of memory reminded Addie of an incident out of her childhood. Her father had taken her on a trip to visit relatives in Mississippi on a paddle boat, the *Delta Queen*. On board, a darkly handsome man, wearing a white linen suit, with a sparkling diamond stud pin in his silk cravat, had been pointed out to her as a well-known "gambler." To her little-girl imagination, he had seemed a glamorous figure, but her father had told her sternly he was to be avoided as "not our kind." Mr. Stanton's appearance was remarkably like him.

"I'll see to your luggage, Miss Pride; then we'll be on our way to the resort," he told her, offering her his arm. Then they started toward the other end of the platform where the baggage compartment was being unloaded. Before they had taken more than a few steps, a voice behind them called, "Stanton!"

They both halted and watched as a man approached them.

"Mr. Montand!" Stanton greeted him cordially. "I didn't see you. Did you just get off the train from Vallejo?"

"Indeed, I did. I was visiting the Fleischers, looking over their winery and learning their process." The man's gaze moved over to Addie. "I believe this young lady and I were in the same coach." There was a questioning lift to his cultivated tone.

"Allow me," Stanton said. "May I present Mr. Louis Montand, Miss Pride, one of our guests at Silver Springs. Miss Adelaide Pride."

Addie looked into a face that might be considered handsome, but it struck her, despite its even features, as somewhat bland. Soft brown hair waved back from a high

24

forehead, a well-trimmed beard outlined a narrow jaw. His brown eyes were alert and curious.

"I'm sure you'll enjoy your stay at Silver Springs. My sister and I have found it most comfortable, a pleasant place to wait out the completion of the home we're building in the valley." He looked at Stanton and shook his head. "These Californio carpenters and stone masons work at a snail's pace. It would be unheard of in Boston! I'm beginning to wonder if we shall become your *permanent guests*, Stanton."

"Oh, I'm sure not, although there could be worse fates!" he laughed jovially.

"Spoken like a true *hotelier!*" quipped Montand, including Addie in his smile. "Is this your first visit to the area, Miss Pride?"

"Actually, it is my first visit to *California!*"

"Ah, well, we must show you the beauties of the valley, then."

"Miss Pride has come to be Mrs. Amberly's companion, Montand," Stanton informed him.

Addie noticed a subtle change in Montand's expression as he darted a quick glance at Stanton. Something she could not discern seemed to pass between the two men at the mention of her employer's name. Or was it her imagination?

The awkward moment passed, and Montand directed himself again to Addie. "Well, I'm sure *you're* not here for your health, Miss Pride, and I hope you will have plenty of free time to enjoy the beautiful surroundings of the resort. I would like the pleasure of showing them to you." He smiled ingratiatingly. "Even my sister, Estelle, who is extremely particular, agrees that Silver Springs is one of the nicest places we've stayed on our travels—especially in the West."

"When will Miss Montand return from San Francisco?" Stanton asked.

Montand rolled his eyes dramatically. "When the stores there run out of merchandise or our bank funds are depleted, whichever comes first!" He threw up his hands in a hopeless gesture.

As both men laughed heartily, Addie felt sure, from the cut of Montand's splendidly tailored clothes, the gold cuff links, and the watch chain across his satin vest, that the latter was not about to happen soon.

"Can I give you a lift back to the resort, Montand?" Stanton asked.

"No thanks. My vineyard overseer is meeting me. I want to go out and see what progress has been made on the house while I've been gone." He turned to Addie, bowing again. "So, then, I'll bid you good-bye for now, Miss Pride, and look forward to seeing you again soon." He tipped his hat and spun on his heel to walk back down to the opposite end of the depot platform.

Stanton settled Addie in his shiny green two-seater buggy, then supervised a porter who was securing her small leather trunk to the back. She guessed he might find the meagerness of her luggage strange. Probably most of his wealthy, health-seeking San Franciscans arrived with handsome matched sets of luggage. However, she was coming as a "paid companion," not as one of the guests, she reminded herself. A fact that the gallant Brook Stanton seemed to overlook, for he treated her as if she were a member of Queen Victoria's court.

After tipping the porter, Stanton took his place beside her in the smart buggy, smiled at her, lifted the reins, then they started off at a quick trot down the street from the depot.

"I'm sure you are going to enjoy your stay in Calistoga, Miss Pride. Accommodations at Silver Springs Resort are of

26

the very best. I pride myself on giving my guests luxurious rooms and amenities that compare favorably with any of the finest resorts in the east—some in your own state of ... Virginia, isn't it, Miss Pride?"

"Yes," Addie answered. "How did you know?"

"I'm a connoisseur of accents." He smiled disarmingly, then added, "I'm a Southerner myself, although I've lived away from my native land for a good many years. I was born in Savannah, raised in Tennessee."

Addie glanced at her companion's aquiline profile, thinking how nice it was to find a fellow Southerner so far from home. It made her feel easier and warmer toward him. Up until now everything had seemed so strange, so new to her. Most of the people she had encountered on her trip almost seemed to have foreign accents—harsh, nasal, or twangy.

"You could not have come at a better time of year—Fall is one of the most pleasant seasons here, although our climate is extremely mild year-round and considered very healthful with just enough rainfall to keep our air fresh and clean and uncontaminated with some of the unfavorable elements in our cities."

Addie listened while she was busy looking from left to right as they turned onto the main street, which the sign indicated, she noted with some distaste, was named *Lincoln* Avenue.

Both sides of the road were lined with small stores of various types, interspersed with shade trees, some now beginning to show fall colors. It looked on the whole like a quiet but pleasant little town.

"And the resort itself is full of interesting, enjoyable things for our guests. Of course, most come for the wonderful treatments, which are even better than the great European spas, if I do say so myself. But besides that, we have a number and variety of social and cultural events, dances, musicales, lectures, poetry readings. Some of our guests have been well-known authors themselves. . . . I would name them but most wish to remain anonymous while vacationing. And that is another thing about which I pride myself—honoring my guests' wishes, whatever they are. Our motto here at Silver Springs is that our guests are all treated like royalty."

They passed a building under construction. Stanton pointed with his buggy whip. "That is one of my newest projects. I'm building an opera house. Here I plan to invite some of the greatest internationally acclaimed artists of the opera and theater to perform. It is almost completed. I've ordered carpets from India, carvings from Italy, furniture from France. It will be a showplace. Opera buffs from San Francisco will buy season tickets and flock here. . . ."

Addie realized that Brook Stanton was a true entrepreneur, a man of ambition and vision. She had been in the company of so many defeated men in the last few years, men who had lost their zest, their hopes, and dreams. It was refreshing to meet someone so full of enthusiasm and ideas.

Addie was totally unprepared for Silver Springs Resort. She hadn't expected anything nearly so grand. As Stanton's high-stepping, gleaming black horse trotted through the gates, Addie saw a sweep of velvety green lawn. It was beautifully landscaped, dotted with sculptured flower beds, bright with a mixture yellow, bronze and russet chrysanthemums, marigolds, and deep purple stattice. A winding gravel drive serpented through the parklike grounds. It led to a white Colonial-style building with white pillars and green shutters. A balcony fronted the upper story, and a deep verandah circled the lower floor.

"This is the main building where many of our social events are held. There are some guest rooms upstairs, but you and Mrs. Amberly are lodged in one of the cottages," Stanton told Addie as the buggy came to a stop. "First, I'll

show you the lobby before I take you over to your cottage."
He pulled out a handsome gold watch and consulted it.
"Mrs. Amberly still has at least forty-five minutes before
she's finished with her treatment. One of the bathhouse
assistants will escort her back to the cottage, and she'll rest
for a half hour there, so there's plenty of time before you
have to begin your duties." His eyes twinkled as they
regarded hers.

He got out and came around to help her down from the
buggy. Then he offered his arm, and they walked into the
lobby together.

Addie looked around with surprised pleasure. She wasn't
sure what she had expected, but nothing like this. She had
never dreamed Silver Springs Resort would be this luxurious. Brook Stanton seemed to sense her reaction and stood
beside her for a few minutes, looking pleased.

The lobby was furnished tastefully: pale green painted
walls gave it a restful atmosphere, graceful furniture was
placed in small conversational groups around the large
room with many windows, curtained in sheer lace, draped
in cream taffeta swags, letting in the filtered afternoon sunlight.

"Now that you've admired my pride and joy sufficiently,
I'll escort you to your cottage," Stanton told Addie teasingly. Back in the buggy, with the horse slowed to a walk,
they proceeded around a flower-bordered circle over to a
group of white cottages, which all had peaked roofs and
small, elaborately fretted porches.

"Here we are then," announced Stanton, braking the
buggy. He sprang lightly out, then came around to hold
out his hand to assist Addie down. As if by some silent call,
a young man in a short green-jacketed uniform appeared to
unload and carry Addie's trunk inside.

Stanton took off his hat and bowed slightly, saying,
"When Mrs. Amberly has completed her treatment at the

bathhouse, one of the attendants will accompany her back here. In the meantime, may I suggest you make yourself comfortable? I'll have some refreshment sent over, and perhaps you can rest a bit before dinner. I trust you will find everything to your liking. If you have need of anything—anything at all—simply ring the bell, and one of our chambermaids will come at once."

"Thank you, Mr. Stanton, you have been most kind, most gracious."

"My pleasure, I assure you, Miss Pride." He bowed again and left.

His manners were so perfect. Why was it he reminded her so strongly of the "riverboat gambler" her father had strenuously told her to avoid? Even at age eleven, Addie had thought the man dashingly attractive—just like the illustrations of the swashbuckling pirate in her storybook. And without doubt, Brook Stanton resembled him. Was Stanton also a gambler? And would her father have warned her against him as well?

Chapter 3

The front door opened into a small parlor. Stepping inside, Addie looked around with immense pleasure. She had been on the road for so many weeks, dealing with all sorts of discomforts, inconveniences, and all manner of accommodations from wretched to passable, that this cottage was a welcome change. Lace-trimmed curtains hung at the shuttered windows. The furniture was not as elaborate as the furniture in the lobby, but it was in excellent taste. A love seat and two armchairs were placed in a conversational arrangement, and fresh flowers in cut-glass vases were set on the marble-topped table.

An archway led into a narrow center hall, with a door at its end and two doors on either side. The door at the end was a bathroom, equipped with modern conveniences and a white porcelain tub mounted on claw-footed legs. The other two must be the bedrooms.

She knocked lightly on the closed door but, receiving no answer, assumed this must be Mrs. Amberly's bedroom. The door opposite had been left open, and in that she saw her trunk had been placed.

In there everything was light and fresh. The sleigh bed of bird's-eye maple was banked with ruffled pillows, and covered by a white embroidered coverlet, which matched the curtains at the windows. Outside, the garden was bright with autumn flowers, and Addie could see the blue ridge of mountains beyond. An armoire, a bureau, and a washstand of the same golden wood, a small desk and chair, and a comfortable upholstered armchair completed the furnishings.

Addie circled the room. She looked at everything and stopped to touch the soft, clean towels on the rack beside the washstand. She picked up the lavender-scented cake of soap in the fluted dish and sniffed it appreciatively. What luxury! After last night, how glorious it would be to wash off all the gritty soot, grime, and dust of the train.

She was tempted to use the tub in the pristine bathroom, but she was not sure she had time to do so before Mrs. Amberly returned. Meeting her employer was a rather daunting thought. What if the woman hated her on sight! That was too foolish a thought to waste any time about. Whatever happened, she had signed a year's contract with Sophia Amberly, only to be broken if Addie proved dishonest, immoral, or committed anything deemed injurious to her employer's reputation or property—none of which was likely to occur. Still, Addie wanted to freshen up so that she could look her best.

Untying the veil, she took off her bonnet, then unbuttoned the tiny covered buttons of her basque, unfastened the hook and eye of her waistband, and stepped out of her skirt. She unlaced her corset and tossed it aside. It was a relief to be rid of the whalebone stays for a few minutes. What an instrument of torture! Stupid! How cruelly the current fashion dictated the ideal woman's waist to be twenty inches or less!

Pulling out her hairpins, she shook her hair down and dug into her valise for her brush. Bending over, she brushed her hair until it crackled. She fastened it back from her face with a ribbon, then poured water into the bowl and began to scrub away the residue of her journey until her clean skin glowed and tingled. Quickly she rewound her hair, drawing it up into a figure-eight chignon at the nape of her neck.

The surprising warmth of the November weather prompted the decision to unpack something lighter weight to wear.

She unlocked her trunk and lifted the lid. On top of her neatly folded petticoats was a tissue-paper-covered square. She hesitated a few seconds, knowing what it was. Then she slowly unwrapped it and drew out a silver-framed photograph. For a long tender moment, she looked at the picture of the handsome young man, resplendent in his newly acquired Confederate uniform. Lt. Randolph Payton—how proud he had been the day he rode over to Oakleigh to show off the splendid spotless tunic, the yellow silk sash, the gilt epaulettes, his then-unused sword. And how tragically soon that uniform was battle soiled, blood-soaked when he fell, his horse shot from under him, himself mortally wounded, at Antietam. . . .

Gazing at the clear-eyed, untroubled face, Addie felt a hard lump rise into her throat. Feeling a deep sadness for all that he represented, all that was lost, a mist of tears blurred his confident smile. . . .

What had Aunt Susan said over and over? "We must put the past behind, forget, and go on—" Addie shook her head, saying to herself, "Auntie's wrong. If I did that, who else would remember him? If *I* did—it would be like Randy never existed. I don't want to forget him—or anything else. It would be like saying it had all been for nothing. I can't. I won't."

Holding it a minute longer, Addie studied his image, then put the picture on the top of the bureau beside her silver-backed dresser set. Determinedly, Addie continued unpacking, putting away her things in the bureau drawers, and hanging her dresses and jackets in the armoire. Then she emptied her valise. In it were the three books she had traveled with: her small leather Bible, the George Eliot novel *The Mill on the Floss,* and her journal.

For some reason, Addie suddenly thought of the tall stranger at the train depot. Would she ever see him again or learn who he was? An involuntary shiver passed through Addie as she thought of that uncanny sense of recognition she had had when their eyes met—as though they had met and known each other somewhere before—almost as if he had been waiting for her to arrive!

What foolishness, like a schoolgirl's daydream. Sternly, Addie jerked herself back to reality, reminding herself that she was nearly twenty-six and long past such silliness. She put the three books on the bedside table and took out a cotton blouse with a tucked bodice and demure collar and cuffs, suitable for her new position as "paid companion."

She had just added her mother's cameo brooch for a finishing touch when she heard voices and footsteps outside her open window coming up on the cottage porch.

"I hope all this is doing me some good!" a high-pitched female voice complained. "What possible benefit is it to soak three times a day in that bubbly mineral water, I'd like to know—it's bad enough to have to drink that stuff without then being steamed in it like a lobster—"

"Well, ma'am, Dr. Willoughby is convinced that these treatments are *very* beneficial, and you will feel like a new person entirely when you leave here in the spring—," a quiet confident voice replied.

Addie stood quite still in the center of her bedroom. Should she go out and introduce herself right now? Or should she wait until Mrs. Amberly was back in her own bedroom? Possibly she was in some measure *dishabille* if she were returning from treatments at the bathhouse. Caught in anxious uncertainty, Addie asked herself if it would seem too forward if she did. Or if she hesitated and did not make her presence known to her employer, would Mrs. Amberly think she was sly or devious or worse still, awkward, without social graces?

As she hesitated, she heard huffing and puffing, the shuffling of slippered feet along the hallway; then a door was unlocked, opened, then closed again.

Addie let out her breath slowly. For the moment, the decision had been taken out of her hands. She felt, however, that she should speak to the attendant, let her know she had arrived, and perhaps ask her what she should do about meeting Mrs. Amberly.

Opening her door, she waited until a white-uniformed figure emerged from the other bedroom and came down the hall.

"Hello!" the rosy-cheeked, middle-aged woman greeted Addie. "I'm Letty, the maid assigned to this cottage, as well as one of the bathhouse attendants. You must be Miss Pride. Mrs. Amberly's expecting you. In fact, she's been fretting, wondering when you'd get here. I guess she was expecting you sooner?"

"Well, transcontinental travel does have its drawbacks!" Addie declared with a smile. "The trains don't always leave on time or get there when they're supposed to either. I've come from Virginia and there were quite a few unpredictable delays along the way."

"I suppose so. I came when I was little girl with my family in a wagon train, so I don't remember much about it. I was only three years old, but I know my poor mother said never again. And she never did."

"Should I go in to see Mrs. Amberly now?" Addie asked.

"I'd give her a few minutes, if I were you. I helped her get dressed, but I wouldn't disturb her right away." The woman lowered her voice. "She's probably having her little toddy." She gave Addie an elaborate wink. "Strictly against doctor's orders, of course. But *at the prices,* who's going to stop her?"

Addie did not know what to say to this unexpected piece of information.

"Well, I best be on my way. My day's done. And I suppose *yours* is just beginning. Good luck, dearie. I think you're going to need it."

With this, Letty went out of the cottage, leaving Addie wondering what awaited her beyond the closed door at the end of the hall.

Chapter 4

*A*ddie knocked tentatively on the door and heard a voice whose tone was to become familiar in the days ahead. "Yes, it's open. Come in."

Addie hesitated a second before turning the knob and entering the room. It seemed to be empty with curtains drawn. The room was shadowy. Addie took a few steps further, looking around for the person who had spoken. Then someone said sharply, almost accusingly, "Well, so you've come."

Addie whirled around to see a large, round figure seated in the corner in a chair, feet propped up on a hassock. A grossly fat woman, overdressed in a tasseled, bell-sleeved purple taffeta of enormous frills, pleats, and braided trim. Her small pig eyes were almost lost under the puffy lids. Her small flat nose and down-turned mouth were bracketed by ballooning cheeks. Addie's immediate first impression of her employer was the woman's resemblance to pictures she had seen of the aging English Queen Victoria.

"Mrs. Amberly?"

"The same," came the curt reply. "And *you*, miss, I presume are Adelaide Pride."

"Yes."

"Well, first things first, I suppose. I am here because of my health—very precarious—I have dropsy, a swelling of the tissue, as you can see, as well as rheumatism—all of which I have been told—practically promised by Mr. Stanton, these mineral water baths and so on—will cure!" She gave her head a little shake, setting the ruby and diamond pendant earrings swinging from her drooping earlobes. She waved one pudgy, heavily ringed hand impatiently. "But I've heard that kind of fairy tale before at other spas in Europe, as well as back east. I'm simply hoping the California climate will help."

"I'm sorry," murmured Addie, not knowing what else to say.

"You needn't be sorry. I don't like people who talk a lot of nonsense. Now, let's get your duties straight. I do need help walking to and from the main lobby—the attendants fetch me and bring me back from the bathhouse after my daily treatments. So, there really isn't that much for you to do, so I expect you to spend your time profitably. I like to be read to, so you will avail yourself of the local library, which Mr. Stanton assures me is well supplied, and get me my hometown newspaper, which comes by train from San Francisco. It's a week late, but I still like to keep up on things—stock market report and such.

"I want you available if I want something extra—morning and evening snacks, that sort of thing. I have a hard time hobbling around on these poor feet. That's the reason I don't like being waited on, but I do like to have what I want when I want it." She pursed her lips for a moment before continuing. "Do you play cards, whist? You may have to fill in if we cannot get a fourth, or if some of the guests I've been playing with should leave—that's always a possibility. If my health improves, I may want to take some short side trips—to the Lake Country or Saint Helena. You would see to those arrangements. I may think of some other things, but for the present that is all, I suppose." Mrs. Amberly frowned. "I dislike change, and my cousin Ella was my companion for a number of years, but when I decided to come out West, she refused to accompany me. Afraid of Indian attack, she said! Ha! Can you imagine such stupidity in this day and age?" Mrs. Amberly looked disgusted. Then she jangled the jeweled necklace that hung around her neck and lifted the magnifying glass attached to it and checked a watch pinned to her shelf-like bosom with a diamond bow knot. "It's almost time for dinner and since I move slowly, we better get started."

It took Mrs. Amberly a number of attempts and several minutes to heave herself out of her chair. Addie had not known whether to move forward to assist her or wait until she was asked. Mrs. Amberly was an uncertain quantity just now. Addie realized she would have to bide her time, learn to know when to offer help or when to resist the urge to do so. Mrs. Amberly seemed easily offended, so that, at the moment, tact seemed the best thing.

Once on her feet, Mrs. Amberly leaned heavily on Addie's proffered arm, and they made their slow, ponderous way across the courtyard to the dining hall.

Mrs. Amberly made little attempt at conversation, even omitting the questions about Addie's trip that one might expect out of ordinary courtesy or even curiosity. Instead, she kept up a running commentary, mostly negative, on the other guests at Silver Springs as they entered the dining room.

All through the long dinner, Addie was more and more appalled by her new employer's comments on everything and everybody, from their waiter to the other guests dining in the large, windowed room. Everything she said was critical or sarcastic. She complained about the service, and declaring that her meat was too rare, sent it back; when it was brought back, she said it was "burned to a crisp." It didn't take Addie long to realize Mrs. Amberly was a selfish, self-centered person who cared little for anyone but herself.

Addie had noticed the curious looks in her direction from the other diners and knew she was under speculation. As they were finishing their dessert, two of the other guests, the Brunell sisters, Elouise and Harriet, stopped by the table. Mrs. Amberly was saccharinely sweet and amiable. Of course, since Addie's presence could not be ignored, an introduction was unavoidable and done with very poor grace. Addie stifled the rush of resentment, finding it galling to be introduced as "my hired companion." From the Brunells' rather startled reaction, Addie realized that designation put other guests at Silver Springs in an awkward position of not knowing exactly how to treat her. She felt humiliated and inwardly outraged by it.

Addie was relieved and grateful that almost immediately after the Misses Brunell had left, Brook Stanton came over to the table.

"Good evening, ladies." He included them both in his smile. "I hope you are finding everything satisfactory."

Mrs. Amberly immediately became a different person. Simpering coyly, she waggled a fat finger a him, saying, "So where have you been the last few days, Mr. Stanton? None of us have seen you."

"In the city on business."

"Visiting some lucky ladies there, I'll wager." Mrs. Amberly screwed up her small mouth into a smile she must have thought looked teasing but only looked malicious.

"Afraid not, Mrs. Amberly. You give me credit where none is due. Rather they were several portly gentlemen with whiskers and beady eyes, inclined to be more parsimonious than gracious." His eyes moved admiringly over to Addie. "It seems I must return to Calistoga to be in the presence of charm and beauty."

Mrs. Amberly darted a glance at Addie, and for a

moment, her mask slipped. As Brook turned toward her again, she quickly rearranged her expression. Only Addie had caught the look of open indignation. In the snap of a finger, she knew with alarm and surprise that her employer was capable of petty and unprovoked anger.

She had no time to dwell on the realization, however, because some of the other guests leaving the dining room passed by and nodded to Mrs. Amberly, saying, "Come along, we're ready to play."

Brook took that as a cue. "I'm sure you must be anxious to get to your regular game, Mrs. Amberly, and I'm also sure Miss Pride must be weary from her day's travel, so suppose I escort her to the cottage this evening for an early retirement. Later, when you are finished with your game, Mrs. Amberly, I'll see you safely there."

Mrs. Amberly seemed as if she were about to object, but Brook had already moved to her side and was assisting her from her chair. He continued a smooth line of pleasant conversation as the three of them strolled out of the dining hall and over to the main building.

They left Mrs. Amberly at the door of the game room where card tables were being set up, and Brook, with Addie on his arm, went out the front entrance. It was a beautiful evening, mild, with stars overhead sparkling.

"Calistoga welcomes you with one of its lovely evenings, Miss Pride. We sometimes get early fog this time of year in the valley, but not tonight."

They walked along in silence. Addie realized suddenly that she *was* very, very tired. But also that it was an emotional weariness rather than physical.

Her mind was numb, and she could think of nothing to say to the gallant Mr. Stanton and thought he must think her either rude or completely lacking in the minimal social graces. That, however, did not seem to be the case because before leaving her at the cottage porch, he said, "You are going to bring something to Silver Springs that I hadn't realized was missing before you arrived, Miss Pride. Youthful beauty, grace, and a certain instinctive charm that have been sadly lacking among my guests."

A little flustered by this unexpected compliment, Addie murmured, "How kind of you to say so. Thank you."

"Not at all, Miss Pride. I feel we will all be in your debt before this winter is over. Just don't let anything stifle your natural cheerfulness and good humor—" There was a hint of humor in this.

"I'll try not to," she replied, realizing Brook Stanton read Mrs. Amberly like the proverbial book.

"Good! Now, have a good night's sleep. This clear air is the best insurance one could possibly have for complete restoration of body and spirit, I guarantee it," he told her, then laughed. "Spoken like a true innkeeper, right? Good night to you, Miss Pride. Sweet dreams."

With that he gave her a little salute and went off into the night humming under his breath. Addie looked after him thinking Brook Stanton was far more than an innkeeper. He was a man of considerable talents, many of them probably hidden.

Chapter 5

*I*t was after midnight and at Addie's desk the wick of the oil lamp sputtered, the light flickered as her pen moved across the pages.

November 24th, 1870

Only two weeks have gone by and I still face months of putting up with this insufferable woman. And this evening was the worst yet. Usually I just manage to sit out the hours she spends at the card tables until she's ready to be helped back over to the cottage. Tonight, however, one of the "regulars" pleaded a headache and retired, and I was ordered to fill in for her. I find the game not only stupid—to say nothing of the shallow chit-chat carried on between plays—but discussion afterward of every play is so boring. By the end of the evening my head ached. I felt like screaming.

Addie was gripping her pen so hard that the point dug into the paper, causing the ink to splatter across the page. She flung down her pen in frustration, rubbing her aching forehead.

November 27th

Mrs. Amberly pretends she has forgotten her promise to reimburse me for travel expenses. The small fund of cash I brought with me from the sale of some of Mama's jewelry has dwindled alarmingly. Finally I had to mention it, and a more humiliating scene has never been my experience to bear. Mrs. A. acted as though she could not recall such an offer. I was forced to produce her letter in which she *had* made such a statement. Confronted with the evidence she turned beet red, and with obvious reluctance wrote out a cheque, giving it to me like tossing a bone to a dog! I dread to think I may have to go through this sort of thing each month for my salary!

But being able to send Aunt Susan and Uncle Myles a nice sum every month will make up for any cross I must bear in this hideous situation. But very honestly, I feel— trapped! That's how I feel. Perhaps this is the way slaves in the old South felt.

Dec. 2nd

Today I went to the Post Office to mail the money order to Aunt Susan. As I was doing that, I saw the man I first noticed the day of my arrival at the depot. I was standing at the corner getting ready to cross the street when he came down the street mounted on a fine, gleaming chestnut horse. As he passed he lifted the brim of his hat and nodded—as if he knew me! The strangest part is that I felt the same extraordinary sensation I'd had before. That we had met somewhere before, been parted a long time, and were only just now seeing each other again.

It is so ridiculous, I do not know why I even record it.

Involuntarily, Addie shivered. She closed her journal. It had been a long, wearying day, and tomorrow there would be another one to face.

As she got undressed for bed her feeling of depression deepened. How could she endure this year of employment to a woman she had come to dislike heartily. Mrs. Amberly's abrasive personality was bad enough, but her arrogance was worse. Her treatment of the resort employees, the maid assigned to their cottage, the bathhouse attendants, the waiter in the dining room, the desk clerk in the lobby, made Addie wince inwardly. Addie felt embarrassed to be associated with Mrs. Amberly, as though she were, as they say, "tarred with the same stick!"

To counteract Mrs. Amberly's actions, Addie went out of her way to pleasantly address the various employees by name, though she had little opportunity away from the scrutiny of her employer.

Addie lay awake praying for patience. She knew she had to make the best of the bad bargain she had made. She had signed a contract. Her word must be her bond. After all, she was a Pride, wasn't she? The Pride name stood for something. It stood for integrity, truth, and above all honor. She must honor her word that she would stay out the year. Whatever it took—and Addie had the feeling she would be tested far beyond anything life had ever before demanded of her.

Addie determined to try harder to put up with the situation. It was a mere matter of will, she told herself. She would try to be cheerful. If she could not overlook the things that bothered her most about her employer, she would simply grit her teeth and bear it. What else could she do?

Dec. 8th

The weather is still mild with the exception of intermittent days of rain. But the sun seems to manage to come out for a portion of every day at least. My escape from the drudgery of my job and the stress of being around someone like Mrs. A. for hours at a time is to take long walks. While Mrs. A. is at the bathhouse taking her heated mineral water treatments, I leave the resort and walk to town. Calistoga is a small town, very new. The houses look freshly painted and the gardens are a wonder, full of all sorts of flowers, some blooming profusely, even this late. The trees are beautiful, all sorts of ones that I cannot name, but think I shall get a book and try to learn what they are, so many different kinds. It does refresh me to do this. Still I cannot help feeling lonely. As I walk along these pretty streets, I keep thinking, people live in these nice houses, people it would be nice to know, perhaps be friends with, but I know no one except the maids and no one knows me. It has been a long time since I've even heard anyone call me by my Christian name. It is certainly a change from Avondale where I knew everyone and everyone knew me and my family.

The guests at Silver Springs were mostly middle-aged, many of them in poor health, who had come there seeking some recourse in the beneficial mineral water, the heated pools, and the mild climate. There were no young people with whom Addie could make friends, even if her ambiguous position as a "paid companion" made that possible.

Oddly enough, it was Brook Stanton with whom Addie found rapport. Busy as he always was as manager of the resort and many other entrepreneurial projects that occupied him, Brook always seemed to have time to stop and chat with Addie whenever he saw her.

Brook was entirely different from the Southern men she had known all her life, who took affluence, position, and privilege for granted as their right. For all his casual affability, Addie suspected that underneath Brook's charming manners was a driving ambition, perhaps even a ruthlessness to succeed. This he skillfully kept hidden under an engaging personality.

He had great style in everything: his attire, his management of Silver Springs. His insistence on perfection was evident everywhere. The tasteful furnishings in the lobby and lounges, the exquisite table settings in the dining hall, the crisp white linens, the gleaming china, the sparkling glassware, the spotless cottages, and the excellent service all compared favorably with any prestigious eastern resort.

Addie enjoyed her contacts with Brook, who provided her with intelligent, witty conversation—a welcome relief from the usual shallow chatter of Mrs. Amberly and her cohorts. The problem was that she soon became aware that her employer resented Brook's attention to her and reacted to any special notice by him with increased orneriness and petulant demands. Addie soon discovered what a petty, childish woman Mrs. Amberly could be.

At least on Sundays Addie had some respite. The first time Addie suggested church attendance, Mrs. Amberly appeared flustered. It amused Addie to see the inner struggle taking place as her employer debated if she could get away with refusing Addie time off for worship service. Since even the hotel employees were allowed to attend church on Sunday mornings, there was really nothing Mrs. Amberly could say.

Addie wondered if it were not that Mrs. Amberly felt some guilt about not going to church herself. After grudgingly assenting to Addie's going, she rambled on at some length about the impossibility, in her rheumatic condition, of sitting in the hard pews during the long sermon. Addie listened, trying charitably to give the woman the benefit of the doubt, but it occurred to Addie that Mrs. Amberly seemed to have no trouble sitting for hours on end playing cards most evenings. Nevertheless, with the tug of wills finally over, Addie had won the freedom of a few free hours on Sunday mornings.

Sunday morning began like any other morning. Addie rose, dressed, knocked on Mrs. Amberly's bedroom door to see if she was ready to walk over to the dining hall for breakfast.

When her employer appeared, she was puffy-eyed, her cheeks creased from sleeping on massed pillows, her mouth in its perpetual downward pull. Addie greeted her. "Good morning, Mrs. Amberly."

"Humph," was all Mrs. Amberly could muster in response as she took hold of Addie's arm.

"I hope you slept well," Addie murmured the comment

she made every morning as if they were lines she'd learned in a play.

"Tossed and turned all night," complained Mrs. Amberly, as she always did not knowing that sometimes her loud snoring could even be heard through the walls and down the hallway to Addie's astonished ears. When they stepped out onto the little porch and saw the light mist rising from the ground, Mrs. Amberly exclaimed crossly, "I thought the sun was always supposed to be shining in California!"

"I'm sure it will burn off before noon," Addie replied, having noticed this seemed to be the weather pattern of valley days.

Ignoring that optimistic prediction, Mrs. Amberly droned on, "I should have gone to Florida or Italy. It wasn't *my* idea to come here. Now I suspect my nephew must have had some investment here and that's why he persuaded me that *this* would be a good place to spend the winter. It's just like him. He's a sly one, a great talker, he is. Money is what he's interested in most—*my* money most likely—and here I sit shivering in *sunny* California while he—I think he went to Bermuda—but how should I know? He never contacts me unless he's got some scheme for me to invest in— but he don't fool me. No, indeed. Somebody'd have to get up pretty early in the day to pull the wool over *my* eyes— my, but my neck's stiff, and my legs—I dunno whether this whole thing is doing me a bit of good—"

Addie groaned inwardly. Was there no end to this petty whining and complaining? This spoiling of every new day?

Settled at their table in the dining hall, Mrs. Amberly surveyed the breakfast menu with a jaundiced eye while the waiter greeted them and poured them coffee. Mrs. Amberly had been advised to eat lightly before her treatments which were scheduled for ten o'clock. But, regardless of that sage suggestion, after a great show of resignation she would go ahead and order sausage and eggs or griddle cakes.

"Stanton should get a new chef. This food is getting monotonous," Mrs. Amberly said as she shoved the menu back at the patient waiter. "His cook is one of them Chinese, you know. What on earth could a China man know about what *Americans* like to eat, I'd like to know!" She sniffed disdainfully.

To avoid commenting, Addie took a long sip of the steaming coffee. She was often at a loss for how to reply to her employer's innumerable complaints. If she said nothing, Mrs. Amberly stared at her belligerently until she said something.

Luckily, this morning Addie was saved by Brook. He was just entering the dining hall and saw them. As he approached their table, Mrs. Amberly immediately stirred in her chair like a pigeon fluffing her feathers and put a smile on her face.

"Good morning, ladies," he said cheerfully. "You two will be the first to hear my news! I've got a surprise that is going to set this town on its ear and give you a chance to enjoy a performance that brought the crowned heads of Europe to their feet in wild applause!"

"What on earth is it, Mr. Stanton?" Mrs. Amberly asked.

"It's a secret. And until I have all the details I will just have to leave you ladies guessing—but I promise you you're going to be thrilled."

With that he went on his way. Mrs. Amberly's false smile faded and her face slumped into its usual petulance.

"Humph, that man's all bluff!" she said grumpily. "I don't believe a word he said."

To save herself from commenting, Addie took a bite of scrambled eggs. *She* had no doubt that Brook would carry out his promise to set this town on its ear. Whatever his surprise, Addie was anticipating it.

After breakfast Addie left Mrs. Amberly in the lounge to

49

chat with one of her bridge partners and went to get ready for church.

Addie decided there was no longer any reason to wear the "protective" mourning attire she had worn so effectively on the long journey west, and instead put on a walking suit Aunt Susan had made for her from a lovely length of soft wool, purchased in England before the war. It had been put away during the war years when any kind of extravagant show was considered unsuitable or unpatriotic. A skillful seamstress, her aunt had fashioned a stylish outfit for her. The Prussian blue color was vastly becoming, the fitted jacket trimmed with soutache, her bonnet refurbished with new ribbons and a bunch of wax cherries. As a last touch she buttoned up her best pair of gray kid boots with French heels that she had bought on impulse in San Francisco the day before boarding the steamer.

Leaving the cottage, she went down the path around the arboretum, aware of several admiring glances from gentlemen guests out strolling, even though they had their wives on their arm. Flattered, Addie lowered her eyes as was proper, smiling demurely, as she passed them. She had almost reached the gates when she heard footsteps hurrying along the gravel path behind her and a voice calling her name.

"Miss Pride, good morning!"

Surprised, she turned to see it was Mr. Louis Montand, the guest Brook Stanton had introduced her to on the day of her arrival. She had not seen him except from a distance since then.

He caught up with her and asked, "Where, may I ask, are you off to on this bright morning?"

"To church," she replied.

"Isn't it rather a warm day to walk? You look so utterly charming I would hate to see you get overheated."

"Thank you, it's lovely and cool, besides I have this—" She unfurled her silk parasol and prepared to move on.

"Would you mind if I walked along with you? It is a lovely day at that."

Addie hesitated only a second. After all they had been properly introduced, and he was a guest at the hotel.

"If you like," she murmured.

"I've just returned from San Francisco," he told her. "I must say it's nice to be back in this bucolic setting. How are you enjoying being in Calistoga by now?"

Truth or a polite lie? What if she told Mr. Montand how really miserable she had been? But of course that was impossible. Instead, she said, "There is much to enjoy here, the mild weather is delightful, unusual, at least to me, for this time of year, and the scenery is awe-inspiring."

"I believe you are a diplomatic person, Miss Pride," Montand replied, amusement in his voice. "You are not bored, then? Not with the provincialism, the stultifying lack of stimulation at the hotel, the vacuity of most of our fellow guests?"

Addie looked at him surprised by the underlying sarcasm in his comment. "Well, Mr. Stanton has promised us some special sort of entertainment soon," she began, then stopped, remembering Brook had said it was a secret.

"Ah, yes, well, we shall see. Ever since my sister and I came here, he has been saying there would be more social life at the hotel, assured me he is making all sorts of arrangements so his guests will not get bored. I trust you are not bored, Miss Pride?"

Addie was saved from answering as the white-steepled church came into sight. "I must cross the street here, Mr. Montand," she said, gesturing to it with her gloved hand.

"Ah, that's where you attend? I am not a regular church-goer, Miss Pride, or I might be tempted to accompany you," he chuckled softly. "But I hope you will not hold that against me. I would like very much to become better acquainted. Perhaps you could have luncheon with me after church services? I would be happy to meet you in an hour or so? I would be waiting right here when you came out."

"Thank you very much for the invitation, Mr. Montand, but I am really not free to make social engagements. Perhaps, you did not understand that I am employed by Mrs. Amberly as her companion, and as such I must be available to her except for when she has her treatments and Thursdays and now—on Sunday mornings to attend services."

"Ah, I see," Montand looked thoughtful as he regarded Addie. "That must become a rather tedious occupation—dancing attendance on a woman so—" he hesitated as if searching for the right word, "—crippled with arthritis, is it? She did tell me one time just what her ailment was and why she was here—but I'm afraid it slipped my mind." His mouth twisted in a mocking smile.

Addie pretended not to notice. She would not for one unguarded moment reveal her own feelings about Mrs. Amberly or risk having Montand realize she agreed with his accurate if uncharitable assessment of her employer.

His sarcastic remarks struck Addie as ironic because she knew, even though Mrs. Amberly had met them only briefly, she admired the Montands inordinately. She had often mentioned both Louis and his sister, Estelle, telling Addie several times that they were the only people at Silver Springs worth cultivation—"They're *real* class!" Addie had soon learned that Mrs. Amberly had a rating system to designate who at the hotel was worth her time or effort. At Montand's obvious disdain for her employer, Addie felt almost pity. From his words it was clear that neither brother nor sister had any desire to socialize with *her*.

"Well, perhaps another time," Louis said. "I'm so happy I saw you and we had this chance for a little chat. I do hope

52

you will consider dining with me some evening when my sister returns from the city? I would like you two to meet."

The church bell began to clang and Addie said, "I must go or I'll be late for the service."

"Yes, of course, but before you go, I must say your ensemble is stunning; you look absolutely charming, and your bonnet is one of the prettiest I've seen in quite awhile."

"Coming from a gentleman who has just been to San Francisco that's quite a compliment. Thank you," Addie smiled. "I really must go now." She closed her parasol.

Intuitively, Addie knew Louis Montand found her attractive, and her old self-confidence, dampened daily by her ignominious position, re-emerged. She crossed the street aware that Louis Montand's eyes were following her.

Holding her skirt gracefully with one hand, she went up the church steps, knowing he was still watching her. For the first time since her arrival she felt like herself, Adelaide Pride of Oakleigh. As she reached the church door, she lifted her head.

Just as she entered the vestibule, one dainty heel of her new boots caught on the doorstep. She tripped and would have lost her balance, maybe fallen, had not a solicitous usher at the entrance caught her elbow and steadied her.

Blushing, she whispered a thank you. Hot with embarrassment, she was shown to a pew and seated. Trying to cover her confusion she opened the church bulletin she had been handed. When she saw the announcement of the text for today's sermon, Proverbs 16:18, "Pride goeth before destruction, and a haughty spirit before a fall." Addie had to suppress a giggle. How humorously the Lord sometimes admonishes.

Across the street Louis Montand stood watching as Addie mounted the church steps then disappeared through the church door. There was no question about it, Adelaide Pride had an air of quality about her. Something that, in his experience, was rare even in the well-bred young women to whom he had been exposed at the rounds of debutante parties when he was an undergraduate at Harvard. She possessed a natural refinement and understated elegance that he certainly had not met since coming to California. Friends had introduced him to any number of daughters of gold- and land-rich families, hopeful mamas hovering, aware of his enormous wealth and his background. However, none had appealed to him. And Louis was determined he would only marry on his own terms. He must feel something. If not passion, at least there must be real attraction. Anything less would only bore him. If he were going to fulfill his own vision of life here in this valley, he wanted to share it with a woman of whom he could feel proud and who would make other men envious of him, someone who could grace the kind of home that would establish him in this tight-knit community. A woman of beauty, breeding, some intelligence, and ability to understand and appreciate his plans.

Possibly Adelaide Pride could be the one. But what on earth was she doing here with that vulgar social climber? Louis's lip curled in contempt.

Well, he would wait until Estelle had a chance to meet Miss Pride. He valued his sister's opinions and advice although he did not always take them.

A few nights later, Addie wrote in her journal:

I have now been here and in the position of "paid companion" (as Mrs. A. never lets me forget!) a full month. I feel like a prisoner marking off the days of his sentence on the wall of his cell! Never have I met anyone who is so universally unpleasant and rude to anyone she considers inferior, which includes me, along with the hotel employees, the waiters in the dining room, the desk clerk, and maids. I wince inwardly whenever Mrs. A. addresses anyone. Only

54

Brook Stanton and Louis Montand escape her razor-sharp tongue.

Mrs. A. is, in my opinion, interested only in people she thinks are superior in some way. Almost upon my arrival here, she pointed out Mr. Montand saying he and his sister, whom I have not met as yet, were the only guests worth "cultivating." "They're *real* bluebloods," she confided. "From Boston." As if I cared.

Besides, I have discovered that in California what is important is to claim you are descended from "pioneers," the earliest settlers. Just as in Virginia a family who could trace their ancestry to Jamestown was considered among the most prestigious F.F.V. In that case, Letty's, our cottage maid and bathhouse attendant poor mother who came out in 1849 by covered wagon, should be on top of Mrs. A.'s list to cultivate!

To my embarrassment, Mrs. A. pursues Montand and keeps asking him when his sister will be returning to the Springs. Mr. Montand is certainly polite and pleasant enough. I had a chance encounter with him Sunday morning on my way to church.

Dec. 27th

Christmas has come and gone, a more dreary one I have never spent. Well, maybe the ones during the war were worse—in some ways. But at least I was surrounded by family and friends and we all tried to make things as merry as possible under the circumstances.

Many people left to spend Christmas with relatives for a week. The Montands left to spend Christmas in southern California with friends at the famous Del Monte Hotel in San Diego and will not return until after the New Year.

So there were only a few of us left, the Misses Brunell, and several older people, invalids in wheelchairs or walking with canes.

I must give credit to Brook who made things as festive as possible for those guests who remained during the holidays. Brook had a seven-foot cedar tree put up in the lobby, decorated lavishly with glass balls, flittering tinsel, and gold garlands, and each evening tiny lighted candles made the gilt baubles and cornucopias filled with hard candies sparkle. He said it was a custom first started in Germany and brought to England by Queen Victoria's Prince Consort, Albert, and now was becoming a tradition in America. At each table in the dining hall he had placed red candles and a wreath of greens and holly. One evening a choir from one of the local churches came to sing carols, another evening a quartet gave a concert in the lounge. He told me he had planned to give a Christmas ball but with so many guests leaving, it had not worked out.

January 1, 1871

New Year's Day. I cannot believe it is six years since the war ended and my strange new life began. It has all passed so quickly and I don't remember as much about it as I remember about the five long years of the war.

Now I am in a whole new phase of my life and the future is a kind of blur. I cannot imagine what awaits me in this New Year.

I don't know why I even mention this, but a few days before Christmas I saw the man I now call my "mysterious stranger"—again. I was doing a little shopping and saw him coming directly toward me along the sidewalk. For some reason, I became so flustered, I simply ducked into the nearest store. My heart was like a wild bird beating its wings. So rattled, I bought a silk scarf and a pair of gloves I didn't need and couldn't afford.

January 23

My Christmas box arrived from Aunt Susan along with a letter from Emily filled with news of friends and events in Avondale—which now seems to me like another world. Sometimes I ask myself what I am doing here, so far from everything I knew in my life. Just this morning when I was reading my Bible I turned to Jeremiah 29:11 and read, "For I know the plans I have for you, says the Lord, of peace and not of evil, to give you a future and a hope."

How comforting that is; how I wish I could believe it.

One thing of which I'm sure is that what I'm earning is helping provide Aunt Susan and Uncle Myles with a few extra comforts. That thought is worth all I have to put up with in this ignominious position.

PART 2

SILVER SPRINGS RESORT

Chapter 6

*U*pon her arrival Mrs. Amberly had outlined Addie' duties to her. Among them was to read aloud to her. Because of her own love of books Addie assumed this would be one of her easiest tasks. But although Mrs. Amberly sent her on weekly trips to the library to select books, it turned out that newspapers were what her employer most liked having read to her. She loved nothing more than hearing accounts of deaths and disasters; murder and mayhem were her special enjoyment. She eagerly relished the details of survivors' firsthand stories of excursion boat sinkings and train wrecks. Floods, fires, and tornadoes she savored vicariously.

Although her employer's tastes continued to dismay Addie, she constantly reminded herself of her purpose in taking this job, of how important it was that Mrs. Amberly be satisfied with her. Addie determined to give Mrs. Amberly nothing to complain about—not her attitude, nor unwillingness, nor any failure to accommodate.

Addie even conquered her distaste for reminding Mrs. Amberly when her salary was due. This demeaning scene was repeated on the first and fifteenth of every month. It was an ordeal each time, but Addie faced it without flinching. She learned to stand impassively while Mrs. Amberly emitted a small grunt or two, frowned as she wrote out her check. It was for Aunt Susan and Uncle Myles' sake, and for them Addie would have gone through much worse.

Twice monthly Addie walked to the post office and sent off the money order. Knowing how gratefully it would be received made up for all the humiliation in earning it. Afterward she would walk to the library and check out several titles of her own choosing.

One such afternoon, as she arrived back on the resort grounds from town, Addie met Brook. He was smiling broadly and seemed in especially high spirits.

"Well, Addie, I've brought it off!" he greeted her. "Come sit down on one of the benches, and I'll tell you all about it."

Curious, Addie followed him over to one of the white iron-lace benches circling the arboretum and sat down, eager to hear at last what Brook's secret was.

"It's confirmed. *She's* coming. *Della DeSecia!*" he announced triumphantly. "She's just finished a concert engagement in San Francisco, and I've persuaded her to come here for a rest *and*—" he paused significantly, "—*and* to give an informal concert for our guests."

"That's wonderful, Brook. I know how pleased you must be."

"I'm planning to send out invitations to people in town, as well—engraved ones. Make them feel they're singled out to attend." He smiled mischievously. "There's nothing people like more than feeling they're getting into something exclusive. And Madame DeSecia will get what she enjoys most—all the attention, not having to share curtain calls with a tenor she dislikes or a contralto who's jealous of her!" Brook rubbed his hands together gleefully. "Ah, it will be quite an occasion. I shall put on a reception like this town has never seen before—champagne, caviar . . ."

His eyes shone with excitement, his voice buoyant. He

was obviously elated by his accomplishment. It confirmed what Addie had intuitively felt about Brook: when he wanted something he went after it. He let no obstacle stand in his way. She couldn't help wondering what he had offered, what he had promised to get the famous opera star to come.

Brook's eyes took on a kind of glaze as he continued. "You know, Addie, this means the beginning of a dream I've had for a long time for this town. To bring well-known theatrical figures, actors as well as opera stars and concert artists here to perform. It's the perfect place, and if we treat them like royalty—this will become as fashionable as any resort in the east!" He sighed. "I've always loved the theater even though I was brought up in a home that considered it a sin and I was forbidden to go." Brook gave a little laugh, shook his head as if at the futility of such a prohibition. "Of course, I used to sneak out and spend whatever change I could scrounge up—selling newspapers, shining shoes, running messages—yes, my dear, since you might never guess it to look at me now, but I was a little street urchin. And then I'd go to the Saturday matinees. Sit in the balcony; I bought the cheapest tickets, but I loved it all—sitting in that darkened cavern on uncomfortable, moth-eaten seats, with smells all around me—the smell of over-ripe fruit most of the audience brought with them to eat—or throw—along with the smell of the oil lamps along the side of the aisles dimly illuminating them. All that is mixed in with the thrill of theater—yes, I was conscious of all that and yet, the minute the curtains parted and the flickering stage lights came up, I was in another world.

"The stories and songs unfolded before me, even as I began to see the shoddy costumes, be aware of the bad acting, realize that the comedy and comics were second-rate— still—" Abruptly Brook broke off as if suddenly conscious of how much he had revealed about himself. Suddenly the shining little-boy look on his face vanished and his eyes hardened. He gave a short, harsh laugh.

"I assure you my taste has risen from that of a little lad. One of the joys I find in going to the city is seeing great performances—drama, opera. And that is what I hope to bring here to Calistoga. I want to make it so attractive to the leading stars of the stage, concert halls, and, yes, opera—that they will all be willing to come—even consider it an honor to perform here."

As if he realized she was looking at him sympathetically, Brook smiled, stood up, and said less intently, "That's my dream. And I'll do whatever it takes to make it happen."

There was a flurry of excitement the day Della DeSecia was to arrive at Silver Springs. The rumor spread among the guests that she would come before lunch. An unusual number of bathhouse appointments were changed, and plans for drives and other activities were canceled so guests could be in the main lounge to catch a glimpse of the opera star. Although everyone tried to maintain an air of casual indifference, as though she were just any other guest arriving at the hotel, the electricity of anticipation was contagious. Mrs. Amberly was as bad if not worse than the rest, though still expressing negative opinions about the famous diva.

"She's past her prime, you know. Why else would she accept an invitation to come here, this out-of-the-way place, if she could go to some big city and have a huge audience?"

Addie said nothing. Besides, the question was rhetorical. Even so, Mrs. Amberly had no intention of missing Madame DeSecia's arrival. She positioned herself in a chair facing the entrance to be sure to have a good view. When Brook's carriage came up the driveway all conversation in the lounge stopped. All eyes turned toward the front door as Brook escorted Madame DeSecia inside. Her white-gloved hand rested on Brook's arm, and she talked animatedly to him as they walked into the lobby.

Addie thought her the most beautiful woman she had ever seen in spite of Mrs. Amberly's stage-whispered comment, "That color *can't* be *real!*"

Under question was the mass of lustrous red-gold hair visible beneath a hat with a sweeping brim trimmed with lilac blossoms. A lavender suit, with wide satin reveres showed off her figure, voluptuously curved, as befitted an opera singer.

Behind them, scurrying with mincing steps, came a small, thin woman, drably dressed in gray, carrying two hat boxes and a velvet case—containing, one assumed, Madame's jewels. This must be her maid, speculated the whispers behind Addie.

After her was one of the hotel porters laden with tapestried luggage. It was, Addie thought, quite a parade. Impressed, Addie watched as Madame DeSecia, apparently unaware of her audience, swept up the stairway to the suite Addie knew Brook had prepared especially for the use of such celebrated guests.

During her sojourn at the Springs Hotel no one saw much of Madame DeSecia. She had her meals in her suite, and if she had any of the treatments they must have been taken at night or at dawn for no one encountered her coming or going to the bathhouse. However, they did hear her. Sometimes the sound of her vocalizing penetrated the lower floor of the hotel, and everyone stopped whatever they were doing to listen. Even when it was only scales, it seemed remarkable that such a talent was actually on the premises.

At last the date of her concert came. Early in the evening the hotel started filling up. Local people who had received Brook's fancy invitations came dressed in their finest. In the lounge, chairs had been set in two semi-circular rows.

A grand piano brought from San Francisco was placed in shiny, black magnificence at one end of the room. Madame DeSecia's accompanist had arrived two days before, and the room was closed for hours at a time so he could practice.

Since Brook had made such a point that the evening would be the most elegant affair ever held at Silver Springs, Addie decided to wear a dress she had been saving—for what she wasn't sure. But now it seemed appropriate. Excitement flushed Addie's cheeks and brightened her eyes as she got dressed. The velvet basque was the color of a ripe persimmon. Tiny amber buttons marched from where the stand-up collar ended in a V, to the waist. The tafetta skirt was a deeper shade, drawn to the back with a velvet bow from which pleated ruffles cascaded down the back.

Addie spent more time than usual doing her hair, experimenting with a new style; swept up from her ears and held with tortoise-shell combs to a fall of curls in back. On impulse she took out her mother's opal jewelry. She held it, looking at it for a long moment, then after only a second's hesitation, she slipped in the earrings and fastened on the necklace. She then considered the effect in the mirror. Perfect!

When she went to see if Mrs. Amberly was ready, Addie's suspicions of Mrs. Amberly's envy of anyone younger or comelier were confirmed by the look of outrage on her employer's face. Obviously Mrs. Amberly felt it was not suitable for a "paid companion" to look so stylish.

But Addie refused to allow anything to spoil this evening for her. She deliberately complimented Mrs. Amberly on her own dress, a brilliant blue taffeta embroidered with black Brussels lace and jet beads. It had probably cost a fortune, although it would have been worn to better advantage by someone twenty years younger and forty pounds lighter.

For all her disparagement of the probable quality of the

evening's entertainment, Mrs. Amberly insisted on their going over from their cottage nearly an hour before the concert was scheduled to begin. That way they could choose the best seats. Even though embarrassed by her employer's pushiness Addie was glad that they did get seats in the front row.

Mrs. Amberly settled herself fussily. "I hope this isn't like some of the ghastly *musicale soirées* I've attended. Not that I expect much. I think she's probably third-rate. I never heard of her myself."

That fact was not much of a criterion by which to judge the artist, Addie thought, but not commenting on Mrs. Amberly's many observations had become one of Addie's skills.

However, when Della DeSecia entered, looking every inch a diva, no one could have failed to be impressed. She was a vision to behold. Gowned in apricot satin embroidered with crystal beads, the bodice draped to show off her white shoulders and rounded bosom. She held a fan edged in marabou. She glittered from the sparkling tiara nestled in the lustrous red-gold waves of her hair to the rhinestone butterflies that fluttered on her peach satin slippers. When she took her place in the curve of the piano the room hushed to awed silence.

As she began to sing in a clear, glorious voice, Addie felt tingles. The program was varied, beginning with a familiar soprano solo from Mozart's *Marriage of Figaro* and followed by the heartbreaking aria from Verdi's *Aida,* which brought tears to Addie's eyes. After a short intermission, she finished with some lighter selections, "leiders," lovely German love songs, and ended with a song from a popular light operetta.

The quiet that fell after the last bell-like note was sung broke into thunderous applause a moment later. Madame DeSecia took several bows and finally accepted the lovely bouquet of yellow roses Brook presented. Then people began to cluster around her with accolades and compliments. Mrs. Amberly was one of the first shoving her way forward to congratulate the singer. Addie let her go.

Still caught up in the music, which had temporarily lifted her out of the mundane, Addie drifted out into the lobby. She found a corner from where she could still see into the main lounge where a beaming Brook hovered over the singer, surrounded by her enthusiastic fans. Addie smiled to see him so happy at his successful achievement of his dream.

Suddenly something caught her attention. Addie drew in her breath. The towering figure of a man in the crowd. It was *he!* The man of her strange encounters! Seated as they were in the front of the room, she had not seen the rest of the audience taking seats behind. If he were among the invited guests, Brook must know him! Her heart began to thump excitedly. Perhaps Brook would introduce him to her during the postconcert reception, which Brook had promised would be as elaborate and elegant as anything given at the Palace Hotel in San Francisco.

A second glance brought the disconcerting fact that *he* was not alone. Standing next to him was a small, slender woman with masses of light, reddish hair, wearing a gray taffeta dress with a lace bertha collar. His wife? The possibility that he might be married had never occurred to her and caused an unexpected pang of dismay. How silly she had been, indulging in romantic daydreams about a stranger. Embarrassed by her own foolish fantasies, Addie panicked. She did not want to see him. Thinking only to escape she turned away and as she did bumped directly into Louis Montand.

"Careful, Miss Pride!" He regarded her quizzically. "Where were you going in such a hurry?"

"It was just a little stuffy," Addie improvised quickly. "I thought I'd get some fresh air."

"Come, then," Montand said, putting a strong hand under Addie's elbow. "I'll find us a nice, quiet spot near a window."

There was nothing Addie could do but accept his invitation. A quick glance informed her the concert crowd was beginning to flow out into the lobby, and she noticed that the alcove toward which they were heading was protected by a large potted palm. Placed just behind it was a small table and two chairs. Here Addie saw she would be concealed from the rest of the room.

Once they were seated, Louis remarked, "A penny for your thoughts, Miss Pride. I was observing you before I spoke to you, and you looked quite lost in another world—at least for a few minutes."

Addie's face grew warm and she wondered how long Montand had been watching her and what her expression might have revealed. She tried to keep her voice casual. "Oh, I think I was just still under the spell of the music. It was truly beautiful, wasn't it?"

"Yes, I suppose it was. Although I must admit music is not my forte. I'm sure I'm sadly lacking in true appreciation of it. Visual beauty attracts me more." His eyes made an appreciative sweep of her. "And to digress for a moment, may I say you are looking very beautiful this evening, Miss Pride."

Addie murmured her thanks. Then he continued. "Are you a student of music? Because if you are, I am certainly willing to learn, and if you'd care to give me your critique of tonight's performance perhaps I could be more appreciative."

"Oh, I'd never dare do that!"

"Come now, I imagine you've studied music to show such rapt interest. Do you play an instrument?"

"Like most Southern girls I was made to take piano lessons, so I play a little but not well at all."

Louis smiled at her indulgently. "I believe you are too modest about your talent. *All* your talents."

The lobby began to fill up with people, and the hum of conversation grew louder. Montand turned to look over his shoulder, then raised an eyebrow. "It amuses me how suddenly all these ranchers and farmers and storekeepers have become aficionados of opera. . . ."

Addie realized he was making fun of the townspeople now lionizing Madame DeSecia. She hated sarcastic comments. It was something she had to live with in her daily life with Mrs. Amberly. But she still hated it. Her father had always said sarcasm was the weapon of cowards. Feeling a stirring of dislike for Louis Montand, she looked at him. What was he really like under that veneer of sophistication?

The crowd began moving en masse into the card room where an extravagant buffet had been set up. A long table covered with a Battenburg-lace tablecloth, illuminated by tall white candles, held two large silver urns at both ends containing iced bottles of champagne; arranged down both sides were platters of sliced meats, salads, fruit, and elaborate desserts.

Apparently unconscious he had said anything Addie might not agree with nor approve of, Montand smiled ingratiatingly and asked, "Shall I get us some refreshment? A glass of wine?"

"I am thirsty. But I think I'd like some lemonade instead of wine."

Montand looked surprised but did not insist she change her request. "I'll be right back," he promised getting up.

After he left, Addie, hidden by the wide palm fronds, watched the panorama of the party. People were still pushing and circling around Madame DeSecia, whom Brook was trying to guide to a place where she could hold court as well as sip some refreshing champagne. From the look on his face, Addie knew Brook was satisfied his goal had been accomplished. The evening was the brilliant success he had hoped. Next she glanced around the room to see if she could find the tall stranger and the woman again. But somehow they had merged into the crowd.

Soon Louis was back. He handed Addie her lemonade then sat down opposite her. He raised his glass of champagne in a toasting gesture. "To music and friendship and coincidence . . ."

Lifting hers, too, Addie took a sip. "That's a curious toast."

"Why so? It was impromptu, although I think appropriate for the moment. I enjoyed the music even though I confessed my ignorance of it; friendship because I hope ours will develop; and coincidence seemed altogether in keeping. Don't you agree, Miss Pride, that coincidence brought you and Madame DeSecia and me all to this small town that I don't think anyone ever heard of twenty-five years ago?" Louis smiled, his eyes narrowed. "I am more convinced than ever of what a large part chance plays in one's life. Sometimes the very things one looks upon as misfortune can be the very things that bring the most good fortune and happiness in life."

"Yes, that is sometimes true," Addie agreed.

"You see there was a series of unfortunate events in my early life—our parents died when I was only a little boy. Estelle was fifteen and at once took over my care. She has been almost like a mother to me ever since. And then as a child I was—delicate, suffering from various illnesses. So much so the doctors thought a change of climate might be advantageous to my health. That is how Estelle and I happened to come to California in the first place, seeking the most healthful place to live. And at last we came to the Napa Valley."

71

He took a long sip of his wine. "As you can see it was a very fortuitous decision of Estelle's, for here I became not only hale and hearty but we are—as they say—in the right place at the right time. We found wonderful land with good, producing vineyards. I foresee a prosperous future—all through no planning of our own. Now, do you understand why I believe in the unplanned, unexpected things in life?"

"For you. But I have known people who blame unforeseen circumstances for bringing them troubles and tribulations and—"

"Yes, but then we cannot blame anyone for our failures. Perhaps I should say I believe in such unpredictable causes to a limited degree. Sometimes we must recognize when life has brought us to a place of decision, and we then, using our knowledge, experience, and wisdom, make the right one."

Addie nodded. "Perhaps you are right."

"Take, for example, this property I own. I intend to make it the best known winery in California. I've been assured it is good, hardy stock, and I have been studying European methods of wine making." He leaned forward, eyes lighted with excitement. "I'll show some of these old-timers around here who think they have a corner on the market. I even have a name for it 'Chateau Montand.' Do you like it?"

"It sounds . . . very French."

Louis threw back his head and laughed. "It *is,* and you, my dear Miss Pride, are very tactful. That was the thing I noticed about you at our introduction. *Almost* the first thing." He paused. "I'm building a home on a beautiful hillside overlooking my vineyards. My sister Estelle is in San Francisco picking out some of the finishing details, drapery material, rugs. I've selected most of the furniture, but I felt it needed a woman's touch to complete the ambiance I want."

He looked at her over the rim of his wine glass, reflectively or was it appraisingly?

"I'd like very much to take you out to see the house as soon as it's finished."

There was no chance for Addie to reply to the invitation because just then Mrs. Amberly lumbered up.

"So here's where you've got to, I've been looking all over for you," she said crossly to Addie. Then she quickly altered her tone of voice. "Oh, Mr. Montand, I didn't see you. . . ."

He rose to his feet, bowed slightly. "You must blame me, Mrs. Amberly. I lured Miss Pride away from the crush of people. We were just enjoying a quiet chat, will you join us?"

Addie saw her employer undergo a painful decision. Addie guessed by this time of the evening, Mrs. Amberly's corset was biting cruelly into her layers of fat, her shoes killing her feet. Most certainly she could hardly wait to be in the privacy of her cottage where she could undress, soak her feet, and relax. On the other hand, Addie knew Mrs. Amberly was in awe of Louis Montand, and his invitation was a tempting detour from such relief.

As Mrs. Amberly hesitated, Montand suggested smoothly, "Perhaps the hour is too late? For a music lover like yourself, Mrs. Amberly, as delightful as the evening has been, you are probably emotionally exhausted. So may I escort you two ladies to your cottage?"

Addie could not help admire Montand's adroitness in managing to get out of an awkward half-hour's chat with Mrs. Amberly, a woman he clearly disdained.

Flattered, Mrs. Amberly took the arm he offered and, ignoring Addie, directed her conversation to him. "Mr. Stanton introduced me to Madame DeSecia—what a nice person—so thoughtful, Mr. Stanton, I mean. I thought she was a bit—well, stand-offish, if you know what I mean. And she can hardly speak English. . . ."

Inwardly Addie groaned. Didn't she realize that Della DeSecia *was* Italian, a star at some of the most renowned opera houses in Europe? The fact that this was her first American tour was written in the brochure Brook had had printed for this occasion. Evidently Mrs. Amberly had not read it.

Addie followed Montand's slow progress with Mrs. Amberly through the lobby. Although the crowd was beginning to thin, people were still gathered in small clusters chatting. At the front door, for some reason, Addie turned her head and saw—standing not five feet away—the tall stranger.

He was looking at her with an expression that startled her. Suddenly she knew she was blushing and why. Dazed, her heart hammering, Addie hurried out the door in the wake of Montand and Mrs. Amberly.

As they walked across the grounds she only half heard what Mrs. Amberly was rattling on about. At the cottage porch Montand said in his most gracious manner, "Good night, Mrs. Amberly, Miss Pride. It's been a pleasure. I hope when my sister returns from San Francisco we can have the pleasure of having you two ladies dine with us."

Addie saw Mrs. Amberly's mouth drop open in disbelief. She mumbled something incoherent, then glanced at Addie as if indignant that the invitation she had longed for from the Montands would include her *paid companion!* Inside the cottage Mrs. Amberly shambled off to her own room without so much as a good night to Addie.

As Addie went into her bedroom and shut the door, she felt suddenly let down. Something in the music tonight had struck a resounding chord deep within her. It brought back a memory from the past, one she had almost forgotten. When she was a little girl, maybe six years old, she had been awakened by the voices of her parents' departing guests and the sound of carriage wheels beneath her bedroom window. She had slipped out of bed, run barefoot into the hall, leaned over the banister, and saw her parents dancing in the moonlight shining in from the open front door as her father hummed a waltz. She had watched as they circled slowly ending in an embrace that seemed to go on forever. Addie had tiptoed back to bed feeling somehow assured, safe in their love.

Her old longings for a love like she had seen in her parents, in Aunt Susan and Uncle Myles, even in Emily and Evan, swept over her in a deep wrenching loneliness. Would she ever find it?

Irrelevantly the old adage floated into her mind: "Journeys end in lovers meeting."

Was her journey to California to end in meeting her love? And who was it? Addie thought of the three men she had met since her arrival. Brook Stanton was the first. As interesting and fascinating as he was, Addie could not even consider him a possibility. Brook was a gambler, just like the man on the riverboat, and possibly every bit as dangerous. Louis Montand? He was undeniably attracted to her but—

Then the image of the tall stranger came. Could it be *he?*

Chapter 7

One evening, a few days after the concert, Addie was entering the lobby with Mrs. Amberly when Louis, who was standing at the reception desk with a tall, slender woman, saw them and raised his hand in greeting. After saying something to his companion, he came across the room toward them.

"Good evening, Mrs. Amberly, Miss Pride," Louis greeted them. "What a coincidence. I was just talking about you to my sister." He addressed them both, but it was on Addie his gaze lingered. "Estelle returned from San Francisco this afternoon, and we were just about to dine. Would you ladies care to join us?"

Mrs. Amberly blinked. She opened her mouth, then snapped it shut like a startled turtle. Was she undecided whether to accept the invitation?

Her employer could not have been unaware of Louis's attentiveness to Addie since the night of the Madame DeSecia's performance. Although *this* was the social opportunity Mrs. Amberly had long sought, Addie realized it galled her to receive it through her companion.

She glanced at her employer, watching Mrs. Amberly swallow this bitter pill.

"I realize this is short notice," Louis continued, "but after all, we are fellow guests here, and I say there is no need for formality in this casual atmosphere. Don't you agree, Mrs. Amberly?"

Mrs. Amberly's own eagerness to be seen at the Montands' table overcame the umbrage she *could* have manufactured at such a last-minute invitation.

"Well, if you're sure it won't be an intrusion—"

"Intrusion? Nonsense. It would be a pleasure," Louis reassured, cutting her protestation short. "Now come along, I'd like to introduce my sister."

While this little scene was taking place, Addie noticed Louis's sister, standing aloofly at some distance. She made no move to join them or to add her own to her brother's urgings for their company at dinner.

"Well, if you're *quite* sure," Mrs. Amberly dragged out the words as she glanced into the adjoining lounge. Puzzled, Addie followed her glance, then saw the Brunell sisters seated in there, craning their necks. She then guessed Mrs. Amberly's purpose in delaying. Mrs. Amberly wanted to make sure her card partners witnessed her being escorted by Mr. Montand over to his sister. Assured of that, she took Louis's arm. With some inner reluctance Addie took the other arm he offered.

Estelle Montand very much resembled her brother. Although he had told her she was fifteen years his senior, her brown hair, sweeping up from the same high forehead as his, was untouched by gray. She had the same sharply defined features in a pale olive-complexioned face. The marked difference between them was their eyes. While his were keenly alive, hers were moody and melancholy.

Everything about Miss Montand exhibited expensive taste. She was dressed in a tobacco-colored silk promenade dress trimmed with fluted ruffles, and carried a glossy brown alligator handbag; her pointed shoes were of cordovan leather. From between the reveres of her jacket rippled a jabot of ecru Brussels lace, fastened by a carnelian and gold brooch. Addie always noticed such details because her mother had been beautifully fashionable. Perhaps now that she could no longer afford fine clothing made Addie aware of them more.

"Estelle, may I present Mrs. Amberly, one of our fellow guests."

"So nice to meet you at last," gushed Mrs. Amberly.

"How do you do," replied Miss Montand with weary condescension.

"And this, Estelle, is Adelaide. Miss Adelaide Pride," Louis announced bringing Addie forward.

"Miss Pride." Estelle nodded. "So, you are real after all." She regarded Addie steadily for a long moment before extending her hand. It felt as dry as a leaf, and her fingers only lightly touched Addie's palm, then quickly withdrew. A smile briefly touched her thin lips, and she lifted an eyebrow. "Louis has waxed so rhapsodically about you, I began to believe you must be a figment of his overwrought imagination."

Addie felt the warmth rise into her cheeks under Miss Montand's gaze, and she knew she was blushing.

An awkward pause followed Estelle's comment. Louis was so busy gazing at Addie he lost the thread of conversation and missed his sister's implication. Addie was acutely conscious of Mrs. Amberly's stare.

Oblivious to both his sister's coolness and Mrs. Amberly's suspicious glare, Louis smiled serenely at Addie as if he had brought off some brilliant coup, "Well, shall we go over to the dining hall?"

Miss Montand's remark about Louis's talking about her made Addie uncomfortable. She was positive it was only at his insistence that she and Mrs. Amberly had been asked to join him and his sister. Perhaps Estelle had anticipated dining alone with her brother after being gone so many weeks.

At dinner Mrs. Amberly monopolized the conversation, trying to impress the Montands with long, boring tales of her European travels combined with name-dropping the famous hotels, mentioning some of the world-known celebrities and minor royalty who had been guests at the same time, broadly hinting that she had been acquainted with such personages. Certainly the Montands could see through this pitiful charade.

Didn't the woman have any sense at all? Didn't she know how she sounded? Didn't she realize the Montands would have a good laugh over her when they were alone?

During one of Mrs. Amberly's monologues Addie glimpsed a glint of undeniable scorn in Louis's eyes. Quickly, she lowered her eyes so that she would not have to meet his. She did not want to seem to be sharing in any way his silent mocking of her employer. What troubled her even more was what she saw in his eyes every time their glances met. It was something more than casual admiration, and it gave her pause. Did she want Louis Montand to be so attracted to her?

As the dinner progressed Addie became more and more aware of the subtle undercurrent of resentment beneath Miss Montand's icy politeness. She began to think the dinner would never end when something unexpected happened. Looking up from her untouched plate she saw Brook enter the dining room. With him were a couple. Immediately Addie felt her stomach tighten, her cheeks flame.

The man was the tall stranger who mysteriously intruded her daytime thoughts and invaded her dreams. On his arm was the same woman who had been with him at the concert!

With mixed emotions she saw Brook was approaching

their table bringing the couple with him. Addie clenched her hands, crushing the napkin on her lap.

With his usual cordiality, Brook greeted them. "Good evening, ladies and Mr. Montand. May I present Mrs. Freda Wegner and Mr. Rexford Lyon."

Addie's first reaction was relief. They weren't married after all. Her next reaction was to chide herself. What possible difference could it make to her? As Brook introduced each of them in turn, she was conscious that Mr. Lyon's gaze was as intense and unsettling as during their first encounter.

Carrying on his usual congenial conversation, Brook explained, "Mrs. Wegner and Mr. Lyon are both longtime residents of our beautiful area. Both are vintners. You have perhaps heard of Wegner Wineries and Lyon's Court?"

Addie chanced a second covert glance at the woman. She was perhaps thirty, very slender, looking small standing between the two men. She was not especially pretty. Her face was pale and lightly freckled, but her expression was alert and interested, her eyes keen and intelligent. She had a thin nose and a mouth that revealed . . . what? Addie wasn't sure. Perhaps that she had known sadness, suffering of some kind or physical pain. Possibly she was a widow since she was dressed in moderate mourning, a black dress trimmed with white ruching, stylish but not fashionable.

However, her smile was sweet and her voice low and pleasant when she spoke. "I hope you folks will enjoy your stay in the valley."

"Oh, the Montands plan to live here, Freda," Brook corrected her. "They've bought land—adjoining Lyon's, right, Rex? And they're building a magnificent house. Near completion now, isn't it, Louis?"

Louis shrugged. "As long as I keep behind those workers—who tend to loaf off, I'm afraid, if someone isn't riding herd on them every minute."

Addie saw Mrs. Wegner and Mr. Lyon exchange a knowing glance. She recalled what Brook had said about valley "old-timers" being cliquish, not too eager to have "outsiders" move into the valley. Were Mrs. Wegner and Lyon among those who resented the Montands buying up such a large amount of property and settling there?

But of course, nothing of such importance was discussed. A few more pleasantries were exchanged; then they left. Brook accompanied them across the room, seated them at a table opposite, in Addie's direct line of vision.

For the rest of the evening, Addie could not resist a few glances their way. She found herself distracted by their presence, curious about their relationship. Were they lovers or just friends? Or somehow related? Was Mrs. Wegner in mourning? If so, was it for a husband? Or a close relative? Although they seemed deeply involved in conversation, they did not seem to have the aura of romantic intimacy.

Addie did not have much chance to spend dwelling on the situation at the other table. She was too much aware of the tension she felt at her own table. Every time Louis addressed her, Mrs. Amberly darted her a sharp look. Louis made no effort to hide his interest in her. It was as if tonight, with her introduction to his sister, Louis felt free to express his attraction to her openly.

Addie had come to know her employer by now. She could almost read Mrs. Amberly's mind from the speculative glances she was casting at her. Was she debating whether or not to nip it in the bud or use Louis's interest to *her* own advantage?

Finally the meal ended and Miss Montand, pleading weariness from her trip, left them in the lobby to go to her room. Mrs. Amberly's bridge partners were waiting, and after thanking Louis profusely for dinner she departed to the card room.

"May I escort you to your cottage, Miss Pride?"

"No, thank you. I must stay until Mrs. Amberly has finished her game. She has some difficulty walking and needs assistance after sitting for so long."

A look of distaste passed like a shadow over Louis's face. He started to say something then changed his mind. "I meant what I said about wanting to take you out to Chateau Montand as soon as it is completed. The furniture and other things Estelle ordered this trip should be arriving soon, and when the interior painting is finished it will be ready to show and to move into. . . ." He paused significantly. "I *do* very much want *you* to see it."

Not knowing exactly how to respond to the emphasis in his words, Addie murmured something that she hoped was appropriate, and they said good night.

Later, alone in her room, Addie opened her journal. Maybe by writing down her mixed feelings she could sort them out. First the facts. Tonight she had learned her tall stranger was a native of Napa Valley, a rancher and vintner. This fourth encounter had left her even more confused. There was no doubt that something unexplainable had taken place between them on each occasion. But tonight he had been in the company of Freda Wegner. This was the second time *she* had seen them together. Were they more than close friends?

Feb. 14th

Well, at last, Mrs. A. has achieved her goal. She has met Miss Estelle Montand, *the sister!* It was as cool a meeting as one can possibly envision. I had the distinct impression that Miss Montand would rather the introduction had never taken place. I was a bit taken aback by the invitation to join them at dinner, which was all Louis's idea.

The most *unexpected* incident occurred after we were all seated. Brook escorted a couple into the dining hall, and when I saw who they were, I was quite startled. It was *my stranger*. Well, perhaps that is an exaggeration. It was the man I saw the day I arrived here. It all came back to me.

That feeling I had as I stepped off the train that he was there to meet me! Of course, it is all foolishness. But still, I had the exact same sensation tonight when we were introduced. His name is Rex Lyon.

Sitting at her desk, in the lamplight, Addie dipped her pen into the inkwell ready to continue writing. But she found it hard to go on. Pen poised above the pages her mind wandered hopelessly.

Then she began to think of Louis Montand. It was impossible to ignore his interest. Certainly he was charming, worldly, and sophisticated. However, his relationship with his sister was puzzling. Was it natural to be so deferential, so dependent on his sister's opinions, eager for her approval? Why had it been so important to him for Estelle to meet *her?*

In spite of any effort Mrs. Amberly might make to associate with Louis's sister, Addie felt sure Estelle would discourage any overtures of friendship. Also Addie sensed Estelle's disapproval of Louis's interest in her.

Addie put down her pen and closed her journal, her thoughts too disjointed to write more. Why should it matter at all what Estelle thinks? It was fairly apparent that her status of paid companion put Addie in a different social class than the Montands. *Why should I care?* she thought.

Estelle Montand? Aloof, cold, snobbish. Did Addie recognize those unlikable traits in Louis's sister because she herself had the same ones? Addie had to admit she often felt superior to others. Is that what she had seen in Estelle Montand that she disliked?

God help me, she thought, *if I am like that!* She knew she looked down on Mrs. Amberly, thought her lacking in social graces, mentally groaned at her murder of the King's English, her ignorance and malapropisms.

Addie flipped open the leather journal again and quickly

wrote in the date and printed boldly in block letters BEWARE OF PRIDE. PRIDE IS THE MOST DANGEROUS OF ALL FAULTS!

She undressed, put on her nightie, and picked up her Bible. The habit of reading a verse or two before going to sleep instilled early in her life still held. She knew the Scripture she needed tonight but she wasn't quite sure where to find it. Thumbing through the pages she came upon Obadiah. *Obadiah?* Addie stopped short. She stared at the chapter heading. Guiltily she realized she didn't even know such a book was in the Bible. It was short, only two pages.

Addie had been taught a rule of thumb in searching Scripture for guidance. That was to start reading until a certain line of a verse struck you or "quickened." If and when that happened, that was the particular lesson God was trying to teach you at that moment.

With this in mind Addie began to read. It took only a few minutes to read through the entire book of Obadiah. But two lines seemed to speak directly to her: "The pride of your heart has deceived you" and "As you have done, it shall be done to you."

Thoughtfully, Addie shut the book, blew out her lamp, and got into bed. She knew she often had a critical spirit, tended to make snap judgments about people—like her judgments about Estelle Montand and, yes, Mrs. Amberly. It was something she needed to guard against.

Lying there in the darkness, the verse she had first sought still eluded her, but the odd ones she had discovered in Obadiah kept echoing through her mind. That's what God wanted her to learn.

Addie's self-declared indifference to Estelle Montand's opinion and its effects on her, she soon discovered was wrong. Contrary to what she had thought, the arrival of Louis's sister *did* make a difference in Addie's life at Silver Springs.

After the night they dined with Montands things took an unexpected turn.

In the first place, Mrs. Amberly set out on a campaign to cultivate Estelle in ways that humiliated Addie. Mrs. Amberly seemed always on the lookout to waylay Estelle, corner her, trap her in a conversation or with an invitation. Mentally gritting her teeth, Addie had to stand by, dying by inches of embarrassment, while Mrs. Amberly, undaunted by Estelle's coldness, pursued her. If Miss Montand could not avoid her, Mrs. Amberly would summarily dismiss Addie, sending her away on a contrived errand—"Do see that the maid picks up my laundry, Miss Pride" or "Go to the post office, I need stamps" so that she could enjoy Miss Montand's forced company by herself.

It was doubly humiliating because it was obvious that Miss Montand could not endure Mrs. Amberly. Why could Mrs. Amberly not see that herself? Addie was terribly aware of unconcealed dislike in Estelle's eyes that included Addie as well as her employer.

Meanwhile, Louis Montand was not around the hotel as much as usual. He spent more and more time out at their property overseeing the finishing of the house. To her surprise Addie found she missed him. At least his company had helped pass the time during Mrs. Amberly's long evening card sessions. Louis was interesting, had many witty stories to tell about his travels and experiences. At least it was a welcome change from nightly being subjected to the overheard carping conversation of the bridge players.

Soon both Montands began to leave the hotel early in the morning to go out to their house, often not returning until dinnertime. It was usually in the evenings that Addie saw Louis in the dining hall. Of course, he was always with Estelle, and often they were accompanied by Milton Drew, their lawyer, or their architect, Leland Parks. But Louis always stopped at Mrs. Amberly's table to pay his respects.

One such evening, Louis told them he and Estelle would be leaving the hotel in a matter of days to move into their house although it was unfurnished except for the rooms they would be occupying.

At this Mrs. Amberly wagged a pudgy finger at him playfully. "Now, Mr. Montand, I hope you won't forget *us* once you're all settled in—for we shall miss *you* dreadfully here at the resort. You and your sister are such an asset to this place."

Addie clenched her jaw and moved the silver at her place nervously. How could Mrs. Amberly be so gauche? But Louis managed to handle Mrs. Amberly's obvious angling for an invitation and get a message to Addie as well.

"Certainly not, Mrs. Amberly. In a community this size I am sure we shall run into each other often." His eyes sought Addie's as he added, "I have no intention of allowing the pleasant acquaintances I've made here at Silver Springs to be neglected."

Later that evening Brook ambled into the card room where Addie was at her usual place waiting out Mrs. Amberly's card game. He pulled up a chair beside her. Leaning close he lowered his voice confidentially. "I couldn't help overhearing Louis Montand's reply to your dinner companion's *imploring* him not to forget his friends at Silver Springs once he moves to his grand new chateau!"

Addie knew Brook well enough to detect the half-teasing, half-serious note in his voice. She smiled but made no comment.

"He's quite taken with you, you know," Brook went on, regarding her closely, as if to see how she reacted to this statement.

"Oh?"

"Oh, yes, indeed. I'd say, quite taken." Brook still observed her shrewdly. "He's asked me all sorts of things about you. In a very gentlemanly way, of course. I told him

86

I only knew what I'd observed. That you were—apart from being beautiful—every inch a lady, with an impeccable character, and from a long line of blue bloods from one of the first families of Virginia."

Addie had to laugh. "Brook, you're incorrigible!"

"Why? What do you mean? Wasn't I right? You are an aristocrat of the first water, aren't you? Or have you come here under false pretenses?" He pretended to act very shocked.

"I suppose I could have and gotten away with it. California is a long way from Virginia." She smiled. "I guess anyone could make up any kind of background and no one would be the wiser."

"How true. And I imagine a good many people do just that. Who knows? Mr. Montand himself might be an impostor. As well as his very proper sister. Maybe they are both fugitives with a dark mysterious past, buying all that property and building this mansion on a hilltop with ill-gotten money. . . ." He paused. "What is it they say?—Nothing is as it seems, much is smoke and mirrors and magic." Then he laughed and got to his feet. "Who are *they*, anyhow? Everyone is always quoting *they* but no one seems to know who *they* are."

"Oh, Brook, what a treat you are! You always make me laugh."

"Good! Life is too serious. As *they* say—" He looked at her for a few seconds more. "Nevertheless, it is true, you know, Louis Montand has serious intentions toward you, Miss Pride. Mark my words, you'll have a proposal from him within a very few weeks if not sooner, or I'm greatly mistaken."

"You *are* mistaken, Brook," Addie said firmly, positive of her intuitive feeling that Louis's sister would have to approve of any choice of a bride Louis made and that Estelle did not approve of her.

"Wait and see if I am or not. If I were giving odds—" Brook grinned.

"I don't believe in gambling," she cut in with pretend primness.

"Then take a sure tip from an experienced gambler and bet on it."

"You're impossible, Brook!" Addie shook her head, and he sauntered off.

As it turned out it was Brook who provided Louis with the opportunity to issue Addie a very special invitation. Since the Montands had stayed at Silver Springs Hotel during the eighteen months of construction of their house, he announced he was giving them a farewell dinner party.

All the hotel guests were included, and to Addie's pleasure and pain, upon entering the dining room that evening, she saw Rexford Lyon among the local invited acquaintances of the Montands. She assumed it was because now they would be neighbors, since the Montands' property bordered Lyon's Court land. Her first pleasure at seeing him was followed by dismay when she saw Freda Wegner was also present.

Addie was angry at herself that the thought that they might be more than friends caused her such dismay. He was a stranger! What difference should whatever they were to each other make to her?

However, the minute after she entered the dining hall and he saw her, she was sure he had started over to her when Louis, seeing her at the same time, intercepted and came to her side.

"You're sitting beside me, at my right, in the place of honor, at my request!" he told her, smiling. Taking her arm he led her over to the large, exquisitely decorated table and held the chair for her. As he took his place next to her, he whispered, "I haven't had a minute alone with you for weeks—the dragonfly is always hovering."

Addie looked at him, startled, wondering if he meant Mrs. Amberly or his sister. Of course, he meant Mrs. Amberly. Louis and Estelle were singularly devoted. Only occasionally had she noticed the slightest suggestion of irritation on his part of something Estelle said or did.

To her surprise Brook escorted Freda Wegner over and seated her beside Addie. He leaned down between them. "I wanted you two to get to know each other. I have a hunch you could be great friends."

This could be an unexpected opportunity. By some tactful questioning Addie thought she would be able to find out just what Mrs. Wegner's and Rex Lyon's relationship was. However, there was not much chance for a personal exchange. The gentleman on Freda's right monopolized her throughout most of the meal while Louis did the same to Addie. Besides, as master of ceremonies, Brook demanded everyone's attention as he held forth with flowery speeches at intervals between courses, waxing loquaciously about the future of the valley, Calistoga in particular, and how wonderful it was to welcome newcomers like the Montands who would add to its prosperity and the renown of the region.

Brook was an ebullient host, and the dinner party was his version of a Roman banquet. The food was superb; merriment and laughter were as plentiful as the champagne that flowed like proverbial water as frequent toasts were offered and drunk.

The round table at which they were seated provided accessibility to everyone and much cross talk was possible. As the evening progressed Louis, flushed and excited with the prospect of moving at last into his long-planned house, with a successful future almost assured, became more and more exhilarated.

In contrast, Addie became more and more remote. Louis, who had been verbally possessive at the beginning of the meal, became engaged in earnest discussion about the best kind of grape vines and methods of production with a local vintner on his left.

Seated at a some distance from Rex Lyon, Addie was careful to avoid looking directly at him. However, if she inadvertently glanced his way, he seemed to be gazing at her. It was as if they both were aware of something that neither of them understood.

After dessert—brandied peaches in meringue shells—the plates were carried away and coffee was brought in. Brook rose to his feet again and, tapping his fork on the crystal goblet for quiet, he made a closing speech.

By this time it was past midnight. After Brook's words, everyone began rising from their places, moving toward the lobby, and preparing to leave. Louis was finishing up a conversation with the man beside him when Freda touched Addie's arm.

"We didn't have a chance to get to know each other better, as Brook hoped we would, did we? Too much going on!" She gestured to the crowd. "But I would like very much for us to become friends. Would you be able to come visit some afternoon? I could send a buggy for you."

"How kind of you. Yes, I would enjoy that. I am free on Thursdays."

"Good, I'll send a note to confirm. Good night." Freda pressed Addie's hand and went to join Rex Lyon who stood at the door as if waiting for her.

Again Addie wondered about them. Rex had only nodded, acknowledging their previous introduction, but made no move toward her. Of course, Louis had been at her side all evening. Still, Addie felt oddly disappointed that he had not even come to speak to her.

Addie had no time to dwell on her feelings because Louis

leaned toward her, saying, "Estelle is tired and wants to leave, so I can't take you back to the cottage. I'll send a note. I want to bring you out to the house, want you to be our first guest. I want to have some time with you away from all these greedy-for-gossip eyes. I feel we are like goldfish in a bowl here—," he made a wry face, "—especially with your *bodyguard* nearby."

He took her hand, held it. He might have continued holding it while looking meaningfully into her eyes if Estelle had not tapped him on the shoulder.

"Do let us go, Louis." Her voice was heavily laced with fatigue—or boredom? "It is very late, and I'm afraid I'm starting a migraine." Then added in a pained voice, "I'm *sure* Miss Pride will excuse you."

Chilled by Miss Montand's steely stare, Addie at once said, "Of course."

As the Montands left, Addie looked around just in time to see Rex Lyon and Freda go out the door. For some reason she felt ridiculously abandoned.

Chapter 8

True to her word Freda sent a note to Addie the day after the party to invite her to spend the day at the Wegner Ranch the following Thursday. Delighted, Addie immediately wrote back accepting the invitation.

A few days later, one evening just before her card game, Mrs. Amberly sent Addie back to the cottage for a pillow for her back. As Addie re-entered the lobby with the pillow, Brook came out of his office near the reception desk and motioned her over in a curiously secretive manner.

"What is it?" she asked curiously.

He looked mysteriously excited.

"My dear Miss Pride, or Addie, as you've now permitted me to address you." He spoke in a low tone of voice, and Addie felt instinctively he was up to something. "I hope I am not presuming on our friendship when I say I have always ascertained you to be a young woman of considerable courage, foresight, maybe even a little recklessness—or perhaps that is the wrong word. Certainly *adventurous*. Else why would you have vouchsafed to cross the country via the newly constructed railroad—alone—to accept, sight unseen, a position with an unknown employer and come to this valley hidden in the hills, about which you knew little or nothing?"

"Just what are you leading up to, Brook?" Addie asked warily, recognizing his persuasive methods in full force.

He put one hand to his heart, affected an innocent expression. "Up to something? Me? You think I'm about to make a preposterous proposal?"

"Perhaps," Addie said doubtfully.

Brook's eyes twinkled. "What makes you think so?"

"The grand inventory you're making of all my supposed virtues, which, I must say, you are grossly exaggerating."

"All right, I'll tell you straight out. I'm thinking of initiating a new treatment here, one that will not only be beneficial to my guests' health but may have amazing rejuvenating effects."

"Rejuvenating? Don't tell me you've discovered the Fountain of Youth right here in Calistoga?" Addie demanded in mock amazement.

"Well, perhaps not precisely. However, our mineral water *is* widely accepted as having positive health potential and restorative qualities. My idea will combine those benefits with an ancient Indian cleansing and purification ritual."

Addie put her head to one side and speared Brook with a suspicious look. "And what has this got to do with *me?* And my so-called adventurous spirit?"

Brook hesitated a split second, then said in a rush, "I want *you* to be the first to benefit from it."

Addie gasped, "You want *me* to be your guinea pig?"

"That's hardly the word for it."

"Well, I don't know what else you'd call it."

"I'm offering you a chance to be the first woman—the first non-Indian woman—to experience this treatment, to reap its myriad benefits."

"You're serious, aren't you?"

"Quite." He paused, watching for her reaction, then

93

continued. "I want you to tell me honestly what you think of it, whether you feel other women coming here would enjoy it, be happy about the results. If you agree, then I believe I'll have something to offer here at Silver Springs Resort that not even the most famous expensive resorts of Europe can offer people in search of health, renewed vigor, and beauty." He paused again. "Will you help me by taking the treatment?"

"What does it involve?"

"A mud bath. Now don't look shocked—," he cautioned her. "The baths are a mixture of the purest organic soil and volcanic ash and mineral springs water. The Indians of this valley came here for hundreds of years to bathe in the natural hot springs. The healing qualities are world renowned." He held up both hands as if to ward off any protest on Addie's part. "It will be absolutely private. The native Indian woman I've consulted will be there to assist you. She knows every phase of the routine. Addie, I promise you it will in no way cause you any embarrassment or discomfort. In fact, you'll feel absolutely marvelous."

Addie looked at Brook suspiciously.

"Trust me, Addie, I wouldn't suggest this if I weren't sure you'd enjoy and benefit from it."

"When will this great experiment take place?"

"Since it will be—at least, for the present—*our* secret, I suggest we plan it for the same time as Mrs. Amberly is having her treatment at the bathhouse. That will eliminate any questions on her part and any explanations on yours. You'll not be under any pressure and be able to relax and enjoy it."

"I don't know, Brook—"

"*Believe* me, Addie, you will *love* the results."

"I'll think about it—"

"What's to think about? I promise you a unique, pleasurable experience. Just say you will."

"Oh, Brook, can't it wait? I'm in a hurry, Mrs. Amberly's waiting for her pillow, and—"

"Please, Addie, I assure you, you will thank me for giving you the opportunity—"

"Oh, for pity's sake, Brook!" Exasperated, Addie laughed. "All *right!* I give in!"

"Great! Thank you. Tomorrow I'll come for you at the cottage and escort you myself," Brook said triumphantly and went out the front door, whistling.

Suddenly Addie had the feeling of being observed. Turning, she saw that Mrs. Amberly was standing in the archway of the card room. How long had she been there watching? Watching her with Brook. As usual, Brook had used wild gestures to make his point, talking with his hands as he tried to persuade her. She had probably been equally emphatic in arguing against it. How must the scene have looked? What kind of interpretation might Mrs. Amberly have put on their conversation? Addie could only guess.

"What kept you so long?" Mrs. Amberly scowled.

"I'm sorry," was Addie's only reply. Why should she explain when clearly Mrs. Amberly had seen that Brook had delayed her.

Mrs. Amberly grabbed the pillow and waddled ahead of Addie back to her waiting card partners without so much as a thank you.

Addie thought she had become used to her employer's surliness. Nonetheless, she still resented it. She hated the feeling of having to account for every action. She knew she had to accept she was Mrs. Amberly's employee and all that went with it. But she didn't have to like it.

Addie went into the card room and seated herself not far from the card players. She took out the needlepoint she brought along to pass the time on these interminable evenings. She felt upset. Not because she had agreed to participate in Brook's experiment—although that might turn out to be a foolish mistake. It was her own ignominious situation that she chafed against.

Paid companions were not unlike the governesses Addie had observed growing up. Many Southern families sent their sons up north to be educated, but for their daughters they hired Northern governesses. Even as a young girl Addie was sensitive to their ambiguous position in the wealthy households in which they were employed. They were neither fish nor fowl. They took their meals with the family but were not treated as either relatives or guests. Mostly they were ignored. Even their influence in the schoolroom, where they should have received respect, was minimal. Southern parents, for the most part, considered their daughters' education of minor importance. A girl's future depended on making a good marriage, becoming the bride of someone in their class. *That* was her priority. Her attendance at a party or ball at a neighboring plantation *always* took precedence, even when it meant weeks of no lessons. This often left the poor young teacher wandering like a lost soul by herself in a deserted schoolroom or empty house. Governesses were never invited to accompany their charges to any of the parties or other events, nor were they ever included in the ones given at the home where they were employed. Addie had often looked at these women with pity, never dreaming that one day she would be in a similar position.

Recalling those days, Addie realized now these young women were probably of good family, perhaps even from backgrounds as privileged as her own, but fallen on hard times so that they were forced to earn their living. Certainly these Northern women were better educated than most of their Southern sisters. They probably had a wealth of ideas, interests, and intelligence to contribute to social occasions.

Yet they were pushed into the background for years—the best years of their lives.

How sad to be within sight and sound of pretty clothes, parties, music, dancing, and good times and not be allowed to enjoy them. They probably had been the same age as Addie was now, or perhaps even younger! After all, once you passed twenty-five you were on the brink of spinsterhood, and, if unmarried, a few years later you would be considered completely without hope!

Worse even than being relegated to the sidelines of social life would be—especially for someone as independent and proud as Addie—being obliged to be conciliatory, never expressing an opinion. Governesses must have lived under the constant fear of offending and being dismissed. That would have been a real threat if, like Addie, they might have had elderly parents or relatives dependent on part of their small salaries.

That was her own problem, the Sword of Damocles hanging over her own head. If she lost her job with Mrs. Amberly, it would mean the difference between the few comforts the money sent Aunt Susan and Uncle Myles provided or deprivation.

What a lot she was learning, understanding, now, if that was any consolation! Didn't Shakespeare write "sweet are the uses of adversity"? Perhaps this year would be richer for its very poverty than she could have predicted.

The next morning after Mrs. Amberly had gone for her regular treatment, grumbling as usual to one of the bathhouse attendants, Addie waited anxiously for Brook. He arrived almost immediately as though he had waited for the coast to be clear. He was in a jovial mood as he walked with her to the far end of the grounds where the last guest cottage was located, and there he left her.

"All right, Addie, everything's all set." He took her hand and raised it ceremoniously to his lips and smiled. "Enjoy!"

With some trepidation Addie went up to the cottage door and knocked. Almost immediately it was opened by a short bronze-skinned woman with straight dark hair drawn from a center part into a braid down her back.

"Good morning, Miss Pride. My name is Oona," she said in a pleasant, low voice. She smiled as she motioned Addie inside. The interior of the cottage was nearly empty. It was one of the most recently built ones, and it was not furnished like the others.

"If you will disrobe, miss," the woman suggested gently.

"Disrobe?" echoed Addie thinking perhaps she had better not. "Why?"

"For the treatment. For the mud bath." The woman parted plain white canvas curtains and revealed a tublike wooden structure filled with a dark gray mixture from which a vapor was rising causing herb-scented steam to fill the small room.

Addie swallowed. "I'm to get in *that?*"

The woman smiled, her teeth very white against her swarthy skin. "Oh, yes, miss. It's very nice," she assured her. "May I help you undress?"

Addie had half a notion to bolt out the door but then she remembered Brook's reassurances together with the fact that she was rather pleased he considered her progressive enough to try something as new and startling as this.

Shyly Addie let the woman unbutton her blouse and assist her out of her skirt and petticoats, chemise and pantaloons. She then wrapped Addie's hair in a soft cotton towel and showed her how to place herself into the tub. First to sit on the wooden ledge, then holding onto handles on either side, to swing her legs over. Slowly Addie felt herself sink into the warm, gritty, moist "mud," which was, the woman told her, a mixture of mineral water, volcanic ash, and various natural herbs. The woman then packed it around and over her body from her neck to her toes. To Addie's absolute astonishment it felt wonderful.

There was a curved pillow cradling her neck and head, and Oona placed a folded cool cloth over her forehead and eyes, saying soothingly, "Now, just relax."

At first the weight of the warm mud seemed to press too heavily on her bare body. Gradually, however, Addie *did* lose all track of time and seemed to drift and float. She could almost feel all the knots of tension that had become a constant in her life—since becoming Mrs. Amberly's flunky—seep away in a kind of glorious euphoria.

"Time now to get out," Oona said just as Addie felt she was almost going to sleep.

Getting out was a bit harder than getting in had been, but with Oona's help Addie managed. The mud still clung to her body, and Oona led her over to a wooden stall where, with a hose, she freed her from most of it.

"Now, miss, you bathe." She opened a door into a rather Spartan bathroom and assisted her into a deep white porcelain tub filled with the bubbling mineral salts water. With a large sponge Oona scrubbed her back then handed the sponge to Addie for her to do the rest of the cleansing herself. This part of the treatment felt great too, stimulating and energizing. Maybe Brook actually *had* happened on an idea that would become a unique part of anyone's visit to the resort.

Oona soon reappeared and held out a huge towel for Addie to wrap herself in as she stepped out of the tub. "You like?" Oona asked hopefully.

"Very much."

"Now time to rest." Oona led her into another room where there was a small cot. She helped Addie stretch out, then she placed a light blanket over her, tucking it in on all sides, as one might tuck in an infant. Again a cool damp cloth, wrung out in some sweet scented water, was placed across Addie's eyes and forehead. Then Oona left quietly, leaving Addie to sleep dreamlessly.

Addie wasn't sure how long she had been there when she felt Oona's gentle touch awakening her.

"Sorry, miss, but Mr. Stanton told me to have you back to your cottage by noon."

"Oh, my goodness! I can't believe I spent the whole morning like this!" Addie leaned up on both elbows, feeling a little dazed as Oona helped her into a sitting position.

"I help you dress," offered Oona, and Addie saw she had brought her clothes into the room.

Walking back across the grounds toward the cottage she was surprised to see a dark green one-horse carriage in front of her cottage. As she approached, Louis Montand got out and started toward her.

"I've been looking everywhere for you!" he said with a slight frown of annoyance. "I was afraid I'd missed you. I was just about to try driving up and down the streets of town searching for you."

"I was. . . .," Addie began, wondering how she could possibly explain where she had been or what she had been doing for the last hour.

Then she saw Brook striding toward her. As he came up to her his glance was roguish. "My, but don't you look especially radiant this morning, Miss Pride," he greeted her, grinning from ear to ear. "Indeed, I would say positively glowing, wouldn't you agree, Mr. Montand?"

"I would indeed," Louis said.

Addie could hardly keep from laughing, but she gave Brook a "You, rascal!" glance and murmured a discreet "Thank you."

"It must be the wonders of our climate here at the Silver Springs Resort—even the air has a certain quality!" Brook made a circular gesture with both hands as if embracing the universe. Then he looked at the carriage and let out a low whistle. "That's a splendid vehicle, Mr. Montand. New is it?"

"Just delivered to me yesterday," Louis said proudly running a hand possessively along the narrow strip of gold trim. "Rubber-rimmed wheels," he pointed to the bright yellow spoked wheels.

"It's certainly a fine-looking carriage. Haven't seen one like it in the valley," Brook said decisively. "Well, I must be off. Good day to you both." He nodded and walked away.

Louis turned back to Addie. "Miss Pride, I drove over this morning hoping I could entice you to drive out to the house with me? Have lunch?"

"I'm sorry, Mr. Montand. But I can't. I have only one day a week free, Thursdays."

"Tomorrow? Well then, we'll make it tomorrow. Shall we plan that tomorrow I'll come for you and we'll drive out to the house?"

"Again, I'm sorry. But I have already accepted an invitation for this Thursday."

An annoyed expression came over Louis's face. At first she thought he might demand to know with whom she had made plans. But his good manners prevented such a breach of etiquette.

"*Next* Thursday, then?" It was more a statement than a question. "I want so much for you to see the house—"

Over his shoulder Addie saw Mrs. Amberly and her bathhouse attendant approaching. When she saw who was with Addie, Mrs. Amberly immediately quickened her step, waving her hand and calling, "Oh, Mr. Montand, hello! How nice to see you. I've been wondering about you and your sister—"

Louis stifled a groan, rolled his eyes before he turned to reply to Mrs. Amberly.

She was huffing and puffing as she came up to them. "So

what brings you over to Silver Springs from your lovely new home?" she asked coyly.

"To see if I could persuade your charming companion to take a drive with me," he said blandly.

Mrs. Amberly's hopeful look vanished as she realized the invitation did not include her. Her disappointment showed on her face. "Well she can't," she snapped. As Louis lifted his eyebrows, she must have realized how rude she had sounded because she quickly changed her tone of voice. "I'm afraid, Miss Pride will be very busy. I have a lot of correspondence for her to take care of for me this afternoon. Now, if you'll excuse me." She glared at Addie, then went past them onto the porch, leaning on the attendant's arm. The cottage door banged.

Addie dared not glance at Louis whom she sensed was amused at the woman's behavior. To avert his saying anything derogatory about her employer, Addie hastened to say, "Thank you anyway, it was most kind of you to ask."

"*Next* Thursday, then, please," Louis persisted.

Addie had some real reservations about encouraging Louis's attentions. But she was angry at the high-handed manner in which Mrs. Amberly had jumped in and refused Louis's invitation for her. Addie was furious, in fact. She may as well be a servant! Then she thought how it would annoy her employer if *she* got to see Chateau Montand first! On impulse, knowing hers was not the noblest of motives, Addie said, "Why, yes, that would be lovely." Later she worried that she had acted against her better judgment.

Louis looked enormously pleased which soothed her conscience a little. But not much.

After the noon meal, on the way out of the dining hall, Mrs. Amberly stopped to chat with someone and Brook followed Addie outside.

"Well?"

"Well what?" she asked innocently.

"You know very well what! How did the experiment go? Did you like it or what?"

Addie squinted her eyes, wrinkled her nose, and shook her head, "Ugh, awful!"

His face fell. He looked so startled, so taken aback that Addie could not contain herself. She burst out laughing. "I'm sorry, Brook! I was teasing! It was ... words fail me. You are right—it is a unique experience. Once women get over the initial shock of getting into that gooey mess, they're going to love it."

Brook flashed a triumphant smile. "I *knew* it. Now, I've got to build a special building just to house the tubs, the resting rooms, and then I have to train attendants—it will take time and money—lots of money." He frowned, "But that's usually not a problem. It's selling the idea to the right people." His grin broadened. "Thank you, Addie, you're a trump."

Addie watched him walk away, his hands in his pockets, whistling like a schoolboy. What other new idea was he dreaming up now?

Chapter 9

After breakfast on Thursday morning Mrs. Amberly began to give Addie a list of errands she wanted done when Addie interrupted politely. "Excuse me, Mrs. Amberly, you must have forgotten this is my day off. I've been invited out to Mrs. Wegner's today for lunch. She will be coming for me in a few minutes. Maybe I can take care of these things tomorrow? Or if there is something urgent, perhaps we could send one of the hotel employees to town for you?"

Mrs. Amberly's mouth went slack. Her face creased with annoyance. "Seems like every time I want something done it's *your* day off."

"It is only one day a week, Mrs. Amberly. Thursday," Addie reminded her quietly.

"Humph," Mrs. Amberly, unappeased, grunted. "Where did you say you were going?"

Addie felt like retorting, "That's none of your business." But she controlled the urge and answered calmly, "To Freda Wegner's, Mrs. Amberly. You remember, the lady we met the evening we were having dinner with the Montands?"

"Oh, yes! Her! The widow woman who runs her own ranch and winery!" Mrs. Amberly sneered.

Addie stiffened at Mrs. Amberly's reaction. As though Freda ran a tavern or worse! She pressed her fingers together tightly, willing the inquisition to be over so she could be on her way.

Looking like she had taken a bite of a green apple, Mrs. Amberly pursed her lips and said, "I don't know whether I approve of your cultivating friendships on your own. You realize, *don't* you, that what *you* do, where you go, who you associate with reflects on *me*."

With effort Addie checked her rising indignation. What right did Mrs. Amberly think she had to talk to her this way? But she managed to keep her voice cool as she replied, "Even servants are free to go where they please and choose their own friends, Mrs. Amberly. And you need have no fear of my association with Mrs. Wegner reflecting badly on you. She is a respected citizen of this town, well-known to Mr. Stanton as well as Mr. Rexford Lyon, whom you also met the same evening. Besides they were both *invited* guests of the Montands to their farewell party."

This seemed to silence Mrs. Amberly momentarily although she still looked sullen.

"Now, if you'll excuse me, Mrs. Amberly, Mrs. Wegner is probably waiting for me." Addie turned to leave.

"Just a minute, young lady," Mrs. Amberly called her back. "Don't forget if I wasn't paying your expenses here you wouldn't even have the opportunity to meet people of the class of the Montands. . . ."

Literally biting her tongue Addie left the room. Outside in the hall she could still hear her employer muttering. Sending up a desperate plea for patience, Addie hurried to her own room to get her bonnet and shawl. By the time she was halfway across the grounds she saw Freda Wegner in a small "piano-box" buggy coming through the Silver Springs gate.

As they set out from town Addie noticed the countryside

just beginning to take on the look of spring. A pale green aura softened the bare branches of the trees on either side of the road leading to Freda's ranch, berry bushes showed their tiny white star blossoms. As they passed the hillsides of vineyards, Addie exclaimed, "It's so beautiful," pointing to the fields, golden with blossoming mustard plants.

"As well as good for the earth. The mustard will be plowed under, but it enriches the soil, giving it needed nutrients for the grapes."

Soon they turned off the main road onto a narrow winding one marked with a sign that said WEGNER WINERY. Freda's house, a yellow frame Victorian, was cradled in a wooded dell surrounded by oak and eucalyptus trees, behind it a vineyard planted in precise neat rows sloped down the hillside.

Freda reined the horse to a stop in front of the porch, trimmed with decorative white wooden lace. A smiling, swarthy man in work clothes, whom Freda addressed as "Rico," came from around the back to take the horse and small buggy to the barn and Freda invited Addie inside.

From the small entrance hall she led the way through sliding doors into a small but elegantly furnished parlor. Luxurious green ferns hung in the bow window and fresh flowers filled the room with scent and color.

"What a charming house."

"Thank you. I enjoy it myself. Since I don't have much company, that's so nice to hear." Freda gestured to one of two armchairs covered in flowered chintz. "Do sit down, Miss Pride."

"Please call me Addie—most of my friends do."

"Well, then, Addie you must call me Freda, because I'd like us to be friends. Would you like tea before lunch? Or perhaps a sherry?"

"Oh, tea would be fine."

"I hope that my asking if you'd have wine didn't shock

you? Here in the valley, it's very appropriate for a vintner to offer the fruit of her vine to guests. Of course, I'm still not used to my status." Freda shrugged. "You see, I'm the first and only woman vintner in the valley, probably in California, and it's something I never dreamed I'd be when I came here as a bride, believe me."

Freda walked over to the door and called down the hall. "Elena!" In a few minutes, a pretty, dark-haired girl with huge, black olive eyes, small gold hoops swinging from her ears, stuck her head in the parlor door.

"Please bring us some tea, Elena, and since it's such a lovely day, I think you could serve us lunch out on the side porch. Would you like that, Miss Pride—I mean, Addie?"

"Oh, yes, that would be delightful. I can't get over how warm it is here in March—like summer really."

"Good. Then we'll eat out there, Elena," Freda told the maid then seated herself. "As I was saying, running the vineyards and winery by myself was the last thing I ever imagined myself doing. We came here shortly after our marriage, mainly for Jason's health. The climate was recommended as beneficial, and we found it so. But Jason had a dream. He was the last of his family, you see. His father had recently died, and he had an inheritance. He wanted to put down roots of his own, something for the children we hoped to have. . . ." An expression of sadness moved across her thin face.

Freda halted as Elena entered with a tray. She smiled shyly at Addie and set it down on the low table in front of her mistress. After the girl left Freda poured the tea, saying, "So, we bought this ranch. We were told that some fine French vines were already planted on the land. Everyone who seemed to know told us that good root stock, such as we'd purchased was half the battle in the successful growing of wine grapes."

Freda handed Addie her cup, offered her cream and

sugar. "Of course, we were neophytes at the whole business, so we took everything at face value. In time we found that it also takes knowledge of the land, care, cultivation, and patience." She stirred sugar into her own cup and for a moment seemed thoughtful before going on.

"We had all the enthusiasm and excitement of youth, but Jason did not have the physical strength necessary for what we'd undertaken. He would be up at daybreak, work in the fields along with some of the Californios he hired to help. Eventually his health broke and he was very ill. I had to take over much of the overseeing of the vineyards and—" She gave a deep sigh "—I tried to keep Jason's spirits up; one of the side effects of tuberculosis is often depression."

"That must have been very hard," Addie commented gently.

"It wasn't easy but . . . ," Freda paused, then continued matter-of-factly, "women are brought up to believe we cannot do certain things. It's etched on our inner selves from the time we are given a doll instead of the interesting set of building blocks our brothers receive. We're told over and over we can't calculate or decipher—in other words, not to even dare dream of all sorts of wonderful things, barred to us simply because of our sex.

"My husband, thank God, was not of that school. He didn't distrust or fear the fact I was intelligent. He gave me credit for good judgment, and he was not afraid to give me responsibility—when he was alive. I believe he trusted that if something happened to him, I'd carry on what he had envisioned here. . . ." She sighed. "Of course neither of us imagined it would come so soon."

Freda's mouth tightened visibly, and Addie did not press her further, sensing that further talk about Jason Wegner's death would be too painful. Freda paused. "Even after Jason died things would have been all right. We had had two years of good grapes. The winery had the possibility of producing a superior vintage. Then—disaster struck! Phylloxera."

"Phylloxera?"

"A hideous blight on the vines. A voracious microscopic louse, usually hidden beneath the soil. It destroyed all our French grapevines. American rootstock is resistant because of years of exposure, but the European varieties were susceptible to it, and we had mostly the French kind." She took a last sip of tea, then set down her cup. "I don't know what I would have done without the help and support of friends. Especially Rex. Rexford Lyon. You met him the other evening at Silver Springs when we went there to dine."

At the mention of that name Addie's fingers tightened on the delicate handle of her teacup. Of course, Freda had no idea that there was no need to remind Addie who Rex Lyon was. Not a day had gone by since her arrival at the Calistoga depot that Addie had not thought of him. Perhaps now she'd find out exactly what his relationship to Freda Wegner was. She leaned forward half-dreading what Freda would say next.

"Even though Rex never wanted to come back to the valley, never wanted to be a vintner, he is very knowledgeable, very dedicated. A double family tragedy brought him back to run the vineyards and winery. Lyon's Court wines are famous throughout California. He took up the reins and has done a wonderful job." Freda paused, then said thoughtfully, "It's strange, isn't it? How sometimes Providence brings us to a place, into situations we would never have chosen on our own, but in the end, that place or situation turns out to be exactly what was supposed to happen?"

After a moment, Freda said thoughtfully, "I worry about Rex though. I don't think he's very happy."

Whatever else Freda was going to say about Rex was interrupted by Elena's coming to say lunch was ready.

On the porch during lunch the conversation turned to other subjects. Complimenting Freda on the delicious dessert of luscious strawberries piled on sponge cake covered with sweet whipped cream, Addie learned that growing flowers and fruit was one of Freda's many other interests.

"I love it here in the valley. Everything I enjoy is here in abundance," Freda said enthusiastically. "It's very different than the life I lived in the city before I was married." She told Addie that she had been the only child of an indulgent widowed father. She had been reared to marry well, to marry someone in her own set so that they could take their place in society. "But the best laid plans and all that," Freda sighed. "Jason's health was the reason we came here in the first place, and now I can't imagine living anywhere else. There's so much freedom. Especially for women. Can you see me wearing this any other place?" she laughed and got up to model what she was wearing. "See the skirt is divided so I can ride horseback astride instead of sidesaddle." She showed how the brown twill skirt was cleverly made. "It's wonderful for all the things I like to do—like squatting and kneeling when I'm gardening and of course horseback riding. I'll give you the pattern if you'd like."

The two young women found they had much else in common besides flowers, fruit, and fashion. They discovered a mutual love of reading, both novels and poetry, as well as an enjoyment of music. They were discussing their reactions to Madame DeSecia's concert when they saw a small one-horse trap coming up the winding road to the house.

"Why, it's Rex!" Freda got up, went to the porch railing, and waved. "How nice."

Addie clasped her hands tightly together, her heart tripping within her starched blouse. She closed her eyes for a

110

second, trying to draw a long breath. When she opened them Rexford Lyon stood at the top of the porch steps.

"You remember Miss Pride, Rex; we met her with the Montands at Silver Springs hotel. I told you on the way home from their party that I was going to ask her out. . . ."

Addie did not hear what else Freda told him. She was too conscious of his slow smile, his eyes acknowledging her. It was almost as if he was saying, "Of course I know her. I feel as if I've always known her." In reality, she heard his deep, mellow voice say, "Yes, indeed, I remember. A pleasure to see you again, Miss Pride."

The words spoken in quiet courtesy fell on Addie like a caress. Oh, foolish, foolish girl! She felt as though she were swimming in deep water, trying desperately to reach shore. She felt as if she might drown. Get hold of yourself! Say something!

"Good afternoon, Mr. Lyon."

"Rex, you'll stay awhile?" Freda asked. "Have some coffee with us, won't you?"

"That would be fine, Freda, thank you." His eyes never left Addie.

"Good, I'll go make some fresh."

Freda immediately disappeared carrying the coffee pot, and Addie was left alone with Rex.

He lowered himself into one of the white wicker armchairs, settling himself more comfortably. He took off his wide-brimmed hat and put it under the chair. Addie was suddenly aware of everything about him: the high-bridged nose, the strength of his jaw, the curve of his mouth, the tawny streak of hair, the narrow white line on his forehead against his tanned face, probably made from wearing his hat out in the sun. She was even conscious of the combined scents of leather, sun-bleached cotton, and tobacco that emanated from him.

She felt nervous perspiration gathering in her palms.

111

Attempting to appear composed, she sat up straighter, wiping her hand surreptitiously on her skirt. With her hands demurely folded in her lap, Addie tried to catch one of the random thoughts floating through her head with which to start some sort of conversation.

Rex seemed utterly unaware of the internal havoc he was causing. In contrast he seemed completely at ease. It was he who broke the silence that had fallen at Freda's departure.

"So, Miss Pride, how do you like California by this time?"

"It is very different—at least different from where I came from, what I'm used to. But then, I have only twice been out of the state of Virginia, so I haven't much to compare it with. It is very impressive, very *big!* Almost overpowering—the trees, the hills!"

"And the people? Do you find them very different as well?"

She thought a moment, wondering how honest she should be. He was looking at her with those clear gray eyes as if he was really interested in hearing what she had to say. It gave her a welcome sense of freedom to be frank and not merely polite.

"Yes, I think so. Much more outspoken, direct. I'm afraid Southerners tend to be—well, careful not to reveal too much of themselves, to not always say exactly what they mean—especially to strangers. Westerners do not seem to have that same wariness, I guess you'd call it."

"Does that bother you?"

Addie considered that for a few seconds.

"It takes some getting used to. But I believe that's all to the good. To mature, a person should be exposed to other ways of thinking, acting. Otherwise you become narrow in your outlook. It's important to take people as they are. Not to put them through the filter of your own prejudices or the way you may have been taught things were, to find out for yourself. . . . Oh dear, I am going on."

112

"Not at all. I find it fascinating how someone coming from another part of the country sees things, sees *us*. You see, I was born here. I've never lived anywhere else. Never traveled outside California. I wanted to, meant to but . . ." He paused; then clasping his hands in front of him on his knees, he leaned toward her. "Please, go on."

"What I was trying to say is that I'm used to—you might call it a polite tip-toeing, not coming right to the point about anything." She laughed. "I don't know what my relatives would think of my dissecting them like this and particularly to a stranger."

"I hope not to be a stranger long, Miss Pride," he said earnestly. "I would like very much for us to be . . . friends."

The hesitation before the word "friends" caused an unexpected little flutter underneath Addie's heart. Then suddenly, Freda entered with a tray on which was the silver coffee server and cups. The conversation became general, with Freda and Rex discussing local matters.

Finally, Rex reached for his hat and stood. "I should be going and leave you ladies to your visit. I'm afraid I barged in uninvited and—"

"Not at all, Rex. You know you're always welcome here," Freda assured. "Besides I was going to drive Miss Pride back into town. She tells me she has to be back by four."

Rex fingered the brim of his hat. "May I . . .," he began, "perhaps, I could do the honor? And save you a trip, Freda. Since I was on my way into town anyway, I would be happy to take Miss Pride back to the hotel."

Freda looked askance at Addie who did not know where to look. Her heart had already jumped hopefully at Rex's suggestion.

"Is that all right with you, Addie?"

"If it isn't too much trouble—for Mr. Lyon, I mean."

"Not at all, a pleasure, Miss Pride."

The trip into town went all too fast although it seemed to Addie that Rex had slowed his horse as much as could be considered reasonable without walking him. The conversation was confined mostly to Rex pointing out the various vineyards along the way, telling Addie the names of the owners. Very conscious of the forced intimacy of the small buggy, Addie made only casual comments.

Addie felt both relief and regret when they reached Silver Springs. She still could hardly believe she had spent even this brief time with Rex Lyon.

"Thank you very much, Mr. Lyon," Addie said as he handed her down from the buggy.

"It was *my* pleasure, Miss Pride," he protested. His fingers closed around her hand, holding it tightly, as if he wanted to say something more. "I wonder if—would you like—may I . . .," he began.

Before he could finish, Addie saw Mrs. Amberly and the Brunell sisters come out onto the verandah of the main building. With them was Louis Montand. Their expressions were frankly curious when they saw Addie and Rex together.

Aware that she was being stared at, Addie withdrew her hand from Rex's while wondering if this scene would become tonight's topic at the card table. "Thank you again, Mr. Lyon."

Ignoring the group on the porch Rex asked, "Perhaps, I could call some afternoon?"

Rather breathlessly, Addie explained, "I'm not sure, Mr. Lyon. I'm rarely free to make plans. You see, I am employed as a companion and my time is really not my own—"

"Yes, I understand that. But surely—you have some time off. Some other Thursday?"

Even as Rex was speaking, out of the corner of her eye Addie saw Louis sauntering toward them. Before she could say another word he was within hearing distance.

"Good afternoon, Lyon," he spoke cordially to Rex, then turned to speak directly to Addie. "I hope I'm not intruding. But I've been waiting for you. Mrs. Amberly informed me you were visiting at the Wegner ranch. I was about to drive out there and escort you back to the hotel. I had to see you because I had something important to tell you."

Louis glanced at Rex as if to imply that this was going to be a private matter and the gentlemanly thing for Rex to do would be to leave. He paused, obviously waiting for Rex to do so.

Rex frowned slightly, but showed no irritation. He said to Addie, "Well, I must be off. It was a pleasure to be with you, Miss Pride. Have a pleasant evening." With a nod to both, he got back into his buggy and drove away, leaving Addie annoyed at Louis for interrupting. It had been a very unsatisfactory parting. She only hoped Rex would get in touch with her.

Louis's voice dragged her back to the present moment. Observing her closely, Louis said, "What I came to say, Addie, is that I'm sorry but I have to break our date for next Thursday. I have to go to San Francisco for a few days on business. I have to complete arrangements about hiring workers for our harvest. When I arrived here looking for you, Mrs. Amberly told me that Stanton had announced that tonight's dinner is going to be served early because there is going to be a magic lantern show for the guests, 'The Land of the Pharaohs.' It's supposed to be excellent, and Mrs. Amberly has kindly invited me to have dinner with you two. I hope that suits you?"

What else could Addie say but, "Of course."

He held out his arm. "Shall we join the others then?"

Having no alternative Addie took the arm Louis offered. She wished she had known before about the dinner hour being changed and the magic lantern show. It would have been a perfectly acceptable thing to invite Rex to stay for

115

it. It would have been a way of thanking him for bringing her into town. But Louis had cleverly finessed that.

As soon as Addie was seated at the dinner table, Mrs. Amberly said acidly, "I thought you spent the day with Mrs. Wegner. But I see you must have made other plans after you left this morning."

All the relaxed enjoyment of her day faded under Mrs. Amberly's caustic tongue. The rest of the dinner hour was a strain with Mrs. Amberly succeeding in monopolizing most of the conversation.

Later, while watching the magic lantern program, Addie allowed her mind to wander back over the afternoon at Freda's. Freda Wegner had all the qualities Addie admired: courage, determination, faith. She was what Aunt Susan would call a woman of character. Her aunt often remarked that how we deal with adversity defines who we really are. It was reassuring to see living proof that any challenge can be met with faith and belief in our God-given strength.

After the program, Louis walked her and Mrs. Amberly to the cottage, said good night, and left. Addie felt worn out. The evening had been tiring. It had been an effort to keep up the polite and mostly artificial conversation while pretending not to catch Louis's subtle innuendoes. His over-attentiveness made her uneasy. How could she discourage him when Mrs. Amberly was so obviously encouraging him—for her own reasons, of course. Still, as her employee, Addie could hardly avoid him if Mrs. Amberly made him so welcome.

She went to the window and looked out. Moonlight painted everything a luminous silver. The glass dome of the arboretum glistened like a giant jewel against the deep blue of the mountains in the background.

Old feelings of longing swept over her. In a few short years the age of thirty loomed ahead of her—the end of youth. Would it also be the end of possibly finding an enduring lifetime love?

She thought of Rex Lyon, remembered what Freda had told her about him. The family tragedies that had brought him back to the valley. That she thought he was unhappy. Why? she wondered. A broken romance? An impossible love affair? What was in his past?

How strange that their paths kept crossing. This time, not at a distance. They had sat together, talked, exchanged ideas, their hands had touched. Again she had experienced that eerie sense of recognition.

Addie sighed, closed the curtains, and got ready for bed.

Chapter 10

$\mathscr{A}$ddie's personal tour of Chateau Montand was postponed. From the prestigious San Francisco hotel where he was staying, Louis wrote a note saying that his business in the city would take longer than he had anticipated and that his return to Calistoga would be delayed.

Within a few days she received another note. In it Addie thought she read some irritation between the lines. While he was away, without consulting him, Estelle had set the date of their housewarming party and invitations were already printed ready to be sent. Since many of the preparations and arrangements still had to be completed, he would regretfully have to forgo the pleasure of seeing her until the night of the party. He would, with her permission, come to escort her and Mrs. Amberly out to their housewarming.

A week later, when, as usual, she and Mrs. Amberly stopped in the lobby to check for mail before going to the dining hall for the noon meal, Addie's formal invitation was in her box. She opened the envelope, noted the date, then put it in her handbag. Mrs. Amberly finished a conversation with one of the Brunell sisters, then asked the clerk for her mail. When *she* found *hers* in her box, her reac-

118

tion was jubilant. She made a great show of displaying the handsomely engraved card to the Brunell sisters. From *their* reaction it was clear they had not been invited and they walked off in a huff.

Later when Addie and Mrs. Amberly were seated at their regular table in the dining hall, Mrs. Amberly placed the envelope prominently in front of her plate with a self-pleased smirk at having been singled out over most of the other Silver Springs guests.

"I don't suppose you could do my hair, could you?" she skewered Addie with a calculating look. "I doubt if there's a decent hairdresser in this size town. I'll have to check the livery stable see if I can rent a carriage; their house is quite a distance from town, you know."

"Louis said he would send his for us," Addie said quietly.

Mrs. Amberly's jaw dropped. "What do you mean—for *us?*"

"He enclosed a note in my invitation assuring me we had no need to worry about transportation—he plans to come in and escort us to the party."

Mrs. Amberly could not hide her chagrin that Addie had received such special treatment from people with whom *she* had tried so hard to promote a friendship. Making no attempt to conceal her pique she pouted for the rest of the meal refusing to speak. She would have been even more affronted had she known that the only reason *she* was included was to make sure Addie would come.

Her annoyance at the situation displayed itself in various ways almost up to the evening of the housewarming. Addie could do nothing right nor could anyone else. Nothing pleased, nothing suited, nothing satisfied. If Addie had not become used to such childish behavior, she would have been at the end of her rope. But she had learned it was best to ignore Mrs. Amberly's fits of temper and maintain her own composure. She refused to let a selfish old woman

119

spoil her own anticipation of what promised to be an interesting evening.

Addie had to admit she was curious to see the Montands' mansion at last. She had certainly heard enough about it. From what she knew of Louis and observed of Estelle this party would certainly be an outstanding occasion.

It had been a long time since she had been to such an occasion, had a chance to dress up, and to look forward to an evening of music and dancing. It had been even longer since she had felt young and lighthearted.

Addie was glad now she'd given in to Aunt Susan's urging her to bring a party dress. "You just never know when you'll have an opportunity to wear it. Better be safe than sorry." It had been her wise advice. Against Addie's protest the dress had been packed in her trunk. Now a week before the Montands' housewarming, Addie took it out from the layers of tissue, shaking out the dried rose petals in which it had been packed, filling the room with the nostalgic scent of summer gardens.

The dress had a history of its own. It had been made for her to wear at the ball at Oakleigh to formally announce her engagement. But then the war had come, and within months Ran had been killed and the dress packed away unworn.

Addie examined it carefully. It was in perfect condition, still lovely—a rosy-gold satin with a net overskirt embroidered with gold thread, the rounded décolletage outlined with stiffened net ruffles edged with ecru lace.

Of course, she would not be wearing it with a hoop or layers of starched petticoats underneath as she would have in 1862. Nonetheless, the gown itself was so beautiful that perhaps no one would notice it was somewhat passé. Her mother's opals in their delicate gold filigree setting would be exactly right with the color of the dress. Excitedly she put in the earrings and fastened the clasp of the necklace, then studied her reflection in the mirror.

Aunt Susan, bless her heart, had tucked in appropriate accessories as well: a small beaded evening bag, a lace and ivory fan, elbow-length kid gloves in their original box—never worn either. Addie smiled, feeling like Cinderella and that Aunt Susan was a veritable fairy godmother.

"I'll do you proud, Auntie!" Addie promised as she whirled around the room a few times holding out her skirt. "At least for one night I'll be Adelaide Pride again! Adelaide Pride of Oakleigh!"

She laughed at her own silliness but her happy mood lasted up until the night of the party when she donned her finery again.

Mrs. Amberly had somehow managed to find someone to "do" *her* hair and was closeted in her bedroom the whole afternoon. When she finally appeared, Addie had to employ rigid self-control not to betray her reaction to her employer's appearance. Mrs. Amberly looked like a walking jewelry counter. Her dress was ruby-red taffeta; her plump shoulders were bare except for a tulle stole. An elaborate coiffeur sparkled with brilliants and the rest of her shone with an array of diamonds, from a huge sunburst brooch on her breast to bracelets and rings.

Fortunately, Addie was not required to comment. It had taken Mrs. Amberly so long to assemble herself that it was already late when one of the hotel maids came running over to breathlessly tell them that the Montand carriage and driver had arrived and were waiting for them.

Brook, splendid in evening clothes, was standing outside the main building. He gave them a sweeping bow, complimenting them both extravagantly. But it was Addie on whom his gaze fixed. With a practiced eye he made a kind of inventory of her—not missing a detail—his approval apparent.

Mrs. Amberly was panting from hurrying and it took both Brook and the Montands' man to assist her into the barouche. Then Brook held out his hand to Addie, murmuring, "Absolutely beautiful, Miss Pride. If I'm not mistaken, tonight will determine Montand's decision—"

Addie sent a quick anxious glance toward Mrs. Amberly, hoping she had not heard this. But she was fanning herself from the exertion of getting settled and had not overheard.

"You look like a fairy princess," Brook said, his glance took in the fire opal necklace and earrings. "Are those the crown jewels?"

"They *are* heirlooms. They belonged to my mother."

"Perfect."

"Thank you, Mr. Stanton. I trust we'll see you later?"

"Indeed, yes. I wouldn't miss it." Brook's expression was enigmatic. What his real feelings were about coming to the Montands' party she could not guess. Did he feel the Montands were outdoing even *him* with this lavish affair?

"Save me a dance," he said as he waved them off.

The minute Rex entered the Montand house he saw Adelaide Pride. She was standing in the front hall talking to Louis. The glow from the glistening crystal prisms of the chandelier overhead sent dancing lights upon her dark hair. Her dress, a golden color of some filmy material shot with gold threads, reminded him of a sparkling champagne.

She looked so beautiful that momentarily he was stunned. It had almost physical impact, as if he had been thrown from his horse, his breath knocked out of him.

Rex had been undecided whether to come to this party tonight. He did not like Louis Montand. That was probably unfair because he did not really know the man. But he had heard some unsettling rumors that made him suspicious of Montand's motives for coming to the valley, taking over the Caldez ranch. But at the last minute he had decided to come, if just to avoid another solitary evening.

He had not been sure *she* would be here tonight. He had hoped she might be—had been almost afraid to hope—but was grateful for whatever had brought him here tonight. He took a few steps into the foyer, surveying the scene, then stood absolutely still.

At that very moment, as if drawn by some invisible cord, Addie turned her head and saw him. Instantly her heart turned over. She felt that same uncanny sense of recognition, leaving her again breathless and confused. Nervously, she unfurled her fan, trying to listen to what Louis was saying to her.

"I may have to devote myself to my guests tonight. Estelle has already warned me I must circulate, not spend too much time with one person more than another." He pressed her hand to indicate who that one might be, then continued, "Feelings in these provincial towns are easily hurt, she tells me. And I suppose she's right. People get offended, imagining slights where none were intended." He gave a little shrug. "Since we have to live here and there are people I may need—I must heed her admonitions." He smiled beseechingly. "I hope you understand?"

"Of course," Addie nodded, distracted, more aware that Rex was approaching than of what Louis was saying. And what did that matter to her anyway? The only thing that mattered was that Rex Lyon was standing in front of them waiting to speak. Addie felt almost dizzy.

"Good-evening, Montand," Rex said; then his glance moved to Addie, and he held out his hand. "Miss Pride, how very nice to see you again."

"Nice you could come, Lyon," Louis replied. "I was just telling Miss Pride my attention must be spread around among my guests this evening. It would be a favor to me if you would look after her until I can get away from receiv-

123

ing my new arrivals. The music for dancing has begun. Perhaps you could escort Miss Pride onto the dance floor?"

Rex looked down at Addie, thinking how lovely she was—those sherry-colored eyes, shadowed by dark, curving lashes—how luscious the glow of her skin, how sweet the tantalizing scent of her fragrance.

"I would be most happy to do so, if Miss Pride would do me the honor?" Rex assured him, his eyes brightening.

Behind her Addie heard a familiar high-pitched voice and turned her head to see Mrs. Amberly holding Louis's sister by the arm, her face pushed up into Estelle's, talking rapidly. Addie saw Estelle cast a look in Louis's direction. She assumed the Montands must have secret signals to use in awkward social situations because Louis immediately excused himself and went to his sister's rescue.

Left alone with Rex, Addie grew strangely calm.

"Would you care to dance?" he asked.

"Yes, indeed, thank you." Addie took his arm. Together they went across the hall to the drawing room where the furniture had been pushed against the wall, the rugs removed, and the floor highly polished for dancing.

A waltz was beginning to play. Rex led her out to join the gracefully spinning couples. He was a surprisingly good dancer Addie discovered. She had seen the way he rode a horse, seen his long-legged stride, his purposeful walk, but none of these had given a clue to his skill on the dance floor.

It had been so long since she had danced that Addie felt a little unsure of herself. At first she was too aware of Rex's hand on her waist, her hand in his. Then the music took over, and she fell in step with its rhythm. They circled the room several times, then reversed, all in perfect time with the three-quarter beat, gliding, whirling, as though they had danced together before in some other time, some other place. She felt as though it were a dream, floating on the rippling waves of the lighthearted music rising and swelling around her. For the first time in ages Addie allowed herself to be happy.

In the middle of a promenade Addie spotted Brook; he looked dashing and debonair as he stood in the archway of the hall. He must have just arrived for he was divesting himself of a white satin-lined cape. Seeing her, he smiled and gave her a little salute.

When the music ended they were at the end of the room near the bow windows, and Rex suggested, "Shall we catch our breath for a few minutes?"

"Oh, yes, let's," Addie agreed. They went over to one of the alcoves to sit on the velvet cushioned seat. Through the open window a cooling breeze brought in the fragrance of flowers.

Rex sat down beside her, looking at her so seriously and thoughtfully that Addie was compelled to ask, "Why are you staring at me so, Mr. Lyon? Is something wrong? Perhaps I have a fly on my nose or something?" She playfully brushed at an imaginary insect on the tip of her nose.

"Oh, no!" Rex said quickly. "I was just thinking how I nearly didn't come this evening and . . ." He hesitated for a long moment. "I just happened to think how many times that sort of thing has happened to me. Like the day I saw *you* for the first time—at the train depot. I hadn't planned to ride into town that day, either—"

"However, I'm very glad I *did* come." He made a sweeping motion with his hand. "This is quite a party, isn't it? I believe everyone in the valley is here, besides a few others I don't recognize."

"I understand Louis and Estelle invited friends from San Francisco, as well."

"Do you know them well—the Montands?" Rex asked.

"Well, they have been staying at Silver Springs for quite some time while this house was being completed. And you

125

know, my employer, Mrs. Amberly, stayed the winter so we have seen a great deal of them."

"It must seem dull to them after the life in the city, although Montand declares he wants to become a vintner." Rex shook his head. "Vineyards and winemaking are mostly family businesses here. That's how I happen to be here." He paused, frowning slightly. "I never intended to come back. I had planned to be a journalist, I had just started getting my feet wet, so to speak when . . ." an expression of infinite sadness passed over Rex's face ". . . my father died unexpectedly and my older brother was killed in an accident—and there was no one else to take over the business my great-great-grandfather had started."

"I know, I'm sorry. Freda told me something about it."

"It's a strange feeling to be the only one left in one's family."

"Yes, I quite understand. You see, I too am the only one left in *my* family," Addie surprised herself by confiding. "Two of my first cousins—boys I grew up with—were killed in the war, and both my parents are dead."

She realized Rex was the only person to whom she had told anything about her personal life since coming to California. His eyes softened, and he nodded as if no words were necessary to convey his sympathy. A brief silence fell between them, but it was not an uncomfortable one. Rather, it was an empathetic one; the unspoken acknowledgment of a mutual experience of loss seemed to bind them closer together.

After a moment, Rex asked, "Would you care for some refreshment? A glass of wine, perhaps?" He lifted one eyebrow and smiled. "Although, I can't vouch for its quality. I don't believe they're serving Lyon's Court vintage. And since Louis hasn't brought in his first crop yet or produced his estate bottled wine, it isn't Chateau Montand either." Rex leaned closer and said in an exaggerated whisper, "It's probably some inferior French champagne—" He shrugged. "But as they say, beggars can't be choosers!"

Addie laughed, delighted to see this unexpected side of Rex who had, before now, always seemed serious.

"What are you two finding so funny?" a voice asked and a smiling Louis stood before them.

Addie and Rex exchanged a conspiratorial look, silently agreeing Louis might not think a joke about his winery altogether humorous.

Not waiting for an answer Louis asked, "May I interrupt? I'd like to take this lovely lady on the dance floor and then in to supper."

Rex got to his feet slowly as though reluctant to surrender her to Louis. Addie stood up, feeling slightly dazed to have had her conversation with Rex so abruptly interrupted. But after all, Louis was their host. She could hardly refuse a dance.

"Did I tell you how absolutely beautiful you look tonight?" Louis asked as soon as they were dancing. "You know how a rare jewel looks in the right setting? That's how it is with you. Your sparkle, your delicacy, your grace is submerged in a place like the Silver Springs Hotel—it's not worthy of you, it does not do you justice. I can imagine the background you come from and how you fit there—that's why I wanted to see you *here*—in a setting I have created. I imagined you here. And it's just as I knew it would be—perfect."

Louis's dark eyes glowed with fiery sparks that seemed to burn into Addie. His intensity made her uneasy. The things he was saying. She looked at him warily. Of course, he was excited at the success of his party, probably overstimulated. Possibly he had drunk a great deal of champagne—responding to toasts of well-wishers as well as priding himself on the brilliant success of the party.

Louis's hand tightened on her waist as he swirled her

127

around to the romantic music of a Viennese waltz. "Tonight I have to share you—I don't really mind—it is very gratifying to see the envy in other men's eyes that *I'm* dancing with you! You do know you are the most attractive woman here, don't you?" He paused. "Of course, you don't. You're not the type of woman who is self-absorbed. You are different from most of the women I've met." Louis smiled. "Utterly charming. I find you absolutely fascinating. Even your name. Pride. It suits you somehow. Miss Adelaide Pride of Virginia."

Addie began to feel uncomfortable but did not know how to stop Louis. They circled the room again and then the music ended. Addie started to step away but Louis's hand on her waist prevented her.

"I'd like to ask you a great favor. I know we have not known each other very long, but I believe—at least, I *think*—we have become well-acquainted even in this short time. May I call you Addie? And, of course, *you* must call me Louis. After all, we're living in California now. And Californians, I've learned, do not stand on formality."

Addie was caught off guard. But before she could reply she caught sight of Estelle standing in the doorway, waving her fan to attract Louis's attention.

"I think your sister wants you."

"Ah, no!" Louis swore under his breath; then still holding on to Addie he walked over to where Estelle stood.

"Louis, it's time to announce supper. I hope you can relinquish him for a few minutes, Miss Pride?" She gave Addie a pinched smile, then took Louis by the arm as if to lead him away.

"I'll be with you in a minute, Estelle," he said rather brusquely. She looked annoyed but left and Louis turned to Addie.

"*We're* eating supper together. I'll just make the

announcement and be right back. Here, sit right down and I'll join you shortly."

Rex was nowhere in sight and had not mentioned supper, so Addie simply nodded and let him lead her over to a secluded corner to wait for him. A few minutes later he came carrying two plates filled with all sorts of delicacies: bay shrimp, creamed potatoes, fresh asparagus, and tiny hot rolls. Following him was one of the servants carrying a bottle of champagne and two glasses. After they ate, while the band tuned up for the last dance, Louis took it for granted that this would be his. Addie realized the evening was coming to an end and she had not had another dance or chance to talk again with Rex.

People began saying their good-byes, thanking their hosts and leaving. Louis settled Addie on a love seat in the small parlor adjoining the foyer to wait for him while he and Estelle saw off their departing guests. "I hope you aren't too tired, but I can't leave to take you and Mrs. Amberly back to Silver Springs until everyone else is gone."

"Of course, I understand. I'll be fine," Addie assured him.

Louis had hardly gone to join Estelle in the hall when Rex appeared at her side.

"I wanted to say how much I enjoyed being with you tonight, Miss Pride. You did say you were free on Thursdays, didn't you?"

"Yes—," she began but before either of them could say more, Mrs. Amberly came along, her face showing both annoyance and curiosity. Rex bowed and murmured good evening to her. She gave him a curt nod then turned to Addie.

"Go get my cape, I'm too tired to move," she said plunking herself down on the love seat.

Addie rose at once. She looked uncertainly at Rex, wondering if he was going to say anything else. But Mrs.

Amberly's presence seemed to have placed a pall on further conversation between them.

"Well, good night then, Miss Pride, Mrs. Amberly," he said, bowed again, and walked into the foyer.

"Well, don't just stand there," Mrs. Amberly said irritably, "I'm chilled. Hurry up."

Addie hurried off, half hoping Rex might still be in the hall and they would have another chance to speak. But to her disappointment, he was nowhere in sight. She noticed the last guest was saying good night to Louis and Estelle. By the time Addie emerged from the room off the hall where the ladies' wraps had been left, Louis was waiting. Mrs. Amberly's mood had undergone a miraculous transformation. She now appeared to be all smiles and compliments about the party to the Montands.

Within minutes they were heading back into town in Louis's smart barouche. At the cottage, while he bade Mrs. Amberly a courteous good night, Louis captured Addie's hand. To have withdrawn it would have been awkward, but it made her extremely uncomfortable. Finally Mrs. Amberly left them alone. Immediately Louis brought her hand up to his lips.

"Do you have any idea how proud you made me this evening, Miss Pride—Addie? You looked so lovely, and it delighted me to see you so happy."

His words set off an inner alarm in Addie's mind. Why on earth should Louis feel proud of her? She gave her hand a gentle tug, and after a second he released it. "It was a wonderful party. Thank you very much for everything. I must go in now."

"Yes, of course. But you never really answered the question I asked you earlier. Can we drop the *Mr. Montand?* I would like very much if you would call me Louis. . . ." He paused. "I think of *you* as Addie—and I think about you a great deal. . . . So may *I?*"

Addie hesitated. To use each other's Christian names was a step toward intimacy she was not sure she wanted to take with Louis Montand. But she could not really think of any reason to say no, without being rude. After all he had certainly shown her every courtesy and kindness. With some inner reluctance she said, "Why, yes, if you'd like to."

"I *would* like. Thank you, my dear. I'll be in touch. Don't forget I want you to come out to Chateau Montand when it is not crowded with people, so you can see it for yourself, see the beautiful home I've created."

He still made no move to leave. Feeling a little uneasy at his lingering, Addie moved toward the door. "Good night, Louis."

"Good night, Addie. I'll see you soon."

Inside her room Addie heard the carriage drive off, and she gave a sigh of relief. She hoped she had not given Louis Montand any false impressions, no reason for him to assume—whatever it was he was assuming about her.

But Addie didn't want to think any more about Louis Montand. She wanted to think about—other things. Tonight had been like being caught somewhere between the past and present, music, dancing, laughter. Addie felt as though she were on the brink of something wonderful. What was it? Were her feelings about Rex Lyon her own imagination or did they have any basis in reality?

Estelle Montand was waiting for Louis in the small parlor when he returned from taking Addie and Mrs. Amberly back to Silver Springs. She stiffened visibly when she heard him humming as he came in the house. She frowned.

"Ah, Estelle, you didn't need to stay up on my account!"

"I wanted to. I wanted to discuss our party. How do you think it went?"

"Splendidly, splendidly!" Rubbing his hands together in

obvious satisfaction, Louis asked, "Shall we have a nightcap while we share our comments?"

Not waiting for an answer he went over to the liquor cabinet and brought out a cut-glass decanter from which he poured two glasses. He handed one to his sister then sat down in one of the damask upholstered chairs opposite her. He raised his glass then took a sip.

"So, you delivered that dreadful woman back to the Springs." Estelle gave a little shudder. "I thought we were rid of her once we left the resort. Why on earth did you invite her?"

"Because, my dear Estelle, if I hadn't, I couldn't have invited the delightful Miss Pride. There was no alternative. And I decided not to deprive myself."

Estelle felt a quick little twinge of alarm. So her brother's interest in the charming Southern woman was still strong. At first she had thought it was simply infatuation. Darting a speculative glance at Louis, Estelle said carefully, "Of course, she *is* attractive."

"*Attractive?*" Louis sounded incredulous. "Why, she's downright stunning." A smile played around his mouth as if he were contemplating an image of her. "She is also intelligent, charming, and completely captivating.

Estelle tried to keep her tone casual. "Well, of course, I didn't have a chance to get to know her while we were staying at the Springs. I was too busy trying to avoid that terrible woman whose secretary or companion she is—"

"Well, you'll *have* the opportunity very soon, Estelle. I want to have her out as soon as possible. I want her to see everything—the house, the gardens, the grounds, the winery—*really* see it, not like it was tonight, filled with people, but as it might be—as a home."

Estelle had a sickening sensation. So things had gone *that* far! At least as far as Louis was concerned. And that woman probably saw him as a "good catch," someone to rescue her from her menial position. *Well, we shall see about that!* The question was, was it too late for *her* to do anything about it? Perhaps not. But to her brother she said mildly, "Yes, that's a nice idea, Louis. Perhaps in a week or so when we're more settled."

Perhaps all she needed was a little time.

Chapter 11

The day following the Montands' housewarming party, Mrs. Amberly was out of sorts. Her feet were swollen from squeezing them into too-tight, fashionably pointed shoes the night before, and she had indigestion from indulging in the bay shrimp and salmon mousse, the chocolate eclairs and chilled champagne at the lavish buffet. She stayed in bed most of the morning, and in the afternoon she sent Addie into town to buy her some patent medicine and some peptic pills at the pharmacy.

The next day she had recovered sufficiently to give Addie a new shopping list, which now included her favorite confection—caramel covered walnuts. That afternoon while Mrs. Amberly was napping, Addie walked back into Calistoga to take care of another number of errands.

It was a springlike day. Addie was glad to be out in it and away from the strident demands of her employer for a few hours of freedom. She decided to enjoy it. As long as she was in town, she decided to go to the library and select more reading material. Books were Addie's sometime alternative to needlepoint to offset the boredom of the long evenings while Mrs. Amberly played cards. If she didn't occupy herself somehow, Addie found herself inadvertently listening to the shallow conversation, inconsequential comments, and trivial gossip of the players. It amazed her that these people, affluent enough to come to this luxury resort, had so little to absorb and interest them. The place reverberated with undercurrents. Casual remarks were sometimes misconstrued, resulting in feuds when guests magnified small slights into insults so that some of the guests did not speak to each other and others took sides in the most ridiculous way.

Of course, Mrs. Amberly was in the middle of most of it. She relished hearing both sides of any battle, relaying what had been said, fueling the flames, so that some unintentional action would be blown into a full-fledged war.

Addie managed to stay clear. She never let herself be drawn into any discussion of the other guests by Mrs. Amberly. Her reticence threw her employer into sullen sulks, but she eventually gave up trying to bring Addie into the conflicts.

Well, she wasn't going to worry about any of what went on at the hotel, Addie decided, not today. It was a beautiful day, the kind of day when one should only think happy thoughts. It was the kind of day when anything could happen.

"Miss Pride!"

Startled, Addie turned in the direction of the voice calling her name and saw Rex Lyon waving to her from across the street. Grinning broadly, he whipped off his hat. In a minute he was crossing toward her. He was a little out of breath when he reached her.

"Hello! This is a bit of luck. I was just thinking about you. . . ."

She had to laugh. He was so boyishly candid. No proper greeting, no polished manners, just direct.

"I mean, I was trying to think how to . . . well, I was planning to send you a note. I didn't want to just come by the hotel. I might not have picked the right time—a good time for you, with your job and all—" He stopped abruptly, then asked, "Are you in a hurry? Could you have a glass of cider or some ice cream—at the candy shop down the street?"

"As a matter of fact, I was headed that way. I have to get some caramels for Mrs. Amberly." She almost giggled as she added, "She's feeling a little under the weather."

"The very thing. Caramels will do the trick," Rex responded straight-faced.

They both laughed and they walked down the sidewalk together.

At the drug store Addie purchased a pound of caramels while Rex got them glasses of chilled apple juice, and they sat down at one of the small, round marble-topped tables.

"I really enjoyed the other night," he began looking at her with steady gray eyes. "At the Montands' party. You know I almost didn't go. Or did I tell you that?" he smiled a little sheepishly. "I said a lot of things the other night. I can't remember talking so much. Not for a long time at least." Then abruptly he asked, "Do you ride?"

"Yes," Addie answered. "But I haven't ridden for quite awhile; there wasn't the opportunity. . . ." Her voice trailed off. She could have told him more, explained that they had horses at Oakleigh; then the war came and the horses were needed. Actually, her father had volunteered them for the Confederate Army. How could she tell Rex all this? How could she tell how bitterly she had wept when her beautiful little mare Phaedra was led away? Oh, she wanted to be patriotic, but it was hard. After all, she had been hardly more than a child—at sixteen, heartbreak, whatever the cause, is still heartbreak.

Rex did not seem to notice her hesitation. He waited and when she did not go on, he said, "The reason I ask is because I've just found out some friends of mine are here in the area. The man, Rob Baird, is someone I knew when

I lived in Monterey, down the coast. We both worked on a newspaper there and then again in Oakland before I came back to the valley two years ago. . . ." He paused, frowning, as if the background of the friendship was too long and complicated to get into at the moment. "Anyway, he hasn't been too well, getting over a bout with pleurisy I understand, and he's come up here for the milder climate—actually he and his wife are camping out in the hills above town, and I'd very much like you to meet them."

Addie raised her eyebrows. How very odd. Camping out? What did that mean? Every day she seemed to hear something new and startling about western ways.

"I can bring you one of my horses. I know just the one and we could take a picnic." He looked at Addie with a kind of mischievous twinkle in his eyes. "It might be a welcome change from all the formality of the Silver Springs dining room. What do you say? How about next Thursday?"

Addie took a few seconds to decide. It was an unusual invitation. But she lately had developed a taste for new experiences. Her curiosity was aroused by Rex's description of his nonconformist friends. Why not?

"Yes, I'd like to—very much."

They finished their drinks, and Addie suddenly became conscious of the time. She consulted her watch pinned to her jacket. "I have to go," she said, gathering her small packages and standing up. "Mrs. Amberly will be waking up from her nap soon and expect me to be there."

They walked out of the shop into the afternoon sunshine.

"I'm glad about Thursday," Rex said. "It's all set then?"

"Yes, I'm looking forward to it," she told him knowing how much she was.

"Well, good-bye."

"Until Thursday."

He seemed not to want to be the first to turn away so

Addie finally said good-bye again and started walking up the street toward the hotel, knowing that Rex was probably watching her. At the same moment she became aware of two figures across the street. The Misses Brunell! *They* quickly turned their heads as if window-shopping at the millinery store. But Addie was sure they had seen her and Rex Lyon come out of the pharmacy, stand talking together. She was just as sure they would report it to Mrs. Amberly.

She didn't care. Addie lifted her chin defiantly. She was entitled to a life of her own—even if it was only on Thursdays.

She walked on, but her steps slowed as she got closer to Silver Springs. It *was* strange that she and Rex had run into each other today. Sitting opposite him in that little sundries shop had seemed so natural. They had talked as easily as if they had known each other a long time. Even the other night at the Montands' party, their conversation had not been the light exchange most social ones usually are. They had told each other important things about their lives. It was as if it was important to find out as much as possible about each other as quickly as possible. And that day at Freda Wegner's, he had asked her *real* questions about how she felt and thought. He had treated her like an intelligent woman whose opinions were worth listening to, as if he had actually wanted to get to know her as a person.

Was it all her imagination? She hardly knew him. Was she being foolish? How could she tell whether he was what she imagined? Maybe it was just an infatuation, a physical attraction—the way his hair fell on his forehead, the impatient way he had of brushing it back, the humorous mouth, the strength of his jaw.

In sight of Silver Springs gate, Addie stopped suddenly. Standing under the shade of a large oak tree, she was almost overcome with a longing for a love that had no beginning and no end. All her life she had been waiting for someone to come into it who would accept her as she was, know her, love her, look at her the way Rex Lyon had looked at her today.

Addie drew a long shaky breath. Today in his eyes, Addie thought she had seen what she'd been searching for all her life.

As he rode back from town, Rex Lyon's mood was elated. The chance encounter with Adelaide Pride had lifted his spirits enormously. Since the day of her arrival in Calistoga when he had happened to be at the train station and he had felt that strange stirring in his heart, she had lingered hauntingly in his mind. He could not rid himself of that uncanny sense of having known her somewhere before. Until the other night at Montand's, there had only been two other brief meetings. To run into her this afternoon when he had not even planned to come into town seemed just luck. Or was it Divine coincidence? His mother had always told him, "Nothing happens by chance." Now, Rex was becoming a believer.

Today they had talked at length and he had drummed up the nerve to ask her to go with him to see his friends Rob and Nan Baird. For the first time in a long while a curious ripple of anticipation coursed through him; next Thursday seemed a long time off.

At the sign LYON'S COURT, Rex turned his horse into a lane lined with majestic eucalyptus trees standing like sentinels on both sides of the road leading up to a turreted stone building. The house his French great-grandfather had built in this California hillside was modeled on a chateau in his village in France. The rays of the late afternoon sun glazed the diamond-paned windows with a lustrous gold and gave the native stones a silver patina.

He brought his horse to an abrupt halt when he reached

the arched porte cochere, and dismounted, hailing the dark-eyed lad who ran out from under the shade of the oak tree near the driveway. The boy greeted him, "Evenin', *Señor.*"

"Howdy, Pedro. Take Roi to the barn and see that he gets a rubdown and some oats. Then tell your mama I'm home."

"*Si, Señor,*" the boy nodded, rubbing the horse's nose affectionately.

Pedro's mother was the housekeeper and cook, and her husband oversaw the vineyard workers. The Hernandez family were Californios, descendants of the first Spanish settlers who had come here long before the Gold Rush in '49, before the vineyards even. As a girl Maria had worked for Rex's mother and had stayed on after her death to keep house for him.

Rex went up the stone steps and into the house. For a moment the old loneliness welled up inside him. A man should come home in the evening to a fire burning, lights shining, a woman's soft voice, a welcoming kiss, the sound of children's laughter. Not to this . . . emptiness. However, almost immediately Rex seemed to hear the words "not for long" echo in his mind. Was it his imagination or some internal assurance? He felt an odd hope that it might be true.

He walked into the library, the fading sunlight slanted through high, curved windows, and then was lost in the high-raftered ceiling of the large, rectangular room. Rex lifted the cap of a cut-glass decanter on the refectory table and poured himself a glass of cabernet, instinctively holding it up to the light as if to test the clarity of its jewel-like ruby color. Then he lowered his six-foot frame into a deep, worn leather chair, stretching his long legs out in front of him.

His eyes roamed the magnificent room restlessly. Family

portraits in heavy, ornate frames hung on the walls. Rex's ancestors came from the wine-growing regions of France, a family of wealth and influence, producers of a famous Tokay wine. His great-great-grandfather, Gerard Deleon, had been a young boy of fifteen when the French Revolution swept its ruthless path across his country.

Although of noble birth, the young man's sympathies were with the peasants. At an early age he had been disturbed by the plight of the poor. He had often seen coachmen of the aristocrats whip an innocent peasant by the side of the road, and he was disgusted. He despised the merciless brutality rampant at the time. At first, he had seen the Revolution as the hope of the peasants, the class who had no rights, no dignity, no future.

But the reign of terror swung close to home and his own family's name was listed with those sentenced to the guillotine. Helped by English friends, the family escaped to England, bringing only the clothes on their backs and a small quantity of some of their choicest grapevines from the family's vineyard.

They had believed the Revolution would be short-lived and that they could soon return to their native land. But it soon became clear that it would be a long time before they could safely return. Gradually, over the years, in gratitude to their English benefactors, the Deleons became Anglicized. They changed their name to Lyon, their religion to the Church of England; their manners and attitudes soon became those of the country of their refuge.

Gerard decided to go to the new world of America to seek his fortune. He had heard much of the fabulous West Coast as the "promised land" of America. So he traveled across the country on the Santa Fe trail to San Diego, then on up the coast to San Francisco and into the Napa Valley. There he was able to buy land, plant his vines, and establish a vineyard.

141

By 1857 Lyon's Court Wineries were famous throughout California as producing some of the finest wines, comparable to those of France. Gerard settled down, married, raised a family, and prospered. Since that promising beginning, an unfortunate series of tragedies had occurred—the untimely deaths of Rex's father and older brother—and only Rex was left to carry on the splendid legacy his forebears had worked so hard to acquire.

He put down his half-finished glass and went over to the long windows overlooking the sloping hills down to the vineyards. In the afterglow of sunset, Rex's thoughts returned to Addie and the unexpected chain of events that had brought him back to the valley and to meet her.

After his mother died when Rex was fourteen, he was sent away to boarding school in Sacramento where his talent for writing was first recognized and encouraged. As the younger son he had not been expected to follow his father and older brother into the family's wine-producing business. So he had been allowed to follow his ambitions for a literary career.

He had loved the life of a journalist. He worked on newspapers in several California towns, mingling with other young men with the same goals. He became part of a small circle of writers in the towns where he had lived: Monterey, Oakland, and then San Francisco. Then had come the shocking news of his brother's fatal accident. Riding in the vineyards, Philip was caught in a sudden lightning storm, his horse had become frightened, reared, and thrown him, killing him instantly. While the family was still reeling from this shock came another shattering tragedy. Their father died from a heart attack. Rex, home for the funeral, had no alternative but to take over the ranch and the winery.

He had deeply resented giving up his career to take up the reins of a business in which he had no real interest. Now, however, he saw that there might be some unknown reason for everything that had happened, and how he had chanced to be here when Adelaide Pride arrived in Calistoga.

His first sight of her at the train station was etched indelibly on his mind. Even though it had been a few brief minutes he had memorized everything about her. The graceful figure dressed in black, the delicate lift of her chin, the glimpse of rich, dark hair swept up from her slender neck under the little black bonnet. He recalled how she had turned toward him and he saw her lovely eyes—clear, sherry-colored eyes. Then for an unforgettable instant they had looked at each other and something indescribable, yet very real, had passed between them.

Rex ran an impatient hand through his tousled hair. Was he mad? Was it only his own longing that persuaded him to think that? Still, he was sure she had felt something, too, although she quickly turned her head away.

For weeks he had thought about her, wondered who she was, what she was doing in Calistoga, was she a widow, married, single? Then the night he and Freda went to have dinner at Silver Springs, they were introduced. This was followed by indecision of how he could get to know her.

Now, everything seemed to be falling in place. At least, he was getting a chance. What the future held, who could say?

Addie's Journal:

March 16

I haven't written in a long time, but must record something extraordinary that happened today. A chance encounter with Rex Lyon in town resulted in an invitation to go riding with him, up into the hills, to meet some friends! I am overly excited, I'm sure. But we had a wonderful conversation, a real meeting of minds—

PART 3

SILVERADO SPRING

Chapter 12

hursday morning Addie awoke with a sense of excitement. She got out of bed and hurried over to the window to check the weather. The sun was already out; the sky a cloudless blue. A perfect day for a ride up into the hills to meet Rex's friends.

She hummed as she washed and got dressed. Instead of pinning up her hair, she brushed it back, braided it, and fastened it with a slide at the nape of her neck. She put on the divided skirt of sturdy blue cotton she had made from Freda's easy pattern; with it she wore a light blue shirtwaist, over this she slipped on a biscuit brown saxon-cloth jacket. Lastly she pulled on her leather riding boots, which some instinct had prompted her to pack.

Making a final check in the mirror she could not help compare her present outfit to the elegant riding habit she had worn in Virginia before the war. That one had been ordered from a prestigious New York ladies' tailor and cut to her exact measurements. It was made of dark blue fine English wool with a superbly fitted jacket and sweeping skirt. With it she had worn a plush derby, veil, her hair clubbed into a velvet snood.

Ah, well, that had been in another lifetime. This was

now, in California, Addie shrugged, realizing that, for the first time, she wasn't looking back with regret; she was looking forward with anticipation.

Since the day promised to be warm, before leaving the cottage she grabbed up a wide-brimmed straw hat to take along in case the sun got too hot. As she crossed the grounds, she saw Rex just coming up to the main building on his horse and with another one on a lead.

Seeing her, he waved. "Good morning!"

"Good morning," Addie said, coming alongside the cinnamon-colored mare, putting out her hand tentatively to pat the sleek neck. "What a beauty! Did you bring her for me?"

"Yes, this is Gracia. She belonged to my mother. She's a lady's mount, very sweet."

Addie felt complimented that he would bring this horse for her to ride even before he had ever seen her on horseback or known how she could handle a horse. No, it was as if he *had* known. Again she felt that bond between them.

Rex helped her mount and handed her the reins. Addie leaned forward and stroked the silky mane. Then he swung up onto his own horse and led the way out of the resort grounds, then at the gates eased into a canter. Addie followed, intuitively sure that curious eyes were watching. For once Mrs. Amberly had not asked her about her plans that day. Addie felt positive the Brunell sisters had told her about seeing her with Rex in town. But today Addie was determined to leave behind her at the hotel all worries about what people thought or said.

At the end of town, they turned off the road onto a narrower one, hardly more than a bridle path leading up into the hills. The terrain was rough and rocky, so their progress was slow. But this gave Addie a chance to notice everything. The woods on either side were dense with tall eucalyptus and madrone; the ghostly, gray lichen-covered oak trees and redwoods towered lordly over all.

Eventually they came to a clearing where a meandering stream trickled over brown, sun-flecked rocks. Here Rex suggested they stop for a while to let their horses drink and take a rest after the arduous climb.

He took out a suede-sheathed flask of water from his saddlebags, poured some into a small silver cup, and handed it to Addie to drink. The water was cool and refreshing to her dry mouth and throat. They didn't talk, but Addie did not feel awkward about it. It just seemed natural that they both quietly enjoyed the short rest in the shady glen.

After a while they remounted and started climbing the narrow, rocky trail hollowed out by thousands of horseback travelers before them. Gradually it widened and they rode side by side. They passed the stagecoach station and a tavern, and began a steeper climb into the hills.

"It isn't much farther now to where the Bairds are staying."

"Tell me a little about these friends of yours. I accepted your invitation to visit them without receiving a real invitation from them. I do hope they're expecting us? Or at least that they know you're bringing me?"

"Of course, you're invited. When I saw Rob he said come any time. I rode up here the other day to tell them about you . . . well, that we would both be coming."

By the puzzled look on Rex's face, Addie realized he considered her question absurd, as if the protocol and social amenities she had been brought up to believe necessary were unimportant in the West. There *was* a kind of openhanded, openhearted, open-door generosity of spirit that did not stand on ceremony.

"Well, what do you want to know about them . . . the Bairds?"

"Oh, just . . . things . . . so I can get more of an idea what to expect."

Rex chuckled softly. "There's really no way to explain Rob. He's unique, like no one I've ever met before or after. We worked on the same newspaper in Monterey; that's where I met Nan too. She and her family were staying there, and Rob had just arrived from Scotland. Did I mention he's a Scotsman?"

Addie shook her head. "And what did he come to California for?"

"To find Nan. To persuade her to marry him." Another pause. "You see they met in France, at some artists' colony where Nan was spending the winter. They fell in love there and . . ." Rex paused again, then said, "Actually, they are on their honeymoon—"

Addie checked her horse, turned slightly in her saddle, looking at Rex. "On their *honeymoon?*" Addie gasped. "Then, should we be visiting them like this? I mean, aren't honeymoons supposed to be rather private affairs?"

"Well, *her* son is with them," Rex answered matter-of-factly, keeping his eyes steadily upon her, watching her reaction.

"Her *son?*"

"Yes, he's a capital little fellow—about eleven."

"But, Rex . . ." Addie frowned as though puzzled. "Oh, I see, she's a widow."

"Not exactly. She divorced her husband to marry Rob."

This time Addie could not conceal her astonishment. She gave a sharp pull on Gracia's reins, twisted around in her saddle to face Rex.

"*Divorced!* Why didn't you tell me?"

"Would it have made a difference?"

Addie thought a full minute. In her experience divorce was the kind of thing never spoken of, or if it was, in whispers. There was always a sense of shame or scandal about

150

it. A tragedy for the woman even if she were not at fault. Unjust, unfair as that seemed, that's just the way it was. A divorced woman was not even received in the society in which Addie had grown up, much less *visited* and on her *second* honeymoon!

"Answer me, Addie, what difference does it make?" Rex asked. "The Bairds are the same people I told you about. Wonderful human beings. That hasn't changed. Does it make a difference to you?"

Addie could not think of anything to say. She felt troubled. She had never been faced with this situation before.

"What is it, Addie? Don't tell me you have some kind of bias against my friends without even meeting them?" Rex chided gently. "Weren't you telling me—just the other day—that you thought in order to mature one had to grow out of narrow ways of thinking, overcome built-in prejudice, presuppositions about people, and look at each person with an open mind?"

Addie felt her face get warm. "I hate having my own words quoted back to me."

"Well?" Rex raised his eyebrows. "*Isn't* that what you said? Or don't you really believe what you said?"

"Of course," she snapped. "I only meant—well, I guess I was surprised."

"Come on, Addie, don't tell me I've been mistaken in you."

She hated explaining what seemed too obvious. Surely Rex must know that back east, people took an entirely different view of divorce. But Rex's searching gaze was relentless and seemed to demand an answer. She looked down at her leather-gloved hands, twisting the reins, before she began speaking in a low voice: "You have to admit divorce isn't very common, and it isn't considered—that is, not in most places—acceptable."

"All marriages may not be made in heaven, Addie," Rex

151

said quietly. "I think if you knew the circumstances, you'd understand." He waited a few seconds, then said, "If you feel the least bit uncomfortable, Addie . . ." He let the implication dangle.

The very air seemed still. It was suddenly so quiet between them that the buzz of insects in the tall grass and the wind brushing through the evergreens on the hillside even sounded loud.

"No. Of course not. Let's go on."

Addie picked up her reins again, flicking them against the mare's neck and they started up the path again. They rode on a little further in silence until Rex broke it. "You won't be sorry you came, Addie, I know, when you meet them. Rob is a whimsical, warm, generous fellow and Nan—she's different, very creative, vivacious—well, I know you'll like them." Rex reached over placed his hand over hers, saying softly, "I wanted *them* to meet *you*, Addie—I wouldn't have put you in any kind of embarrassing situation if I hadn't been sure you'd be great friends."

She turned and met his intent gaze, struck by how important this was to Rex. In that moment, she also knew it was important to whatever relationship they were destined to have. It only took a second more for her to realize that made it important to *her*.

A little farther on the trail Rex turned in his saddle and pointed down the hill to a clearing where Addie could see a weathered shed, hardly more than a lean-to. "Here we are."

"That's *it?*" she gasped. "*That's* where they're staying?"

Rex grinned, "I told you they are an unusual couple, didn't I? Come on."

The "honeymoon cottage" convinced her the situation she was coming into was stranger than she could have imagined. What kind of woman would agree to spending her honeymoon in such rugged accommodations?

The horses made their way down the precipitous path; the rolling stones under their hooves made it a jolting downward trek. Addie leaned back in her saddle, holding her breath. Before they reached the bottom they heard the sound of a dog barking. When they came in sight of a slant-roofed, dilapidated gray-frame building, a rusty, scruffy-coated dog, looking like a cross between a spaniel and setter, was out on the platform loudly announcing their arrival. Almost at the same moment a man's figure—so tall and thin he looked almost like a shadow against the sun-light—stepped out from the door of what looked like an abandoned miner's shack.

He waved both hands like a windmill and bounded down off the ledge toward them, scrambling down the pebbly path, sliding and slipping as he came. He hailed Rex with a shouted, "Hello, old fellow!"

Rex dismounted. In a few long strides he clasped Rob Baird's outstretched hand and shook it heartily. Their greeting was that of two long-lost brothers. After a few slaps on the shoulders and much laughter, Rex came back over to Addie, took hold of her horse's bridle, and held up his hand to help her down.

"Addie, I want you to meet one of my best friends, Robert Baird. Rob, Miss Adelaide Pride."

Baird made a courtly bow. "Miss Pride, delighted! Welcome to our domain." He raised his head, rolling his eyes mischievously. "Now come to meet the queen of all you survey, my gypsy wife." He gestured to the door of the shack where a small, stocky woman, in an ankle-length denim skirt and striped shirtwaist, stood hands on hips, observing them.

"Hello!" she called. "Glad you could make it. Couldn't have asked for a better day."

The three of them walked toward the shack and Addie got a better look at Rob Baird's bride.

Nan Baird had a strong, interesting face framed by masses of curly dark hair done up quite untidily and tied with a rather frazzled ribbon. Her complexion was tawny, her arms, under the rolled-up sleeves of her blouse, sunburned. She had a pert nose and laughing brown eyes. Her smile was spontaneous and genuinely friendly. But it was her eyes that gave her face a special beauty; their warm brown pierced you with their genuine interest and depth.

"Been picking berries," she told them as they came up to the makeshift shelter, wiggling her blue-stained fingers as if to prove it. "But look what bounty!" she declared, holding up a bucket filled to the brim with glistening blue-black berries.

Rob was all Rex had described: tall, lanky, thin-to-gauntness. His lean, high-cheekboned face was pale in contrast to his wife's tan, and Addie remembered Rex saying he had recently been ill. He wore his hair long, curling around his scrawny neck, and his drooping mustache was scraggly. But in spite of his spectral appearance, his handshake was firm, his voice strong and rich with a Scottish accent.

Lowell, the boy, was a fine-looking, sturdy child with tousled maple-colored hair, sun-streaked from the days in the glorious sun of the hills. He was outgoing without being cheeky. He had beautiful manners, which made Addie concede that even though his mother and new father might live in an unorthodox way, he was as well-behaved and attractive a child as many a parlor mother's pride.

Addie soon saw the truth of what Rex had told her about the Bairds. They obviously adored each other. They were totally unself-conscious about displaying their affection. It wasn't embarrassing to others because it was so natural. Rob's running dialogue with Rex was frequently punctuated with questions to Nan. When he needed confirmation of a date of an event or replenishment of his faulty memory of a name or a place, he'd ask Nan, "Was it not, love?" or "Correct me if I'm wrong, darlin' mine." He always listened intently to any comment she made, and his remarks were sprinkled with direct address to her as "gypsy," evidently an endearing nickname prompted by her Romany looks.

Addie had never before been exposed to such open and easy communication between married people. Her own parents, whom she was sure dearly loved one another, used formal terms of address with each other as did most of her adult relatives. Her mother called her father "Mr. Pride," and her father always called her by the name he used during courtship, "Miss Lovina." It had never seemed odd to Addie. But now, seeing the Bairds made her a bit wistful, a bit envious and longing to know that same kind of sweet intimacy someday herself.

When Rob announced he was famished, Nan immediately declared it was time to eat. His eyes followed her as she moved around briskly, setting up a dining table by placing a wide wooden plank across two large flat stones.

Rex unpacked the wicker baskets he had brought on his horse, two bottles of Lyon's Court best vintage, a half ham, cheese, oranges. Nan produced a loaf of bread she had miraculously managed to bake on their homemade grill oven, and happily declared it all "a feast fit for a king—or a poet." She looked fondly at her husband.

From bits and pieces dropped casually as the three "talked shop," Addie found out that Rob was widely published in Britain, his articles printed in the prestigious periodical *Cornhill*. Although Rob was self-effacing, Nan would not let him get away with false modesty. Apparently Nan thought her husband a brilliant writer.

The conversation was as sparkling as the wine Rex had brought, bright with literary references, plays on words, teasing banter in which Addie surprised herself by joining

155

in, even making some quips herself or retorting to some playful jest or conundrum posed by Rob. He seemed to have an endless supply of stories and kept them spellbound with hilarious incidents of his many traveling adventures. He had come across the country on an emigrant train that should have been the death of such an emaciated physical specimen as he. But it was his indomitable spirit and outrageous sense of humor that had not only kept him alive but alert to the characters who had shared his car, to all the nuances involved in such a journey.

"As a matter of fact, I've just about completed the first draft for a book on the subject!" he laughed. "It should provide me with enough cash so I never have to use that particular mode of transportation again!"

Nan brought out a delicious cobbler that she had also whipped up while Rob was showing Addie and Rex their "kingdom."

There was such a holiday atmosphere about the day that Addie soon fell under the spell of her two unusual hosts and found herself relaxing in a way that was new to her. In fact, perhaps, for the first time since she had come to California, she felt completely carefree.

"Now, both Lowell and Rob must take a *siesta*," Nan declared as she started gathering up the remains of their picnic. When both the gentlemen named began to protest, Nan said firmly, "No arguments!" Her tone was severe. With hands on her hips she regarded them both. "Rob, you *know* you're here to recover your health, and Lowell, if you want to stay up late by our campfire and hear the rest of the story Rob started last night . . . well, you know what you must do!"

Rob threw out both thin hands in a helpless gesture, saying to Addie and Rex, "You see who rules with an iron hand?" He unfolded his lanky frame and pointed up the hill. "Rex, if you want Miss Pride to see the most beautiful view in the world just take her up a ways; there's a peak—not a difficult climb, my dear—," he said to Addie, "but well worth the trouble."

Rex looked askance at Addie who nodded. "Yes, I'd like that, but first I'm going to help Nan."

Nan did not turn down the offer but said over her shoulder to the men, "It won't take long."

Addie followed Nan down a little path to a creek where Nan bunched up her skirts, stooped down, and began expertly scrubbing the few tin plates with sand, then rinsing them in the water that rushed and gurgled over rocks. She cast a look in Addie's direction, then went back to her chore saying, "So what do you think of us, Miss Pride? I suspect a motley crew?"

"Not at all. A happy band."

"I suppose most folks would think we were a bit daft, as the Scots say. But it's done Rob a world of good to be up here in all this clean, pure air, the sunshine." She sat back on her heels and faced Addie. "You know they've given Rob only a year to live?"

"Oh, no! I'm sorry."

"Of course, I'm not going to let him die," Nan said fiercely. "You know people told me I was a fool to marry him. That I'd be a widow before six months. He was that sick when he got to California," she sighed. "But I knew if I'd marry him, he would live. And what choice did I have? I loved him."

Addie said nothing. She had been an eyewitness to the evidence of such love.

Nan placed her hands on her back arching it. "How much has Rex told you about us?"

"Not too much, except that he's very fond of you both."

"Yes, Rex is one of the staunch ones. You can depend on Rex." She gave Addie a long look. "I was married before, you see, to a philanderer, a gambler. Nothing worse than

157

not being able to trust someone. We were separated when I met Rob. I'd taken my children and gone to Europe. I'm an artist and we went to the south of France. I thought our love was impossible, so I returned to America, tried to make my marriage work again. But it was no use. Even the Bible says adultery is a cause for divorce, you know. I left him again and moved to Monterey. Then Rob wrote that he was coming." Nan started piling up the plates. "He was in real bad shape after the horrible trip. I nursed him back, but the doctors . . . well, what do doctors know, when it comes to that?

"Anyway, my husband agreed to give me my freedom. But I would have to file for the decree myself. Desertion was easy enough to prove. I had to sell a painting to pay the lawyer who got my divorce—one of my favorite ones too," she laughed. "But it was worth it. You can see what a prize I got. And he's going to get well, *really* well. We're going to find the perfect year-round climate for his health, and we'll—as they say—live happily ever after."

She smiled confidently then got to her feet. "Come on, let's go. These are finished, and I have to go round up my boys, see they follow my orders. And you and Rex want to go up the mountain."

Rob and Rex were talking in quiet voices when the women came back to the shack.

"Ready?" Rex asked, handing Addie her straw hat.

"Here, you'll be thirsty when you reach the top," Nan said and tossed them each an orange.

Tucking the orange in the pocket of her jacket, Addie followed as Rex led the way out of the small enclosed campground over the rubble of stones and onto a winding upward path.

It was a quiet, still afternoon, the sun warm on their backs as Addie and Rex climbed slowly up to a hillside above the "mountain castle," stopping every so often to look down on that little settlement. At the top was a lovely plateau. Large rocks bounded a cleared space surrounded by dwarf manzanita and madrone. In the cracks and crevices of the heaped-up rocks, hardy wildflowers struggled to bloom, adding unexpected color and scent to the unusual beauty.

Addie sighed a peaceful sort of sigh. She had never felt so tranquil in all the time she had been in California. Shielding her eyes with her hand she looked out over the ledge and saw, as Rob had predicted, a magnificent view of the entire valley. She glanced over at Rex who was leaning his back against a boulder; his eyes were squinted, almost closed. She wondered if he were drowsing.

Addie turned back to the view, unaware that under his half-shut eyelids Rex was observing her, finding her profile much more enchanting to contemplate than the view.

Rex watched as Addie took the orange from her pocket, turned it over in her palm once or twice, then began to peel it. Her broad-brimmed hat had fallen back, hanging by its ribbon around her neck and the sunlight sent sparkles through her dark hair.

In that moment he realized he had fallen in love with her, with this lovely woman who had appeared in his life, out of some dream, here in Calistoga, where he had not wanted to return. "God works in mysterious ways" passed through his mind like a confirmation.

Suddenly a fierce longing to tell her what was in his heart gripped him. But he knew it was too soon. To make such a declaration after so short an acquaintance would frighten someone like Addie, gently reared, not long from the strict social protocols of the East, especially the South. He must bide his time, give her time to get to know him, to know the life of the valley she would have to learn to live if—if—

He wanted so much to share everything with her, his

159

hopes, his dreams, his accomplishments, as well as his failures and disappointments. He wanted to share his life with her. That's why he had wanted to bring her up here to meet the Bairds, to see him through their friendship. He said her name over and over to himself—Adelaide, Adelaide, my love, my *wife!* The word touched him with a deep sweetness. There was a sense of inevitability about it. Why else had she come from half a world away, across the plains, across the country—to this place and time in both their lives?

As if his thoughts had somehow reached her, Addie turned and smiled at him, and his heart lurched. It had to happen. It had to be. He was determined it would be.

"I like your friends," she said.

"I'm glad. I hoped you would." He smiled back at her. "I was fairly sure you would—being the discerning person you are."

She laughed softly, tipped her head to one side. "What gives you the idea I'm discerning?"

"I could tell—"

"But you hardly know me."

"That's true, not as well as I want to." Rex paused. "I'd like to know everything about you, Addie. So, tell me," he urged. "I'd like to know about you, your childhood, your home, and family."

"Well, there's not that much to tell, really. When I try to think of how it was before the war, it's hard to remember. One tends to romanticize the past, especially a past that is irrevocably gone—forever." She looked wistful. "The war changed everything for us, you see."

"The war all seemed to be happening so far from here— a long way away. We didn't seem to be part of it. California had its own problems at the time—I was working as a reporter covering the gold mines in the northern territory while it was going on."

160

"You should be glad you were." She shook her head. "And it was all such a terrible waste—of men and lives—young women left widows, children orphans, families destroyed—all so needlessly. And what did it really accomplish?"

"Freedom?" Rex's question was gentle. "For the black slaves."

"Yes, perhaps. But also years of bitterness and unforgiveness on both sides," Addie replied. "I know my father was concerned about what would happen to the slaves—after it was all over. He was afraid it would take at least a generation until the country would really be one nation again."

Addie felt her old sadness as she remembered her father. He had been a man of wisdom, vision, and compassion. If he had lived he might have helped bring healing.

They fell silent, each pondering the other's words. Addie considered Rex's comment to her question of what the war had actually accomplished. Freedom, for the black slaves. But in a strange way it had also brought her freedom, she thought with some surprise. For all its devastation, deprivation, destruction, pain, and loss, she had gained a freedom she would never have dreamed of before the war. If the war had not happened, she certainly would never have come to California! Unconsciously she turned and looked at Rex. She thought, *And I would never have met Rex Lyon.*

"Tell me what it was like for you when you were a little girl."

Addie's expression grew thoughtful. "I guess you'd say my childhood was ideal. I had loving parents, doting grandparents, uncles, aunts who cared for me, cousins to play with, parties to go to. But I always felt that . . ." She halted.

"What did you feel? Go on, Addie, tell me."

"Well, it'll probably sound strange, but it was as if I was always waiting for my *real life* to begin, as if there were

161

something missing, that I hadn't found yet." She felt his eyes upon her and she laughed a little self-consciously. "Oh, my, that *does* sound fanciful, doesn't it?" She reached for her hat, straightened it on her head and tied the ribbons.

"I guess we'd better get started back," Rex said reluctantly. He rose, then held out his hand to pull her to her feet. Looking about her, she sighed.

"It's so beautiful here."

"We'll come back another time," Rex promised.

Addie's heart lifted, happy that Rex said *they would* come back, that there would be other days spent together like this.

The sun sent long shadows on the hillside as they left the Bairds' idyllic kingdom hidden away in the hills. Addie could not remember when she had wanted so much to see a day last longer.

Finally they said their good-byes to the Bairds and started down the rocky, winding trail back to town. It was all over too soon, Addie thought. Evening was coming on by the time they reached Calistoga and approached Silver Springs. A sense of melancholy overtook Addie the closer they got to the resort. They walked their horses through Silver Springs gate and dismounted in front of the main building. Rex tethered both horses to the hitching post. Overhead the sky had turned a lavender gray. Tiny pinpricks of stars were beginning to show, and a thumbnail moon shone palely through the trees.

No one was in sight. It was after six, and Addie knew all the guests were in the dining hall. She was glad. She didn't want to see anyone, have anyone break the spell of this lovely day. As they strolled across the grounds toward her cottage, Rex's hand brushed hers, then took it, held it tight. She did not withdraw it. Instead her fingers interlaced with his. She felt the roughness of his palm against her own, the pulse of his wrist beating against hers. When they reached the cottage, Addie slowly relinquished Rex's hand.

"It was a wonderful day, Rex."

He stepped up on the porch beside her. His nearness made her breathless and she dared not move or turn. But then he touched her gently, turning her toward him. "I wish this day could go on forever," Rex said. Addie drew in a deep breath and as she did, he raised her chin with his finger, and for a moment all their unspoken feelings trembled between them.

Then she was in his arms, her face upturned, and he leaned down to kiss her. When it ended, Rex said quietly, "I've been wanting to do that all day. Maybe even longer. Since that first day—Addie. I don't know how to say this—except that now, I think I know why I came back to the valley—"

"Don't!" she said gently, placing her fingers on his mouth. "It's . . . too soon, it's . . . We must get to know each other—give ourselves time."

For some reason Juliet's words to Romeo from the world's most famous romance came into her mind. This was all happening too quickly, too suddenly "like summer lightning."

Slowly Rex let her go, holding her at arm's length.

"Yes, of course, you're right. I won't say any more. For now—"

She felt his fingers press her upper arms and understood how much it was taking him to control his emotion. She shivered slightly.

"I better go in. Good night, Rex."

"May I?" he asked softly leaning down to kiss her again.

"Good night," she said breathlessly and hurried into the cottage, down the hall to her room.

Shutting the door behind her, she leaned against it for a minute, pressing her hands against her breast, feeling her racing heart. She closed her eyes savoring what had just happened, the strength of Rex's embrace, the warmth of his lips on hers.

When she opened her eyes they fell upon the picture of Ran. Were those clear eyes accusing her of faithlessness? Had she in the space of one afternoon forgotten him, what he had meant to her, what they had meant to each other? Had she betrayed him by what she felt for Rex Lyon?

She crossed the room, picked up the framed photograph, studied the face of the man—the boy, really, only twenty when this picture was taken. That was before Ran had gone to war or known its madness or paid its ultimate cost. It was a handsome face, the eyes looking out at the world with hope and confident expectation that life was good and fair and decent. It was a kind face, a gentle one in which she saw no rebuke.

They had been so very young. *Oh, Ran,* she thought, *we never even got a chance to find out who either of us really was—or could become.* If he had come back—but he hadn't and there was no use trying to imagine what would have happened.

Still holding his picture, Addie knew looking at Ran was looking backward, to a time and place, a way of life, that could never come back. Ten years had passed. She was a different person than the girl this young soldier had left when he had ridden away to battle. If he had lived Ran would be different, too, from the man she remembered.

It was time to put the past to rest, to allow new thoughts and ideas and a new self emerge. Carefully wrapping the portrait of Ran in tissue paper, she pulled out her trunk from underneath the bed, opened it, and placed the picture at the bottom.

As she closed the lid she thought of the Scripture verse that Aunt Susan often quoted: Philippians 3:13, "Forgetting those things which are behind and reaching forward to those things which are ahead—" Addie knew she should be thinking about the future. What was her future? Was it here in California? And was Rex Lyon a part of that future?

It was hard to trust her own judgment about Rex. She wished Emily were here to confide in, advise her as she had all the years they were growing up together, sharing secrets.

Unconsciously, Addie put her fingers to her lips, tracing their outline, thrilling again to Rex's kiss. Was what she had felt real? Or had she been swept away by a dream of her own making?

The next morning while Mrs. Amberly was over at the bathhouse Addie took one of her favorite Jane Austen novels and went outside. The weather was spring-like and warm. It would be pleasant to sit on one of the iron-lace benches near the arboretum to read. However, her mind kept drifting from the page to the picnic yesterday. Thoughts of Rex distracted her.

She felt sure he had been about to tell her he loved her before she stopped him. How would she have responded if he had? She wasn't sure, she didn't know. Addie knew he had awakened something in her she had never experienced.

She had had plenty of beaux back in Virginia. But even Ran had not drawn the kind of response from her she felt with Rex Lyon. The more she saw of him, the more she wanted to know, to discover. It was more than his rugged good looks, his outward attractiveness. She knew, somehow, there were layers to him yet to unfold if only she got to know him better. She felt instinctively if that happened—

"Daydreaming, Miss Pride?" Brook's teasing voice made her jump. His shadow fell over the unread page and she looked up into his laughing face. "Lost in reverie? You seemed to be. You have a dazed look in your eyes! Aha! A certain glow—can I guess what gives you that special glow this morning?"

Addie put a finger in her book to mark the page, closed it and gave Brook a mildly reproachful look. "Aren't you ever serious?"

"But I *am* serious. You *do* look especially radiant. Could riding off on horseback with a handsome rancher yesterday have something to do with it?" he asked, all wide-eyed innocence.

"We had a lovely time," she answered primly. "We took a picnic and visited some friends of his."

"Aha! I can guess who they were. Rob Baird and his wife? Correct?"

"Yes, how did you know?"

"They stayed here for a week when they first came from San Francisco. In that cottage over there, as a matter of fact." Brook pointed to the first one in the row. "That is until they moved to a more private, if rustic place—seeking more solitude. They're on their honeymoon, or did you know?"

"Yes, Rex told me."

Brook paused for a moment. "Do you know the circumstances?"

"Yes, if you mean what I think."

"Well!" Brook sounded both surprised and pleased. "I'm very impressed, Miss Pride. Gratified. You have fulfilled my estimation of you. That you are able to see beyond the circumstances that some would not. In fact, some would even condemn."

"To be honest, at first I was a little shocked. But after Rex explained what they had been through, I couldn't help but admire—even envy—them for having such a great love and faith in each other."

"Love endureth all things," Brook quoted, giving her a speculative look. "Would it shock you to know I am somewhat in the same circumstances?"

Addie turned a startled face toward him.

"You mean—you're—?"

"Not divorced. An early marriage—annulled. My fault entirely. Of course, I was too young. We were both too young. Childhood sweethearts. Everyone paired us off early, expected us to . . . even though I was way too unsettled to have ever gotten married in the first place. I always had this reckless, adventurous streak, I guess you'd call it. I wanted to come West, had 'gold fever' like so many did— and my child bride wouldn't come with me. Wouldn't even come join me after I sent her the money." He shrugged. "We were together less than a few weeks and never—well, I don't blame her. By the time I got the papers saying she had the marriage annulled, charging me with desertion, I had already made my first fortune!" He paused, sighed, shrugged. "I'm not proud of any of this, you know. All I can say is that when I came to California, I changed, or it changed me. I'm not the man—or rather the boy—I was then." He stopped abruptly, gave Addie a rueful grin, saying, "Then you would forgive my dark past?" Brook seemed suddenly serious as though it really mattered to him.

"Of course. My father used to say 'to understand all is to forgive all.'"

"Well and wisely put. All that's over and done with, and I believe we should put the past behind us—move on to the next horizon!"

"Of course, I believe that," Addie agreed. "That's what I'm trying to do too."

"Good! And if you're really looking into the future, Addie, you couldn't find a better man than Rexford Lyon," Brook said emphatically. "I applaud him on *his* good taste, as well."

Addie felt warmth rising into her cheeks at this.

"Well, I must be off," Brook said with a sigh. "Must get back to the books, my ledgers. I've been working on my monthly accounts, trying to make both ends meet. A

167

hopeless task, keeping one jump ahead of the sheriff so to speak." He laughed, started away, then turned back. "What are you reading?"

Addie held up the book so he could read the title.

"*Pride and Prejudice.* That's a provocative title. Is it interesting?"

"Yes, it's a good story, but there's a lot of wisdom in it too."

"Such as?"

"The foolish foibles of society, the pretenses people go to great lengths to maintain—in other words, pride and prejudice."

Brook nodded, then quoted, "Pride, the never failing vice of fools."

"And yet there is some pride that is understandable, isn't there?" Addie asked thoughtfully. "Family pride, for instance. I was brought up on that. Being always careful not to do anything to bring dishonor on it."

"I seriously doubt *you* would ever do anything other than heap glory on your family name," Brook declared. "Well, I really must get back. Good day to you. Keep happy, Addie." He strode back toward the main building.

After Brook left her, Addie mused over their conversation. Brook was certainly a man of many facets. On one hand, he seemed always to be in high spirits, confident, assured. No one would ever guess there was a brooding side, a past he regretted, hopes unfulfilled, love lost.

Addie opened her book but somehow she could not concentrate on it. Her thoughts turned again to yesterday, to Rex. The ride up into the hills, the slanting sun shining through the leaves, the smell of sun-warmed grass and of orange—a day to remember always, a day that shone bright with sunshine against the shadows of what lay ahead.

Chapter 13

Taking up her chores as companion to Mrs. Amberly seemed more tedious than ever after the day with Rex and the picnic with the Bairds. That day Addie had caught a glimpse of something new—that life could be joyous and interesting even if it was different, and that happiness was possible in many unexpected ways if it was shared with someone you loved.

In spite of all the Bairds had been through—separation, sickness, sorrow—they had not let it embitter them. They had known disappointment, delays, difficulties of all kinds, the ostracism of society because of Nan's divorce, and who knows what else. They valued each other and what they had found together. It had made Addie see everything in a different light.

Only a few months ago, life had seemed leaden; now it had endless possibilities. How much she had learned, changed, and grown since setting out for California.

More and more she was beginning to believe there had been a purpose behind it all. One that was becoming more and more clear. Rexford Lyon. Was he the real reason she had come?

Thoughts of Rex Lyon were the last she had at night, the

first that entered her mind in the morning. What they had talked about, what they had shared, especially the memory of the kiss lingered.

But the weekend passed without any word from him. On Monday she thought there might be a note suggesting plans for them to spend the following Thursday together. But there was nothing, and Addie felt a slight uneasiness of doubt. Perhaps she had imagined a meaning where none existed? Had his kiss really meant Rex felt something deep and tender and passionate for her? Or had it been only her imagination?

Tuesday morning the desk clerk told her there was mail for her in her box. In happy anticipation she tore open the envelope. But instead of the note she hoped for from Rex, to her disappointment it was from Louis Montand. He asked if he could call for her Thursday morning before noon and bring her out to the new house for lunch with him and Estelle?

Addie debated. Should she wait another day to see if Rex came by or sent a note? Maybe she was expecting too much, being too sensitive. After all he was a busy rancher with a vineyard to oversee, a business to run. He had told her his days went from sunup to sundown. She would rather think he was working too hard to get away than that she had mistaken his interest in her.

For a moment, she held Louis's note. Then with a sigh of resignation she decided to accept that it would be better than spending her day off at the resort. If she remained here most certainly Mrs. Amberly would find some excuse to give her a chore or an errand to run. It would be safer to be gone. After all, Louis was amusing and it would be a distraction from her own nagging worries and useless wondering about Rex Lyon.

April 1

April Fool's Day! I write this because I'm beginning to believe I am the biggest fool imaginable.

Almost a week has passed and not a single word from Rex. I don't understand. Could I have been completely wrong about him? I close my eyes and see the way he looked at me, feel his kiss upon my lips, the warmth of my response—Fool!

Fool to get my hopes up, fool to dream that the "secret desire of my heart"—to love and be loved—was on the brink of happening.

On Thursday morning she chose her outfit carefully, knowing it would come under Estelle's severe scrutiny. The thought of Louis's sister almost took all the pleasure out of her day off, but it was too late now to back out. A glance out the cottage window told her Louis had already arrived. He was standing beside his shiny black phaeton, talking to Brook.

Both men's eyes registered approval as she joined them. Her fawn faille suit was one of Aunt Susan's remodeled creations, but the material was fine and her refurbished accessories were also stylish.

"You look charming as usual, Miss Pride."

"And I believe her stay in our beautiful clime has brought fresh roses to her cheeks and a sparkle to her eyes," commented Brook with a wicked twinkle in his own. His slow wink behind Louis's back reminded Addie of her secret "experimental treatment."

Addie returned the look with a reproving glance while maintaining her air of propriety for Louis's benefit. What an incorrigible tease Brook was!

Louis assisted Addie into the smart carriage, climbed into the driver's seat beside her, then picked up the reigns as Brook waved them off. As they started off at a trot, Louis remarked, "You may have noticed I called you "Miss Pride" instead of Addie as you've given me permission to do. That was for Stanton's benefit. No use setting Silver Springs tongues wagging—at least *not yet!*" He glanced at her with a sly smile.

Louis must not have thought it necessary to wait for her to confirm the remark. Smiling confidently he turned onto Lincoln Road and started toward the center of town.

"I hope you won't mind, Addie, but I have to make a brief stop at the train station before we set out for home. I would have done so before coming to pick you up, but the train was late, and I didn't want to keep you waiting. It won't take but a few minutes. My overseer should be there to receive a shipment. I just want to check with him."

He pulled the buggy into the shade of a leafy oak near the train depot and placed a buggy brick to brake the wheels before crossing the street to the depot.

Addie watched him go, thinking how immaculately dressed and well-groomed Louis always was. Somehow he did not seem at all suited to the life of ranching or owning a vineyard. Addie had noticed how casually clothed other ranchers were when they came into town. Many frequented the gentlemen's lounge at the hotel, and they all had a certain look about them—a rugged, outdoorsy "western" style—like Rex Lyon.

At the thought of Rex, Addie felt a twinge of resentment. She was more disappointed than she cared to admit that he had made no effort to see her since the day of the picnic with the Bairds. Could he actually be *so* busy that he didn't have time even to send a note?

As she sat there waiting, Addie glanced idly about her. Her attention was drawn to what seemed to be an animated conversation—an argument?—between Louis and a shorter man in workman's clothes standing at the end of the platform of the train station.

Her eyes followed to where the man was pointing and

172

she gave an unconscious gasp. She saw a group of twenty or more men squatting on the ground near an open box-car still on the tracks. They were dressed in faded blue jackets, their bare feet were in sandals, their black hair was pulled back into long braids hanging down their backs. Why, they were *Chinese!*

Other than the glimpses she had had of the cook at Silver Springs, Addie had never seen Chinese, except in pictures in books—pictures mostly of plump mandarins or empresses adorned with jeweled, embroidered costumes, long curved fingernails and tiny bound feet, round faces painted white with shining black almond-shaped eyes. These men were not at all like that. There faces were gaunt, sallow, and they looked pitifully thin.

For some reason Addie felt a sick churning in her stomach. A terrible memory flashed into her mind. Once when she was a very little girl she had been in Richmond with her father, riding in a carriage over to visit relatives. They had passed a wagon in which some black men were huddled. As they went by, Addie had seen the same blank, hopeless stare on their faces that she saw now in these Oriental men. Later, much later, she had learned those men were on their way to the slave market.

Involuntarily, Addie shuddered. She blinked as if to erase her memory. Even though she had been brought up in Virginia, her parents had both hated the system of slavery and thought it should be abolished. Her father had been a lawyer, not a planter like her grandfather Pride. Although they spent summers and holidays at Oakleigh, in the winter she and her parents lived in town. Except for Renie, Addie's nurse when she was a tiny child, the only servants they had were Essie, the cook, and Lily, a maid. Thomas, the butler, also served as coachman and her father's valet. Addie had never thought of them as slaves. They were just

173

adults who were black, friends, part of her life. All had eventually been freed.

As she grew older, her father talked to her sometimes about more serious matters. He had been vehement in his denunciation of slavery. "It's a horrible institution. The sooner abolished, the better for the South. It corrupts as much as it demeans human dignity, and has a demoralizing effect on everyone it touches."

Addie remembered that as she could not turn her gaze away from that pitiful group of Chinese. What were *they* doing here in this pleasant little California town?

"Well, now, we can be on our way," Louis said briskly as he got back into the buggy. "Sorry to keep you waiting."

"Who are those men, Louis?"

"Chinese I hired to work in my vineyards. Just came up from San Francisco. I've had some building the limestone cooling caves. Good workers. Hard workers, much better than some of these locals who don't even put in a day's work—" Louis's mouth tightened. "But let's not talk about *that*." He turned and smiled at Addie. "I don't even want to think of labor problems or work today. Today is to enjoy!"

Addie had many questions she wanted to ask about the Chinese workers. They looked sick and undernourished. How could they possibly outwork the well-fed, hardy Californios she had seen in the fields around Calistoga? But obviously Louis had no intention of discussing it.

The countryside out to the Montands' place was beautiful. The winding road was flanked on either side by trees, and acre upon acre of vineyards on the hillside golden with mustard blossoms.

At length, they turned into a lane that led steeply up a hillside. At its crest a large white house gleamed in the sunlight. They entered by a crushed stone drive with yards of manicured lawn on either side edged with flowering bushes. As they got closer to the house Addie noticed a formal garden with circular flower beds.

"What lovely grounds, Louis. It was dark the night of the housewarming party so I didn't see them."

"That's all Estelle's province," Louis replied expansively. "I have no feel for flowers."

He pulled on the reins, and they stopped before the rococo Victorian house, circled with balconies, a deep verandah shadowed by elaborate fretwork. Between the porch posts all along the front were large hanging baskets of pink fuchsias and purple lobelia.

To Addie the three-storied structure looked austere, unwelcoming. Perhaps it was the dark-painted closed shutters on the long windows all across the front that gave that impression.

When Estelle came out to greet them, she was cordial and gracious if cool. But then again, Addie tried to remind herself that Bostonians could not be expected to have the warm effusiveness of Southern hostesses. Addie tried to put aside the feeling that Louis's sister was not all that glad to see her.

"Good day, Miss Montand. What a lovely place you have," Addie said sincerely, holding out her hand, which Louis's sister did not seem to see.

"So much still to be done, I'm afraid," Estelle said with a show of ennui. Then she turned to her brother, saying, "Louis, Manuel wants to talk to you. He's waiting for you. I think it's about—," she checked herself, "He said it was important."

"Excuse me, my dear," Louis said and went back down the porch steps over to where a man stood under the shade of a large oak tree nearby.

"Come along inside," Estelle said to Addie.

Addie tried to forget her initial snub, and giving Estelle the benefit of the doubt that she had not seen her extended hand and had not simply ignored it, she followed her into the house.

As Estelle led her inside, she explained the dimness of the interior saying she had learned it was necessary to close the shutters against the heat of the day in order to keep the house comfortably cool. The spacious entrance hall was paneled, as was its wide stairway in glowing redwood.

The parlor was, although elegant in every respect, almost overmuch. There were scalloped valances about the floor-length windows draped in brocade satin and curtained with starched lace. The furniture was heavy carved mahogany upholstered in emerald velvet. A richly flow-ered carpet covered the floor up to the marble hearth in front of the white marble fireplace over which hung a gloomy landscape framed in ornate gold.

It seemed ironic to Addie that with the abundance of real flowers growing in the yard an arrangement of artificial wax flowers under domed glass was placed on a polished table in the center of the room.

"Louis has excellent taste and is very particular," Estelle said as she moved over to the windows, fidgeted with the tassels, adjusted the tiebacks.

Estelle darted a quick glance her way, as if to see if she was sufficiently impressed. Although her statement seemed to beg some response, Addie could not think of any to make. She had been brought up in a gracious home with the understated elegance of fine English furniture, most of it brought over early in the eighteenth century by her Pride ancestors. She was a little at a loss of how to react to such ostentation.

"Louis told me he wanted you to see the whole house, so we'll indulge him." Estelle spoke with affection not untinged with condescension, a tone she often used in regard to her brother. Estelle moved toward the hall out to the broad staircase. "So, come along, we'll go upstairs."

176

Addie followed Estelle up the steps, noting the flocked wallpaper, the crystal prisms on the globed gaslights at the landing and at the top. As an invited guest, she had never before been asked to inspect the premises. Evidently complying with Louis's request, Estelle was doing the honors with some reluctance.

Addie remembered how Louis's conversations had been sprinkled with insinuating remarks—hinting at some point in time when his mansion was finished, when he was settled on his own estate, of some decision he would make. With even more discomfort Addie recalled Brook's predictions regarding Louis's intentions. With each step she took Addie's apprehension increased.

Estelle proceeded down the thickly carpeted hall, then opened a door at the end. Her voice jerked Addie back from her random thoughts. "This is the master suite. Go in, look around," Estelle urged, stepping back to let Addie enter.

Almost hesitant, Addie walked in and looked around at the lavishly decorated bedroom. Pink cabbage roses bloomed on the wallpaper, matching pink satin draperies hung at the bow window, pink marble tops were on all the surfaces of the dark wood furniture, a mirrored bureau and tables. An enormous, ornately carved bed draped in pink satin dominated the room.

"Louis ordered all *this* furniture himself. It's Philippine mahogany, hand carved by Spanish artisans. The marble is from Italy," Estelle said as she crossed the plush, flowered carpet and opened another door. "Here is the bathroom," she said triumphantly, gesturing with a flourish into what appeared to be a giant seashell. The walls and floor were pink marble. A huge porcelain tub stood on a polished wooden dais. Sculptured gold taps and faucet on a pedestaled wash basin rose like a huge opening flower, thick bath towels monogrammed with an embroidered M hung on a scrolled rack nearby.

Addie *was* impressed. Who wouldn't have been? Certainly no expense had been spared in the completion of Louis's house. To live here with his sister? Or alone? Certainly he had something else in mind with all these luxurious accommodations.

"Louis said you would be staying for luncheon?" Estelle hesitated as if expecting—hoping?—Addie would correct her. Addie felt puzzled.

"Why, yes, at least that is what I understood," Addie replied. Surely Estelle must know that Louis had invited her for lunch. It was hard to believe his sister would be so gauche as to ask such a question, unless . . . Then Addie recalled something she had heard her Aunt Susan say: *A lady is never rude unless intentionally.* Was Estelle *intentionally* trying to make her unwelcome?

"Well, then, I must go consult with our cook." Estelle spoke as if she must avert a culinary crisis. "In the meantime, please feel free to use the facilities to freshen up before we dine. Louis is with his overseer and may be some time coming in." With that Estelle swept out of the room.

Addie moved over to one of the long windows, parted the lace undercurtain, and looked out. Morning sun drenched the lawn—and the vineyards and the hills beyond—with golden light, and for a moment Addie felt a wave of nostalgia for the Virginia countryside. Suddenly she was back at Oakleigh and she felt the tug of homesickness for those other more familiar fields, trees, and views.

She turned back into the room with its ornate furnishings with a sense of loss and disorientation. All at once she felt stifled for air and hurried out of the overdecorated room. At the door she paused in brief confusion trying to recall which way to turn to the stairs. Then seeing the large brooding landscape she had noticed at the top of the landing, she hurried along the hallway and down the stairway.

The front door stood open, and Addie went out onto the

verandah in search of Louis. Standing on the edge of the porch steps she saw him at the far end of the lawn in an intense conversation with a man dressed in workman's clothes. As they spoke the other man punctuated his speech with hand gestures. Was this the Californio Louis said he had "inherited" along with his purchase of the land? Whatever they were talking about appeared important, to do with the vineyards. Addie did not want to interrupt. She turned her attention to the lovely gardens, the circular flower beds filled with blooming plants of all colors, the gravel paths that wound through the Italian statuary and birdbaths artistically placed at intervals. At the end, where the terraced lawn sloped down into the vineyards, stood an elaborate latticed gazebo.

Just then Louis turned as if to walk away from the discussion. Seeing Addie, he raised one hand to wave and started walking toward her. As he came within hearing distance he asked eagerly, "So, did Estelle give you the grand tour?"

"Yes, and it is very impressive indeed."

Looking pleased, Louis took the verandah steps two at a time and stood smiling down at Addie. He took her hand and drew it through his arm. "Well, then perhaps I should show you around the grounds a little. There are extensive orchards as well as the vineyards."

Just then Estelle came out the front door, and Addie said, "Louis is just going to show me your lovely garden, which he tells me is your creation."

"A garden is constant work. There is always much more to be done and our gardener is very slow—" her mouth tightened, "—very stubborn, set in his ways. I give directions but . . ." Estelle shrugged indifferently. Then without thanking Addie for the compliment she spoke directly to Louis, "Don't forget Father Paul is coming for lunch, and Milton should be here soon."

179

"Of course, I remember, Estelle." There was a tiny hint of irritation in Louis's voice. As they started down the verandah steps he explained, "She has invited Father Paul Bernard whom we knew from Saint Helena before we came to Calistoga and our lawyer, Milton Drew, to join us."

Addie thought of the little scene earlier when Estelle had seemed unsure whether she was going to stay for lunch. Did she really *not* know? Or was that an act? If so, why?

"I'm so glad you were able to come today, Addie. To see all this." He gestured broadly as they began strolling through the garden. "It's all turning out just the way I planned. I've been eager to share it with you."

They walked around the gazebo where the graveled paths formed a circle. Addie paused at a pansy bed filled with large purple, yellow, and lavender flowers. Leaning down to touch a velvety petal delicately with one finger, she said, "Everything is picture perfect, Louis."

"I'm glad you find it so, Addie. Next we'll go down to the orchards," Louis said. "If I weren't so determined on becoming the premier vintner in the valley, I think I would cultivate more fruit trees," Louis remarked. "But wine is becoming increasingly popular in America. Cultivating wine grapes will be a lucrative crop. Growers and vintners are bound to have increased prestige. I mean to show all these naysayers that you don't have to be born into a winemaking family to succeed. In fact, eventually, I will have my own dynasty to pass on to my children and grandchildren."

Addie was conscious of the emphasis he put on the words, *children and grandchildren.* She felt him looking at her with special significance but she pretended to be admiring some calla lilies and did not meet his gaze.

They left the garden and turned down a path that led into the bordering orchard planted with precise rows of fruit trees. Louis stopped to point out a peach tree with its greenish yellow globes that would soon ripen into luscious fruit. As Louis examined the leaves of one branch, Addie heard a rustling sound and saw movement at the end of the lane in which they stood. She squinted through the heavy foliage and was sure she saw several blue-coated figures huddled behind some trees at the end. She tugged Louis's sleeve, "Louis, are there people working here? I thought I saw some . . ."

He turned around, a deep frown creasing his forehead. "Where? Oh, yes, those are the workers I employed to build more cooling caves when my first harvest of grapes is ready. . . ."

Suddenly Addie remembered the Chinese coolies she had seen at the railroad station. "What are they doing here, Louis, and why are they hiding?"

"Hiding?" Louis seemed annoyed at the question. "They're not hiding. Most of them speak no English, so they're shy of strangers. Keep to themselves. They sleep out here in the orchard. Cook the strange food they like to eat. But they're hard workers, and I shall put them to good use come harvest time." He patted Addie's hand, which he had drawn through his arm again. "It's nothing for you to concern yourself about, my dear. Come along, our guests will be arriving soon, and I don't want Estelle to be cross with us if we're late for what I presume is a perfectly planned luncheon."

Somehow his answer did not satisfy Addie. Instinctively she felt there was something wrong, something furtive about the explanation. But realizing Louis did not want to discuss it further, she did not pursue it further.

As they walked back toward the house they saw a rickety black buggy coming up the drive.

"Ah, Estelle's good pastor right on time," Louis said with a touch of sarcasm, pulling out his gold watch and

181

consulting it. "He doesn't want to miss what will most surely be his best meal of the week."

The priest was old, his face wrinkled and brown as a nut, but his eyes were bright and shiny as black shoe buttons.

"Welcome, Father. May I present our guest Miss Adelaide Pride. Addie, Father Paul Bernard."

"A pleasure, Miss Pride. I beg your pardon for my appearance," the old man said, brushing great puffs of dust from his shabby cassock and worn boots. "I made some pastoral visits on my way here since I don't get over here from Saint Helena as much as I would like. Many of the places were off the beaten track."

"No apology necessary, Padre," Louis said jovially while giving Addie a wink behind the priest's back.

Addie felt a prick of distaste that Louis would make fun of this obviously nice, sincere minister. It struck her as arrogant and insensitive. But she had no more time to think about it as he was escorting her up the steps into the house where Estelle was entertaining her other guest, Milton Drew.

The three of them went inside where they found Estelle seated in the parlor already conversing with Milton Drew. Introductions were made and the men shook hands.

"Now, shall we all enjoy a friendly libation? Which shall it be a glass of Zinfandel or a sherry?" Louis asked.

Orders were taken and Louis poured the requested wine into tulip shaped crystal glasses already set out on one of the heavily carved tables. While Louis was so occupied, Mr. Drew, a balding man with a pale, jowly face turned to his host. "Your overseer, Manuel stopped me just now, Louis, complained bitterly of your plan to replace local workers with the Chinese you brought in to extend the limestone cooling caves. He is upset, you know. It's never been done here before. It could cause you a great deal of trouble."

"Milton, I realize you have lived in the valley a long

time. You were instrumental in getting me this property and negotiating the terms, and I am most grateful for your expertise in doing so. But I draw the line at being told by you or anybody else, for that matter, most of all by a Californio *overseer,* whom I can hire to work for me!"

Addie saw the muscle in Louis's cheek twitch and could tell he was extremely angry. But when he turned around to hand the filled glasses of wine to each guest, his expression was bland, his smile pleasant, his demeanor cordial. "Now, let's forget about all these unpleasant things and enjoy ourselves," he suggested and lifted his glass in a toasting gesture.

Addie accepted the delicate glass that Louis handed her; then he gave her an indulgent smile as if they two shared a special secret. The thought of the huddled Chinese coolies flashed into Addie's mind, somehow connecting them with the slave market memory of her childhood. Feeling slightly sick, she set down her glass untasted. She knew she didn't want to share anything special or secret with Louis.

Underneath his pleasant-mannered suavity, Louis was as hard as a diamond, calculating and caring little for the feelings of others. She had been appalled at the way he had put down his lawyer, a guest in his home, in front of his other guests, in such a dismissing way. She realized that what she had taken for self-confidence was actually arrogance.

Addie glanced at Estelle, wondering if Louis's sister had been at all dismayed by her brother's behavior. But Estelle had simply asked Father Bernard a question, turning to a less controversial topic. The half-hour that followed was as smooth as silk, although to Addie, the conversation seemed stiffly polite and artificial. Finally the muted sound of a gong echoed from the hall. Estelle stood up and announced they should go in to lunch. Although the dining room was large, high-ceilinged, and opened out onto the verandah that wrapped around the house, it seemed overcrowded. The walls were hung with too many heavily framed gloomy landscapes of the Hudson River school, a huge, carved sideboard took up one side of the room, and the windows along the other side of the room were draped and swagged in maroon velvet. It seemed a shame on such a beautiful spring day that the sunshine was blocked out by drawn lace curtains. Addie felt suffocated by the cumulative effect.

The table was elaborately appointed. There was a plethora of silverware at each place. A centerpiece of twin silver peacocks with sweeping tails on either side of the silver epergne was piled with dripping grapes, purple plums, polished golden apples.

The meal, although elegantly served, was a bit too highly seasoned and sauced for Addie's taste. She could manage to eat only a little for politeness's sake. With the conversation flowing around her, Addie's mind drifted. The lavish lifestyle of Louis and his sister was overwhelming. Luxury had once been an accepted part of her own life, something that her family and others of their class were used to, but it had not seemed so overpowering as the Montands'.

Since the war Addie had not known anyone who could afford to live as they had formerly. Of course, there were despised carpetbaggers, who had come to the defeated South, taken over the big houses, flaunted their wealth. But no one Addie knew associated with them—that is except Cousin Matthew, she thought ruefully, remembering it was *he* who was responsible for her coming to California.

"Addie, my dear?" Louis's voice, slightly puzzled, broke into her wandering thoughts. "Estelle was asking if you are quite finished? We are going to have our coffee in the drawing room."

"Oh, yes, sorry . . .," Addie said looking down at the unsliced pear on her dessert plate.

Louis came around behind her chair to assist her. As they went into the drawing room together he asked in a low voice, "Are you quite all right? You looked—pensive somehow."

She shook her head. "I'm fine, really."

But her day off had not had the restorative effect Addie had hoped. In fact, by the time Louis drove her back to Silver Springs she felt oddly depressed.

They drew up at the main building, and as Louis helped her out he asked solicitously, "Is there anything wrong, Addie? You were very quiet on the way into town."

"Oh, nothing, I assure you. A slight headache. Nothing more. I'm sorry if I seemed uncongenial."

"Perhaps you found the company today dull?" he persisted, frowning. "I wish Estelle had not included Father Bernard and Milton. I'd wanted our lunch *en famille*. I did not know they were coming until—" He broke off. "Next time we'll plan something livelier, more interesting."

Addie did not really want to make any future plans with Louis. Today she had seen a side of him she did not like, a side she had not really been aware of before now. Their walks and talks while he was still a guest at the hotel had been a pleasant enough distraction, but she did not want to encourage any greater intimacy. She was anxious for him to be gone.

"Thank you, Louis. It was very kind of Estelle, a lovely luncheon."

"Good afternoon then, Addie, I'll be in touch."

Seemingly reassured he mounted back into the carriage and drove away.

Addie hurried into the lobby. She wanted to check her mailbox, hopeful there might be a note from Rex. How different her last day off had been spent with *him*. With Rex she had felt at ease, not tense as she had at times today out at the Chateau Montand. She recalled how quickly she had

185

dismissed Brook's assertion that Louis's intentions were serious. Marriage had never been mentioned, yet there had been a subtle change in his attitude toward her today, a kind of possessiveness that alarmed her. Addie was sure there would be a series of tests any prospective bride of Louis's would have to pass. Estelle's approval, of course, would be first, and she did not think *she* would ever get that, did not even want it! Addie shuddered, imagining a life under Estelle's critical supervision.

She checked her mailbox. Still nothing from Rex. Her disappointment was assuaged a little when she saw there was a letter from her aunt Susan. Seeing the familiar spidery handwriting, Addie felt a sudden stab of homesickness. She realized how starved she was for news of home and family. She waited until she reached the privacy of her room to read it, then she tore open the envelope hungrily.

Addie raced through the three thin pages of closely written script. Her aunt wrote just the way she talked. Addie could almost hear her softly accented voice telling of incidents about people she knew, recounting the small events that made up her daily life. It might have seemed like trivia to most, but to Addie it was food and drink.

When she came to the last paragraph tears blurred the lines her aunt had written, "We miss you, dear girl, and California seems a long way away."

Addie let the letter fall into her lap and she stared blankly into her room full of shadows as daylight was fast fading. California *was* a long way away. It was miles and worlds away. The people were different; life here—the way people talked and thought and acted—was infinitely different. Her aunt's letter had brought back so poignantly everything Addie had left that her heart felt almost bruised.

Now, Addie realized what had happened to her during the luncheon at the Montands, why she had found herself so detached from the company, the conversation. It came

186

to Addie that the war and all it had meant to the South, to her family, to herself had only been a distant drumbeat here in California. She had glanced around the table, from face to face, knowing they understood nothing of what she had been through. Through all the violence, the battles, the men who had fought and been killed, this valley had slumbered peacefully, moving from season to season. The war that had cut like a saber swath through Virginia had left the people here untouched. She felt empty and infinitely lonely.

Memory is mysterious. It is like a mansion with many doors, each opening and leading down several corridors, into halls and hidden rooms and even dark closets you may not want opened. Addie thought she had put away her memories of the past, of Ran, of what might have been. Perhaps she had been mistaken. Maybe she imagined that she had seen in Rex Lyon's eyes, felt in his kiss her own deep longing for love, her hope that such a love was possible.

She folded the pages of Aunt Susan's letter and put them back in the envelope. She felt depressed. She did not even feel like writing in her journal. She felt as though she were standing on a precipice over a great yawning void of loneliness, of empty days, maybe even of years, stretching ahead.

Probably she was just tired. The day with Louis and his sister had been a strain. She would have liked a reviving cup of hot tea but didn't feel like going over to the dining hall to get it. She certainly wasn't up to an interrogation by Mrs. Amberly for details about the Chateau Montand. So she would do without.

Addie washed her face, braided her hair, put on her nightgown, and climbed wearily into bed. She fell asleep quickly, slept heavily, but the impressions of her day colored her dreams. The plush draperies, the flocked wallpaper, the velvet upholstery of the Montands' house seemed to close in upon her, clinging to her smotheringly. Distorted images of Estelle and Louis, and lurking in the background the shadowy figures of the Chinese in the orchard, were all seen as if through the cloudy murkiness of a crystal ball.

She woke suddenly, heart pounding, and pushed away the blanket and quilt. She struggled into a sitting position. Perspiration beaded her face, her damp nightgown clung to her; she was shaking. Gasping for air, she told herself it was only a nightmare. But it was a long time before she could fall asleep again.

Chapter 14

The next morning and the two that followed, Addie woke up with the feeling she was plowing through quicksand. Mrs. Amberly seemed more difficult than ever. The necessity of being polite during the forced companionship of the day was bad enough. But biting her tongue, clenching her teeth through the long evenings while she listened to the shallow, pointless conversation at the card table, the gossip rife with rumors passed on with malicious relish—all this was even worse.

Addie was honest enough to admit it was her own inner frustration that made it all seem especially irritating. With each day that passed with no word from Rex, Addie grew more puzzled. Why had he stayed away? Why had he not sent her a note? Was there any explanation? When she thought of those kisses exchanged on the shadowy cottage porch, her cheeks burned. Had she taken too much for granted? Rex had not seemed like a man to play with a woman's affection. What could possibly be the reason?

In contrast, the day after she had been to the Montands', a bouquet and a note had been delivered from Louis. He had written in his flowing script:

Yesterday was one of the most enjoyable days I have spent since coming to California. Without a doubt it was being with you that made it so. I hope we'll spend many such lovely days together at Chateau Montand. Seeing you there made my vision of my home perfect.
Devotedly, Louis

Addie tore the note up. She was glad Mrs. Amberly had been at the bathhouse having her treatment when the note and flowers had come. Addie did not want to satisfy her employer's avaricious curiosity. After her first chagrin at Louis's interest in Addie, Mrs. Amberly began to regard it as a possible path to gain access to Estelle.

Addie did not want to be interrogated—especially about Louis, concerning whom she had more and more troubling questions. Under his suavity, his pleasant manners, there was something unlikable. He had a rapier wit that edged perilously close to cruelty. He had a need to feel superior to others, and in order to maintain that he must make others look inferior. He was often sarcastic—and there was something else she had seen yesterday. When Mr. Drew was expressing some doubt as to the wisdom of hiring Chinese workers, Louis had ruthlessly cut him short with the same kind of contemptuous disdain Addie had seen in Estelle. Two of a kind, birds of a feather—all the old adages seemed appropriate when applied to the Montands.

Louis's note made her vaguely apprehensive. Addie decided she must definitely not encourage him.

Wistfully Addie thought how she would have welcomed Rex Lyon actively courting her. Why could *he* not have sent flowers and such words after *their* day together? Try as she might not to mind, it really hurt.

That afternoon, during Mrs. Amberly's nap time, Addie caught up on some personal chores, some mending, repairing a hem that had come loose, putting a new lace collar on a dress. But her thoughts spun endlessly on the question to

190

which she could not find an answer. Why had Rex Lyon so suddenly dropped out of her life? Was it his work? Or was it his will?

That evening as she and Mrs. Amberly entered the dining hall, to Addie's dismay the first person she saw was Louis. He was dining with Milton Drew. As soon as she and Mrs. Amberly were shown to their usual table, Louis came over.

Immediately Mrs. Amberly went into her act assuming the saccharine tone she always used when speaking to him. "Well, well, Mr. Montand, how lovely to see you. Miss Pride has told me *so* much about your beautiful home, I'm *languishing* for a glimpse of it myself!"

At this Addie flushed with embarrassment. What an outlandish fib! Even under her employer's relentless questioning, Addie had hardly said a word about Chateau Montand. Knowing the sly ridicule with which Louis regarded Mrs. Amberly, Addie refused to meet his mocking eyes and nervously rearranged the silverware at her plate.

Mrs. Amberly obliviously bumbled on. "So, Mr. Montand, what brings you into town this evening?"

"Business, not pleasure, I'm afraid. A meeting to settle some legal details with my lawyer," Louis replied smoothly. His gaze, however, rested on Addie even as he addressed Mrs. Amberly. "But when we're finished, perhaps I'll stop by the card room later and see who's winning."

Mrs. Amberly shook her head coquettishly. "You know what they say, Mr. Montand: lucky at cards unlucky at love!"

"But I'm sure, Madam, *you* have had the good fortune to be lucky at *both*," Louis teased, looking directly at Addie.

After Louis went back to his table, Mrs. Amberly lapsed into her usual complaints about the food and her fellow guests. When they finished they went into the card room. Addie settled herself with her needlepoint for another endless evening. She positioned herself at some distance from

the table where Mrs. Amberly sat with her cronies. She tried
to turn a deaf ear to their chatter, concentrating on the
design on the pillowcover she was making to send to Aunt
Susan. But even as she plied her needle steadily, her
thoughts were of Rex Lyon. Why had she not heard from
him? Addie considered all possible reasons why, making
up excuses for him, imagining how he'd explain it when
she saw him. And when would that be?

She knew it was futile to guess. But she couldn't help herself. Rex Lyon filled her with hope, answered that longing
in her heart. There must be some explanation. From that
first unforgettable moment on the day she arrived, she had
felt *something*—and now, after getting to know him, she
discovered other qualities about him—his integrity, his
intelligence, his gentleness—that appealed to her. What
could be keeping him away?

The evening moved with creeping tempo. Addie willed
herself not to sneak too many glances at the clock over the
reception desk in the lobby nor look at her little gold watch
pinned to her bodice. She knew she could not leave until
Mrs. Amberly's game was finished, and her employer was
insatiable at cards, especially if she was winning.

About an hour into the evening, Mrs. Amberly's acerbic
voice penetrated Addie's boredom, jolting her to attention.

"It's said the widow Wegner's mortgaged to the hilt. Her
husband was no businessman and left a mountain of debts.
They say *he* died under *very* mysterious circumstances."

Her employer was talking about *Freda!* Where on earth
had Mrs. Amberly picked up this piece of outrageous gossip? Addie seethed. She longed to rush to the defense of
her friend. Helpless rage at her position trembled through
Addie.

"Of course, nothing was proven—this being the small
town it is—they all protect one another. *But . . .*" Mrs.
Amberly paused significantly. ". . . I've had it on *very good*

authority that she's used up all her credit, and the bank won't extend her another loan. Several ranchers are waiting until the bank forecloses so they can pick up the land at a low price—which tells *me just* how *loyal* friends *really* are when it comes to a good deal!" Here she gave another dramatic pause. "*But* she has another trick up her sleeve— I'm told . . ."

The Misses Brunell and Mrs. Cranby leaned forward like three scrawny buzzards to pick over the kill.

"To *remarry!*" Mrs. Amberly announced triumphantly. "A rich husband would solve her problems, right?"

She turned, jerking her head to where Louis and Milton Drew could be seen conferring in the adjoining lounge.

"I understand the widow Wegner has set her cap for *him.*" She raised her voice slightly. "With his wealth and class he'd certainly be a catch—especially for a penniless woman."

Addie checked the urge to contradict her suppositions about Freda and Louis. What would Mrs. Amberly think if she knew the truth—that Louis's interest lay closer at hand. Addie smiled ruefully. Perhaps, if there were no Rexford Lyon, even *she* might—*no,* of course not. She would have to be desperate indeed to consider marrying Louis Montand.

"What are you smiling about?" a voice asked and she looked up startled to see Louis standing in front of her. "It must be something pleasant. I could hope you might be thinking of me."

He drew up a chair and angled it so that when he sat down beside her his back would be to the nearby card table and none of the players would be able to overhear what he said.

To avoid answering his question, Addie asked, "Did your business meeting go well?"

Louis frowned slightly. "Ah, well, some small problems— these locals . . ." he started to say something more, but changed his mind. Instead he smiled. "When shall we plan another afternoon together or an evening?"

Before Addie could reply, over Louis's shoulder she saw a tall familiar figure enter the lobby. Then Rex was at the archway, scanning the card room as if looking for someone. Addie's first happy surprise at seeing him was followed by excruciating embarrassment. She almost raised her hand in a greeting when she saw him cross the room toward them. Louis half-turned and followed the direction she was looking. When he saw Rex he stood up.

The four heads at the card table swiveled curiously. As Rex came closer, Addie saw his expression. Anger had turned his gray eyes to burning steel. Suddenly she felt unreasonably frightened.

Rex acknowledged her with a brief nod then spoke directly to Louis in a hard, tight voice, "I have to talk to you, Montand."

Louis lifted an eyebrow. "Now?"

"Yes, *now*. It's important."

"If you insist." Louis shrugged indifferently. "But surely this is not the time nor the place, Lyon."

"I agree. Shall we go into the Gentlemen's Lounge?"

Louis turned to Addie and in a tone that implied annoyance asked, "Will you excuse us, my dear? This should not take long." Then to Rex, "Let's go and be done with it."

Without a glance at Addie, Rex spun around and led the way out, his boots loud on the polished floor. Louis followed more slowly.

Addie froze, every muscle in her body strained. What were the two men going to discuss? Why was Rex so angry? Just then she heard Mrs. Amberly declare, "I always thought there was bad blood between those two. I felt there was going to be an explosion in *that* quarter soon, mark my words. What's their trouble? Land. In California that's what any kind of battle seems to be about. Montand can

194

outbid, outspend Rex Lyon, and he's known for getting what he wants. And he wants the widow's property—I don't think he's willing to *marry* for it, but he *is* willing to pay a high price for it—higher than any of the ranchers around here can scrape up. Especially Lyon. I understand his family's fortune was all turned into the land, no cash. And the widow wants out—she's tired of the drudgery and lonely—although it's said she has plenty of company—when she wants it."

Addie was almost too upset at the moment to pay attention to Mrs. Amberly's ugly gossip. Then suddenly the bone of rumor Mrs. Amberly had thrown for the others to gnaw on came through to her. Could Mrs. Amberly have for once heard something *true?* Addie's hands clutched the canvas-backed needlepoint so tight that the needle jabbed into her finger. She gave a little gasp and looked down to see a small spot of blood rising at its tip.

What *really* was going on between the two men? She *had* to find out.

The card players were too preoccupied with their game and gossip to notice as Addie slipped out of the room. She crossed the lobby and stood concealed by one of the fluted pillars. From behind the swinging louvered doors of the Gentlemen's Lounge she heard raised voices.

"You're hiring Chinese?" Rex's was intense.

"Yes, if that's any concern of yours," Louis replied coldly.

"You're darn right it concerns me. Just as it will the other ranchers. Anything that happens in this valley concerns us all. I'd like to know why you're importing cheap labor when we have plenty of willing workers right here—people who were born in this valley, live here, support their families by working the vineyards, Californios who love the land, take pride in their work, have worked for vintners for years with loyalty and—"

"One Chinaman can work twice as long and three times

195

as hard as any Californio you've got in your vineyards, Lyon. It's a free country. You're free to save money yourself any way you can. Don't tell me how to conduct my business. You run your ranch the way you see fit, and I'll do the same. I'm just trying to make an honest profit on my investment."

"At the expense of the rest of us? At the expense of those poor devils brought here like cattle in boxcars? I was at the station just after they arrived. I saw the conditions in which they traveled seventy miles in the heat of the day—no light, no air, no water—" his voice became heavy with contempt, "—no thanks to you, it's a wonder they didn't die en route. Now, I hear you have them sleeping out in your orchards."

"They're used to a lot worse in their own country—"

"I guess you think the Chinese are less than human. The lowest form of humanity, right? They swarm over to this country like rats. They're only peasants in their own country, why should you care if they're treated decently? Or what conditions they live under after they get here? Just so you get twelve or sixteen hours a day of work out of them."

"I think you've said quite enough, Lyon. I warn you, don't go too far." Louis's voice dropped, attempting a lighter tone. "Come now, let's have a drink together like two reasonable fellows who happen to disagree."

"Drink with *you?* No thanks."

Before Addie could move, she heard the creak of the doors of the Gentlemen's Lounge being pushed open. She shrank back against the post, flinching at the sight of the ironlike expression on Rex's face as he stalked across the lobby. As the slam of the front door of the hotel reverberated, Addie discovered she was trembling.

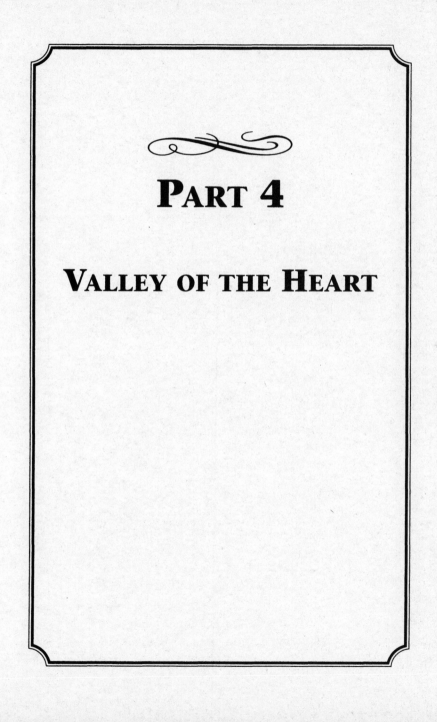

PART 4

VALLEY OF THE HEART

Chapter 15

*A*ddie did not sleep well that night. Louis's soothing assurance that it had all been 'a little disagreement' between the two men—nothing she should worry "her pretty head about"—failed to satisfy Addie. She did not tell Louis how much she had overheard, since that would place her in the awkward position of being an eavesdropper. But when she tried tactfully to find out the real reason, Louis became irritated. He told her he had to be off to Chateau Montand, that Estelle would worry if he was too late.

What bothered Addie more was Rex's coldness toward her. She had seemed to be included in his animosity toward Louis. What could possibly have happened to change his attitude so drastically?

She was awake at dawn, her head aching, her eyes heavy from lack of sleep. Maybe some fresh air, a walk would clear her head. She got up, dressed, and went out into the cool gray morning.

The image of Rex's angry unsmiling face lingered in her mind. The way he had looked at her last night was so different from what she had seen in his eyes before. Or had she imagined it all? After all, she scarcely knew him—one day together was all they had really had. One magical day. Hardly enough on which to build a dream. And yet . . .

Head down, Addie trudged on, heartsore. She had just turned in the gates of Silver Springs when a familiar voice jerked her out of her melancholy reverie. "Whoa there, Miss Pride! Hold on!" She turned to see Brook striding purposefully toward her. "Addie!" he smiled as he came alongside her. "What are you doing out so early on this gloomy morning?"

"Escaping!" Addie tried not to look guilty even though she felt sure Brook knew how difficult Mrs. Amberly was.

"I understand." He gave her a solemn wink. "'One hour of thoughtful solitude may nerve the heart for days of conflict, girding up its armor to meet the most insidious foe,' eh?"

"I'm not sure I recognize that," she said as they fell into step and started walking again.

"Percival, a rather obscure philosopher. I like to collect that kind of quotation, then I can spring them once in a while when it's appropriate, and my friends think I'm erudite."

Addie laughed. "Well, *I'd* think that anyway, Brook. I'm convinced you are very clever indeed." They walked along a little farther. "Now, I'll ask you the same question you asked me. What are you doing out and about so early?"

"Well, I'm going out of town for a few days—to San Francisco first. I need to talk to some of my investors, explain my plans for the race track and other expansions I have in mind." He glanced at her smiling. "In other words you might say I'm going prospecting for gold!"

"You don't look dressed for it!" As usual Brook was impeccably dressed.

He acted surprised. "Don't you know the secret of borrowing lots of money? You have to look like you don't need it!"

"Well, you *don't*. You look as though you owned the world," she told him, surveying his superbly cut coat, snowy linen shirt, silk cravat.

Brook swung his gold-headed cane and his expression became serious. "Well, let's hope the men I'm going to see will agree that Calistoga *can* become the *Saratoga* of the West. If we're going to draw the racing crowd we've got to have thoroughbred horses, attract the top jockeys. It will mean a sizable investment. But well worth it, if I can just convince them." He frowned for a minute. "Let's just hope these men will be willing to part with a great deal of cash—otherwise . . ." He let his thought fade away like the morning mist; then he smiled down at her. "Wish me luck?"

"Of course, I do. Although Silver Springs seems almost perfect just the way it is—if you didn't do another thing—"

"Ah, but then you don't have my dreams."

"Dreams," she repeated thoughtfully. "I guess, maybe—I've seen too many dreams dissolve."

"Don't give up dreaming, Addie. That's fatal. Remember, 'A man's reach must exceed his grasp'—or else, as the poet says, 'what's a heaven for?'"

"Browning. I got that one right, didn't I?" Addie smiled. "I didn't know you also knew poetry."

"But then, dear Addie, there are many things you don't know about me."

"Perhaps in time . . ."

"Time. There is never enough of it, is there? But maybe, if you *did* you'd be disappointed—disillusioned—" He broke off abruptly. "Well, I must be off."

"Will you be gone long?"

"I can't be sure. It depends." He smiled enigmatically. "To quote Will Shakespeare, 'As good luck would have it'—what success I have in my endeavor."

"I'll miss you anyway, however long. The Springs is never the same when you're away."

201

Something curious softened Brook's glance. "And I shall miss you, Addie." Then he gave the brim of his hat a flick, bowed, and nonchalantly said, "*Adios. Hasta luega*," and walked quickly away in the direction of the main building.

Addie watched him go regretfully. She had been tempted to tell Brook about the quarrel she had overheard between Rex and Louis, and ask him if he could guess what it was about. Brook was discreet, but he knew the town well, the undercurrents as well as the rumors and the facts. However, she did not have a chance because Brook had seemed very distracted as though he had other things on his mind today than valley conflicts.

What an enigma Brook was. She had never met anyone like him. Outgoing, congenial as he was, there was much about him that remained mysterious. A few times he had let her see a part of him he mostly kept hidden. Ambitious, creative, impulsive, he had made no secret of his goal of bringing Calistoga prosperity and fame, and becoming a millionaire before he was thirty—whatever that took. This Addie found fascinating.

She sighed. As mercurial as he was, Addie knew she would miss him. His presence around the resort was certainly energizing and gave the humdrum days a needed spark.

However, this time Brook returned as suddenly as he had departed. Going to check her mail one morning a few days later, Addie was surprised to see him behind the reception desk in the lobby.

"Brook, I didn't know you were back! How was the mining? Successful?" she asked teasingly.

He looked blank for a few seconds as if he didn't know what she meant. Then he must have recalled their conversation, and his face broke into a smile—a rueful one. "Not quite as successful as I'd hoped. But as they say, 'thar's gold in them thar hills'—*other* hills. I've still got my plans, just have to dig in another spot."

But there was something in the way Brook spoke that made Addie wonder.

In the next few days the weather turned changeable; there were days of drizzling rain and days of brilliant sunshine. On some afternoons, fog began drifting over the land, moving with eerie swiftness, its misty veil giving a sense of isolation and beauty to the valley.

The damp spring weather had an adverse effect on Mrs. Amberly's rheumatism, and she complained loud and often about how little good the treatments were doing her. Even when the rain stopped and there were several mild days in a row, the sky remained sullen with low-lying clouds, and Mrs. Amberly became vocally irritable, talked of leaving. Then one of the other guests, an elderly lady Addie quite liked for her dignity and aloofness, suggested that she might try a few days in the lake country at the geyser resorts. The air was said to be drier and the weather a little sunnier. Mrs. Amberly began to talk of joining the group of guests from the hotel who were going to make the trip to Lakeport.

At breakfast she told Addie to make inquiries about arrangements. When Addie left the dining hall and started toward the main building she nearly collided with Brook. He was walking toward her, his head down as if in deep thought. He seemed startled when she spoke to him. "Brook?"

For a second he almost seemed to be trying to place her. Then he smiled and held out his hands to her. "Addie! Sorry! I was woolgathering."

"I was hoping to see you before we left," she said.

"Left?" he seemed puzzled.

"Maybe Mrs. Amberly didn't mention it to you, but she's planning to go up to Lakeport to the geysers for a few days.

She's heard it's warmer, less damp up there—" Addie halted, mid-sentence. Brook seemed so distracted. Obviously he had something more important on his mind than hearing about Mrs. Amberly's plans.

"What? I'm sorry, Addie, I guess I'm a little preoccupied today."

"Thinking about racetracks and thoroughbreds?" she teased.

Again he seemed to draw a blank for a minute before giving a short laugh. "Oh, yes, right! Racetracks and thoroughbreds." He paused then said, "I may have to go away again for a few days."

"Oh, are you planning another *gold mining* expedition?"

"Well, maybe, I guess you could call it that." Brook reached for her hands and held them in his. "Good-bye, Addie, in case I don't see you before I leave." He gave her a smile, more tender than his usual roguish one. "You're a very special lady, you know. I wish—" he halted and resumed his teasing way, "—but then you know what they say about wishes—if they were horses, beggars would ride? My wishes tend to run to thoroughbreds—very, very expensive thoroughbreds."

Brook held both of her hands a little longer, then gave them a gentle squeeze before releasing them. "Good-bye, my dear Miss Pride."

Addie watched him walk away with his self-confident stride; then quite suddenly the swirling mist rising up from the ground seemed to encircle then blot him from her sight. For a moment Addie felt an icy shiver course down her spine. A premonition of some sort? Of danger? No, of course not. It was just that it had been a strange sensation seeing Brook disappear like that into the fog.

The arrangements to go on the morning stage up to Lakeport and the geyser resort were made. In a flurry of packing

204

and last-minute decisions of what to take, Mrs. Amberly belatedly remembered she would need cash for the trip, so she sent Addie to the bank before it closed for the day. Addie dropped everything else she was doing and rushed off to town. Just as she reached the bank door, it opened. Rex Lyon was coming out.

Both halted. Blood rushed hotly into Addie's face. The day of the picnic with all its romantic promise, the days of diminishing hope that followed, her disappointment and sense of hurt seemed to culminate in this unexpected encounter.

For a moment they both seemed locked in an embarass-ing inability to speak. For what was there to say? Neither could pass because the other was blocking the way. Speech-less, Addie nonetheless searched Rex's face for a clue as to what he might be feeling. But his eyes regarding her steadily revealed nothing, and his expression told her even less.

But behind that steadfast gaze Addie thought she saw some reproach, disappointment. In her? Why? It was *he* who had failed to pursue what had seemed to begin that day of the picnic. She still did not understand what could have happened to change things. But her pride prohibited the question for which her heart begged an answer. Impris-oned by convention, her smile became fixed.

An eternity seemed to pass in the space of a few moments.

He removed his hat, "Good afternoon, Miss Pride."

"Mr. Lyon." Her voice sounded unnaturally hoarse over the tightness of her throat.

She stood there in anxious uncertainty until he spoke again. "Maybe, you'd be interested to know ..." He hesi-tated, then went on, "Since I saw you, my friends, the Bairds, have had some misfortune. Nan, Mrs. Baird, and the boy, Lowell, both developed diphtheria. I had to help

Rob move them down from the hills, find them a place to stay in town where they could have medical attention and recuperate."

"I'm sorry to hear that." Addie's natural sympathy for the Bairds was countered by her questioning of Rex's motives. Was he telling her this just an excuse? Sick friends or not, if he had wanted to, he could have come by or at least sent a note of explanation. But her years of drilling in social graces compelled her to say, "I hope—are they—how are they getting along now?"

"Yes, much better, steadily improving. In fact, they will be leaving at the end of next week to go to San Francisco and then back east to take a ship to Scotland. Rob wants his family to meet Nan and Lowell."

Addie managed to say something she hoped was suitable. Standing here was becoming increasingly uncomfortable. "If you'll excuse me . . ." She moved to go past him. "I must get to the teller before the bank closes; we are leaving tomorrow on a trip to the geysers, and Mrs. Amberly needs cash."

"Of course." He immediately stepped aside.

In spite of herself, Addie hesitated a few seconds, to see if—hoping that Rex might say something more. But he simply stood there waiting for her to go into the bank. In a surge of wounded pride, Addie swept past him. As she did she heard him say in a low tone of voice, "I wish you every happiness . . ."

At the cashier's cage, heart racing, his words suddenly came back to her, before she actually *heard* what he had said. What did he mean? "I wish you every happiness?" That was the cliché people used when congratulating someone on an upcoming felicitous event—like an engagement or marriage. Involuntarily Addie turned her head to see if Rex was still there. But he was gone.

"May I help you?" came the cashier's impatient voice.

"Oh, yes." Addie turned back, flustered. Tugging her gloves off hands clammy with nervous perspiration, she quickly thrust Mrs. Amberly's cheque through the window for cashing. Distracted by Rex's puzzling remark, she stepped away from the counter. "Miss! Your money!" The clerk's sharp voice bolted her back from her trance.

Addie gathered up the stack of bills and left the bank still baffled by the upsetting encounter with Rex and his enigmatic words.

The next morning was overcast. After breakfast the Silver Springs contingent going to Lakeport assembled outside the main building to wait for Henessey's Stage Line's big six-horse passenger wagon. There was much good-natured complaining about the fog drifting grayly around the verandah posts. Joking remarks about hoping the driver could see his way out of the fog up to the sunnier hills were greeted with laughter.

Addie tried to join the merriment that surrounded her. But her heart was still heavy from yesterday's jolting meeting with Rex. She had relived the incident a dozen times. Accusing herself of stupidity, over and over she thought of things she could have said, how she might have handled it better. But finally she had to admit she had been too much in shock.

She vacillated from frustration to indignation. It was *his* fault it had been so awkward. *He* was the one who should have apologized, made some excuse, given some explanation for not contacting her. Oh, the shame of it! Every time she thought of it she died of humiliation all over again.

In spite of everything that had happened, in her secret heart Addie blamed herself. She had allowed herself to believe that what had taken place between them was special. If it was anyone's fault, it was hers for being such a fool.

Forget it! Forget him! But the old adage was true: Easier

said than done. She had let her heart rule her head. She did not know how long it would take her to get over it.

As she was giving herself all this advice, to her surprise she saw Louis's phaeton, drawn by his high-stepping horse, come through the gate. After parking the vehicle he jumped out and came over to her.

"I've come to see you off," he told her jauntily, then handed her a small basket of grapes nestled in glossy leaves. "Compliments of Estelle."

Addie doubted the gift *was* his sister's idea, and she had to credit Louis himself for the thoughtful gesture. Still feeling she must, she forced an appropriate response. Addie replied, "How kind of her. Please give her my thanks."

A murmur of approval came from the ladies gathered on the porch observing the little tableau. "What a gentleman," "How nice," "*She* should be flattered."

Louis did not miss the consensus of approval, and smiled benignly.

"I hope you have a delightful time but I shall miss you, Addie," he said, looking at her significantly.

Addie was aware that Louis always did the *right* thing, the socially correct thing. It was as inborn as the Boston accent. Maybe there were worse things than being a "proper gentleman." She could not help, though, thinking of Rex's spontaneity, his openness, his "California" naturalness. That seemed a great deal more sincere.

Before her thoughts could slip further along this dangerous line, someone shouted, "Here it comes!"

They all turned to see the big, brightly painted red and yellow stage pulled by three matched pairs of powerfully built horses come through the Silver Springs gate and pull up in front. Buck Henessey, the driver, well-known for his expertise on the mountain roads, climbed down. He was a large, barrel-chested man, with a ruddy complexion, bright blue eyes, and a bushy mustard-colored mustache, which twirled up at either end giving him the look of a roguish pirate. He lifted his pearl-gray Stetson to the group and greeted them jovially, "Good morning, folks! You all are in for the time of your life! So, now, if you'll jest git on board, we'll git goin'."

Since the stage was open, everyone had donned canvas dusters and swathed themselves in protective veiling. To all the many questions asked him, from queries as to the weather, the roads, the accommodations when they reached the geysers, Mr. Henessey gave the same hearty assurance, "Finest kind!"

Because she was the youngest of the travelers and because it seemed proper, Addie volunteered to sit up front beside the driver. It suited her fine since seated up there she would not have to sit by Mrs. Amberly on the twenty-mile trip. As she settled herself Henessey assured her that in that seat she'd get the "finest kind" of view.

Shortly after they left town the day began to clear. They started up the torturous mountain roads. Some of the curves were so short that the lead horses were out of sight on one side as the stage was rounding the other. The sharper the curves the louder the gasps and small cries coming from those in the seats behind. Addie realized they were probably suppressing screams and clutching each other as they swerved around the serpentine road.

Addie too might have been really terrified if Brook had not sung the praises of Henessey. He was the best stage driver around, he had assured her. Sitting beside him on the high driver's seat, Addie was impressed by his dexterity. Even so Addie gripped the hand bars several times and held her breath.

But Buck was a master at what he did; the reins were firm in his grip, his shouts sometimes punctuated by an occasional twirl of his whip, which echoed through the mountain pass like the crack of a pistol shot.

The view of the valley was breathtaking from this height as they ascended the steep grade, and Addie was kept amused by Buck's commentary as they made their way up the narrow road. At one point, he pointed with his whip to an immense, conelike peak that rose sharply up against the now cloud free sky. "That there's Lover's Leap," he told her. "Legend tells that a young Indian couple fell in love with each other but were from different tribes, and their folks wouldn't agree to them marrying, so they come up here—on a moonlit night so the story goes—" here Buck gave her a broad wink, "—and took a flying leap off'n that rock." He chuckled. "That's the valley's own kinda Romeo and Juliet tale, ain't it?" and he roared with laughter.

By noon they reached Lakeport where they were to stay at the inn for two full days. Henessey was to return for them on his way back to Calistoga from Santa Rosa. After the long trip, everyone was eager to try the famous geyser soda springs. The air was crystal clear and dry, the weather mild and delightful.

Addie knew the change of scene should lift her spirits, and scolded herself because it didn't. The memory of the embarrassing incident with Rex in front of the bank blunted her enjoyment. She kept mentally kicking herself for her awkward handling of the situation.

By the second day she did succeed in taking advantage of the exhilirating air and the mild weather. She was also allowed unusual freedom from Mrs. Amberly's carping. Her employer seemed to have found nothing to complain about and was socializing with the new people she met at the Lakeport Inn. Left on her own, Addie tried to enjoy her delightful surroundings and forget Rex Lyon. She managed the first but found the second impossible. He seemed to have lodged himself permanently in her mind—and heart. The question of his changed attitude toward her remained a mystery.

210

The two days passed pleasantly enough and many of the Silver Springs exiles were loath to leave the high, dry climate for the valley, where the damp, foggy weather possibly persisted. Buck Henessey paced, smoking one of his long cigars, waiting while his erstwhile passengers caused countless delays. By the time all the baskets, boxes, and valises had been stowed and lashed securely, it was late when they got started down the mountain.

Since on the return trip Henessey had a helper sitting beside him on the front seat, Addie had taken a seat with the others in the coach. The sight of the man with a shotgun had momentarily alarmed her until Henessey explained the man was an employee of Union Express in Santa Rosa who required it because they were carrying a cash box containing the miners' payroll, a standard precaution, he told her calmly.

All the passengers seemed quieter on the return trip than they had on the way up to the geysers. Two days of the hot spring treatments, long walks, hearty food, and nightly square dances had taken their toll. Heads were nodding and conversation faded away after they were on the road a few miles.

Mrs. Amberly had soon fallen asleep, and Addie stared at the scenery. Lulled by the rocking motion of the stage, she was in a half-dreamy state. She still couldn't seem to keep her thoughts from wandering back to Rex Lyon. Why did something nag at her, keep her from accepting the obvious fact he did not want to continue their relationship? It was just that it didn't make sense. He had told her she was discerning, hadn't he? Well, there was something strange about his sudden turnaround. Something had happened. What, she couldn't guess. Why hadn't she been bold enough to ask him if she had done anything to offend him? Of course, that would have been out of the question. Yet—there had been something—even that day, in the awkwardness of that meeting—something in his eyes, his expression that made her wonder—and that strange thing he had said—"I wish you every happiness." What had that meant? It was as if he never expected to see her again. Bewildered, Addie shook her head.

As they came up the other side of the mountain, Lovers Leap came into view. It brought the legend Buck had told her about to Addie's mind. Would lovers *really* do anything to be together, no matter how misguided? Or were stories like *Romeo and Juliet, Tristan and Isolde,* and all the romantic classics just that—figments of the imagination of some author or dramatist?

Then she thought of Rob and Nan Baird. They were certainly a *real* love story. Thinking of the Bairds, of course, made her think about Rex again. What was it Freda said about him? That he was the most honest person she had ever known. If that were true, how could he have said all the things he had said to her and mean them, and suddenly not call or send a message, a note of explanation for his silence?

Addie remembered what else Freda had said: "Love is always a risk. You open yourself up to hurt, betrayal, and loss." Freda had known her husband had a history of tuberculosis when she married him, that he might die young. She had taken a chance that with her love and care he would recover. He didn't. But perhaps he was given a few years more of life because of her love. Freda said it had all been worth it. Those few perfect, happy years together had been worth what came after—the pain, the sorrow, the loneliness.

Nan Baird felt the same way about Rob. Love was worth the cost, that when you really love someone, you gave yourself, relinquished that inner you, it was worth it. Addie thought of the legend of Lover's Leap. When you put your life and happiness into the hands of someone else—it was a kind of jumping into the unknown. Maybe, some things in life are worth risking everything for and maybe love was one of those.

Or was that just romantic dreaming? Maybe it only made sense when the person you love, loved you in return. She hadn't asked for this heartache. She hadn't wanted to fall in love. It had just happened.

The stage slowed as they started up a steep incline, a precipitous section, steep cliffs and only manzanita and brush to hide the drop to the river far below on one side and on the other side the dense woods. Outside, the day seemed to darken. Addie leaned back, steadying herself against the lurching vehicle as they moved steadily up the mountain.

Then quite suddenly they jolted to a stop. Addie heard shouts, the whinnying of the horses. She sat up straight, clutching the seat handles. The stage rocked precariously, as if the horses were rearing and backing up. Mrs. Amberly, aroused from her slumber and struggling to sit upright, bonnet askew, narrow eyes wide open, grumbled sleepily, "What's happened, what's going on?"

"I don't know. Perhaps a fallen tree's blocked the way."

But before the words were out of Addie's mouth, there was the sharp report of gunshots. She started up from her seat, leaned out, and saw something that turned her blood to ice. A group of three or four masked men on horseback had blocked the stage; their upraised shotguns were pointed directly at Buck.

Addie's heart froze. Every nerve in her body tingled. Even as her conscious mind registered what was happening, another part of her refused to absorb its reality. The cries of the other passengers pierced the air. A loud voice declaring, "This is a holdup, folks!" brought it all to immediate understanding. A stagecoach robbery! The kind she had read and heard about in stories about the "Wild West" was happening right here before her eyes! Her stomach dropped sickeningly, then knotted. She tried to speak but her throat tightened as though she were being strangled. She could neither swallow nor speak. She could hardly breathe.

"All right, Buck, don't try any funny business. Get down, nice and easy—hands above your head, that's right. Nobody'll get hurt if you just do what we say."

The way the man was talking so familiarly to Henessey was almost as if he knew him. Had he known Buck would be driving this stage? Had he and his men been lying in wait at this point to ambush the stagecoach?

This man was on the horse in front. He was evidently the leader. He was wearing a long buff-colored canvas duster, which covered him from neck to the tops of his boots. His face was masked by a triangular blue bandanna, the brim of his wide-brimmed, brown slouch hat shadowed his eyes.

He pulled a long-handled pistol from his belt, and waving it toward the man beside Buck, he ordered one of his men, "Relieve that gentleman of his shotgun." To Henessey he said, "Now, Buck, I don't mean you no harm, so if you'll just hand over the cash box, everything will be just dandy and you all can go on your way." The man had a pronounced drawl, almost as though he were imitating a Southerner or a Texan.

"This is foolishness," growled Henessey. "You're taking' an awful risk. This here fellow is deputized a U.S. Marshal from over Santa Rosa, you'll be in big trouble if you—"

"Don't want to argue, Buck. Don't you worry about us; just do as we say and there won't be no trouble."

In a few minutes, one of the men had climbed up and unbuckled the steel cash box from under the driver's seat and carried it down.

"What about the passengers, Boss?" one of the masked men asked him.

"What about them?"

214

"Cash, jewelry?"

The man nodded almost indifferently, turned in his saddle, then motioning with his gun ordered, "Get them out and line 'em up."

Until now, the passengers had been too frightened to say anything. But as the man, waving his shotgun as though it were a palmetto fan, ordered them out, there were whimperings, moans, and mutterings as one by one people climbed down from the high wagon and stood huddled together against the side of the coach.

"Keep your eye on these two," the leader said sharply to the men still on their horses, indicating Henessey and the deputy. Then he dismounted and sauntered over to where the passengers stood trembling.

"Sorry, ladies and gentlemen, to inconvenience you like this—if you ladies'll just hand over all that pretty jewelry and the gentlemen their wallets and watches, and if you've got a tie pin, that'll be fine. Then we'll be on our way and no one the worse for it."

He gave one of the men a chamois drawstring bag and gestured for him to take it around to each passenger to fill with their valuables.

"This is an outrage!" spluttered Mrs. Amberly who had gone ashen. But as the bag was thrust at her by the man pointing the gun, her fat fingers fumbled at the diamond brooch at the neck of her blouse.

One of the men passengers started to protest, but when the man's gun waved in his direction, he subsided into a terrified silence, unhooked his gold watch chain, and handed it over without another word.

"Those rings too, Madam, if you please," the man continued. "And the earrings as well."

The clinking together of jewels inside the bag was the only sound as one by one the women nervously dropped cameos, pocket watches, ropes of gold chains, strings of

215

crystal beads, pearls, and rings of all kinds into the bulging leather pouch.

Addie's hand trembled as she unfastened the chain from around her neck, with the locket containing her parents' pictures. She held it for a second before relinquishing it, then she slipped out the garnet earrings, undid the cameo brooch. Lastly she drew out the narrow velvet box containing the opals she carried in her handbag and added it to the rest of the loot. The bag now heavy and lumpy, bulged with its horde.

"Thank you kindly, one and all. Be assured your treasures will be used for a good cause," the bandit said politely. He chuckled, drew the leather thongs closing the bag, and backed away from the carriage. He made a slight bow and tipped his hat.

At that gesture, something clicked in Addie's head—it came and went like the flip of a goldfish's tail before she could grasp it. Yet the something—of what she wasn't quite sure—hovered like a hummingbird on the edge of her mind. She tried to catch it, but it slipped away before she could even name what it was that occurred to her.

Then it was over. The horsemen rode away, vanishing into the thick woods. Everyone remained absolutely still until the sound of their horses' hoofbeats on the pine-needled path thudded away. The woods seemed to echo with silence. A collective sigh followed. They were safe. No one had been killed, no one hurt in any way. Then pandemonium broke loose. Everyone began to talk at once, loud voices, interrupting each other as the mixed reactions of fear, relief, and excitement reached a fever pitch. It was bedlam for several furious minutes. Calls for smelling salts mingled with cries of rage, anger, indignation, much of it directed against the driver and the guard. Recriminations, threats, declarations of revenge, demands for retribution,

216

and wails of distress over valuable lost property filled the air.

Addie did not join in with the others. After all, her jewelry had nothing but sentimental value. Hers had no precious stones, no priceless diamonds. She felt a sadness for what had been taken. But they were only symbols of what she had already lost.

Once the immediate danger was past, Mrs. Amberly's howls of rage gained volume and vehemence. Addie winced at the woman's insulting condemnation of the driver for his lack of protection of his passengers during the robbery. She must not have noticed the gun pointed at Henessey's heart the whole time. She included the Union Express clerk in her recriminations, even though the poor man had been reduced to a quivering mass of jelly by the entire episode. His protestations that it would have meant his very life had he resisted did not seem to convince her. The tirade continued unabated.

Gradually Addie simply withdrew into her own confusing thoughts. An indefinable notion kept nagging at her, that there had been something vaguely familiar about the highwayman. Even as Addie told herself it *must* be her imagination, she could not erase the impression.

Finally the coach plodded into Calistoga and pulled to a stop at the sweep of the drive in front of the hotel. When the uniformed employees came out to assist the passengers, they were assailed by the story of the robbery. A whole new cacophony of attacks began, heaping blame on the driver. Henessey finally drove off in fury, leaving the hotel staff to deal with its guests.

Mrs. Amberly's voice could be heard above the rest as she stormed into the lobby demanding to see Brook. When told he was out of town, she stamped her foot in rage and ordered the cowed desk clerk to send at once for the sheriff.

Of the seven passengers, each had a different version of

the robbery story to tell the sheriff, who arrived soon after having been informed of it by Henessey. Listening to the others, Addie began to wonder if she had even been there, the tales grew so tall in the telling. The robbers loomed much larger, bolder, more threatening to life and limb than they had been in reality. Actually it had seemed to her they were a rather orderly bunch, following the low-keyed orders of their leader. But even descriptions of him were so disparate, Addie began to doubt her own impression. But when it came her turn, Addie tried to relay as factual a picture of the bizarre event as she could and even surprised herself that she had remembered it all so clearly.

However, the sheriff was a canny fellow. "Well, now, I'm mighty sorry you folks had to go through such a bad time, and I'm pretty sure I got the picture now. I can't promise anything, but we think we've got a pretty good clue as to who these men are. They've pulled some fifteen or twenty robberies over the past two years. They're well-planned, and they usually happen about the same way—"

"I hope, sheriff, you are going to apprehend these vicious criminals!" Mrs. Amberly interrupted.

"We are certainly goin' to do our best, Ma'am."

"I had some very valuable pieces of jewelry stolen, you know—," she began, ready to repeat her story again. But the sheriff was moving toward the door, nodding his head.

"Yes, Ma'am, my deputy has a description of everything that was taken. We'll let you know as soon as we have any more information. Now, thank you ladies and gentlemen, for your cooperation." The sheriff tipped his broad-beamed felt hat and left, followed by his deputy.

It wasn't until later that night, after Addie, with the assistance of the hotel maid, had helped a still furious Mrs. Amberly to bed, that she had a chance to be alone, to sort out her own reaction to the episode. She felt exhausted but was too wound up to sleep. She had always wondered how she would react to danger. Many times during the war she had wished she were a man so she could do more than stay behind when so many she cared about were on the front lines fighting the invaders of her beloved homeland. The young men she knew never talked about fear. She had grown up believing bravery was the highest and noblest attribute one could attain—to face danger and death and not be afraid.

Now, she had learned that you can be both afraid *and* brave. At least, she had not become hysterical or disgraced herself. Although her throat was dry from fear and her heart banging so fast and hard she thought it might explode during the robbery, she had not fainted, collapsed, nor made a spectacle of herself.

Addie recalled how she had repeated the Scripture, "Thou, O Lord, shall be my shield" during the robbery. It sprung into her mind from the realms of her childhood when as a self-willed, stubborn little girl she had been sent to her room and made to memorize a verse. Addie smiled, remembering that was the only kind of punishment her gentle mother had ever inflicted. Its reward had been a supernatural calm throughout the frightening ordeal.

As frightening as the experience was, it was not only that that made her strangely restless, unable to relax. She couldn't get hold of the fleeting impression she had about the leader of the band of robbers. It kept eluding her. What exactly was it?

First, he had not fit her idea of an outlaw. For instance, there was a theatrical air about him. Almost as if he had been playing a part. And his politeness as he conducted the crime—even if it had a certain mockery in it. He had an air of unquestioned authority that the other men recognized and obeyed. Then there was his voice—had she been mistaken or had she heard it somewhere before? Or one like it? Not a decided accent but there was a slight drawl to it.

Unable to put her troubled thoughts in any kind of order, Addie prepared for bed. After a while she fell asleep, but her slumber was shallow, interrupted by startled reawakenings and confused dreams.

The following afternoon, a very concerned Louis arrived at the cottage. The news of the stagecoach robbery had spread rapidly, even to the outlying areas, and he had ridden into town at once to see if Addie was all right.

"It must have been a terrifying experience," he said solicitously, taking both of her hands in his.

"Actually not as much as one would think, Louis. It was very strange; after the first few minutes, I felt very calm. The leader was so—I know this will sound incredible—but he was so polite, even while he was stealing from us—so gentlemanly—"

Louis frowned. "Then you've heard?"

"Heard what?"

"I stopped at the sheriff's office before coming over here. I wanted to get the story directly from him of just exactly what had happened. I assumed you women had become hysterical and may have been unable to give all the details of the incident, but I thought the driver would have given a straight report and that the sheriff could then tell me exactly what had taken place."

Addie had to suppress her annoyance at Louis's assumption that she, along with the other women passengers, had become *hysterical*.

"And what did the sheriff tell you then, Louis?" She tried to keep from sounding sarcastic, but it annoyed her for Louis to be so condescending.

"Do they know who the robbers were?"

"You say the leader acted *gentlemanly*, right? Well, they suspect the man who robbed your stage was none other

220

than the famous, or I should say the notorious Gentleman Jim. He's been the perpetrator of many successful stage-coach robberies. He seems to have it down to a science—knows when and where to attack—usually he goes for a stage carrying a payroll or the claim payoff of mines, or a bank's supply. He's gotten away with it. A real rascal." Louis shook his head. "But always described as *gentlemanly*."

Addie recalled her own reaction to the masked leader. He had been almost gallant in his manner. Still, something in her memory caught her attention, but Louis was speaking and she lost track of what she was trying to grasp.

"You've had a severe shock. It would be good for you to come out to the house, be our guest for a few days. Estelle agrees with me."

Addie was startled at this. Privately she wondered how long it had taken Louis to persuade his sister to accept what must have been his idea.

"That's very kind of you, Louis, and of Estelle too. But I couldn't possibly come. I have to stay with Mrs. Amberly. She was very upset by all this, and I'm sure she would be most indignant if I went away. She would feel as if I had deserted her when she needed me most."

Louis frowned but finally conceded that this might happen. "Tomorrow is your regular day off anyway, isn't it? I'll come for you early, and we'll take a drive. It will get your mind off all this."

Chapter 16

*O*f course, the robbery was the topic of everyone's conversation that evening and even the following morning at breakfast. Those hotel guests who had not gone on the fateful trip to Lakeport crowded around the ones who had and wanted the story retold. Nothing delighted the tellers more. They were basking in the reflected glory of their experience. As one witty old gentleman commented to Addie, "They'll dine out on this for months—maybe even *years!*"

Addie could not help agreeing with him. Mrs. Amberly was milking the episode for all it was worth. She held court, and each retelling was more embellished with details Addie could not remember. No pistol had even been held to anyone's head, least of all *hers*. Even the driver and his aide were treated with courtesy. But Addie held her tongue. If anyone asked her for her version, she was brief and factual. This seemed dull in comparison to what the others who had shared the experience were saying. Eventually she was not asked for her story anymore.

There was no one Addie could really talk to about it. She wished Brook were back. She knew he would listen. He would help her sort through her fragmented impressions of the robbery, perhaps recall some clue that would aid the sheriff in identifying the robbers.

It was a relief when Louis came to take her for a drive. She was tired of the constant talk of the robbery and hearing the exaggerations that grew larger with every successive telling. As they left Silver Springs Addie lapsed into a reflective silence. They had driven quite awhile before Louis asked, "Why so quiet, Addie?"

"I'm sorry, Louis, I didn't mean to be rude."

"Not rude at all, my dear. It's understandable. You've been through a terrible ordeal; it's bound to have an effect." He reached over and took her hand. "I wish I could help some way."

Louis guided the buggy over to the side of the road, reined his horse, then leaned toward Addie. "I wish I could protect you from anything unpleasant. Take care of you, always. Does that surprise you, Addie?"

Addie drew back a little. "I don't think I—"

"Addie, don't you know? Haven't you guessed what I feel? That I am—*very* fond of you? I haven't said it in so many words. I know you're under contract to stay with Mrs. Amberly until the end of the year. And also I wanted to have my own plans settled, the house completed, the winery under way before ..."

Addie controlled an involuntary shiver. She didn't think she wanted to hear the rest of what Louis was going to say.

"I've been looking for someone with your qualities for a long time. Almost as soon as I met you I *knew*—I couldn't wait to tell Estelle, to have her meet you ..." Louis's hand tightened on hers. "Addie, I have so much to offer you—*want* to offer you."

"Oh, Louis, don't—"

"Why not, Addie? It's true. Maybe, you don't love me now—not yet, but you do care for me a little, don't you? You must. I think we get on very well together. You would

223

enjoy having a home like ours, a position in the community, wouldn't you? You were born to it. I know you would be a grace to my home, be an asset in every way. And I'd try very hard to make you happy."

"Oh, Louis, I'm sure you would. But I—I just haven't thought—"

"If I should marry—*when* I marry, my wife would be mistress of Chateau Montand. Estelle plans to travel extensively in the next few years. She has spent her life caring for me, but once I am happily settled, she would pursue her own interests."

Addie understood what he was implying. In case a sister-in-law in residence would present an obstacle to her, Louis wanted her to know that would not be the case.

"I don't have to have an answer right away—," Louis continued. "Just consider what it would mean to both of us. Think of what it could be like—all your problems, your financial worries, the future—all taken care of for you. That's what I want to do. Please, Addie, think about it, won't you?"

Addie moistened her dry lips with the tip of her tongue and took a long breath. "Yes, of course, Louis. I will. I can't promise you anything but—yes, I can do that."

Seemingly satisfied, Louis picked up the reins again, and they continued to drive. He didn't force her into conversation and try as she might, Addie could think of little to say. Louis's proposal had pulled her wandering thoughts back into the present, to decisions that would soon have to be made about the rest of her life.

Much of what Louis said was true. What he was offering was, actually, an escape. Hadn't she been praying for a way out? Addie knew after she had fulfilled her year's contract with Mrs. Amberly she still had to find a way to earn a living. But how? She wasn't any better prepared than she had been a year ago. She assumed she would go back to Virginia. What then, she had no idea.

Now Louis was giving her a choice. But a marriage without the passion and romance like the Bairds had? To give that up would be giving up a cherished lifelong dream.

But perhaps, after all, life wasn't a love story. The hopes she had allowed herself to have about Rex Lyon had vanished, been crushed. Maybe she should consider a marriage of mutual respect, security, and companionship. Addie knew many such marriages had turned out to be good.

But in her heart of hearts she *knew* she could not settle for that.

After a while Louis suggested he take her back to Silver Springs so she could rest.

Before Louis left her at the main building, he said, "You'll feel better after a good night's sleep. I'll stop by again tomorrow to see you. Estelle told me to be sure and tell you that after the flurry dies down, she insists you come out to the house. She wants very much to get to know you better."

Addie wondered if Estelle knew he was going to propose to her today.

"I don't want to press you, my dear. But I shall be very busy when my first crop is ready to harvest—so I would like to know as soon as you feel you can give me an answer."

"Louis I—"

"No matter, my dear, don't fret yourself," he said quickly. "We have plenty of time to make plans."

"You are very kind, Louis."

She watched him ride away. Louis *was* kind, thoughtful. But marriage? She would have to feel something much stronger for him to seriously consider that.

Glancing at the verandah she saw Mrs. Amberly sitting in one of the rocking chairs, surrounded by a small group. Probably holding forth to those who had not heard the adventure or perhaps were listening to it again. Since Mrs. Amberly's back was to her, Addie saw no reason to make her presence known. It was still her day off, her free day, and she was going to enjoy her freedom as long as possible.

Besides, her head ached. The drive with Louis had not refreshed or relaxed her. In fact, after Louis's proposal, she felt even more tense. Maybe, if she lay down for a while it might help. She would soak a handkerchief with cologne and place it on her throbbing temples.

In her cottage bedroom, when Addie opened her bureau drawer to get one out, she saw, to her surprise, one of Brook's monogrammed handkerchiefs among her own. She remembered that one day when they were out walking, a cinder had blown into her eye, and he had taken his out of his pocket and lent it to her. She had washed and ironed it then forgotten to return it to him. Since his larger one would make a better size headache band, she decided to use his, then give it back later.

Dear Brook! She wished he were back from the city. She missed him. If he were here she knew she could confide Louis's proposal to him. She could trust him to be honest, to help her decide what was the best thing to do.

She poured water into her washbowl, added a few splashes of cologne, then dipped Brook's handkerchief into it. Soaking it thoroughly, then wringing it out, she folded it into an oblong. She lay down on her bed and pressed the fine linen cloth over her forehead and closed her eyes.

It took a long time for her to quiet her jumbled mind. So many questions to which she could not find answers. She longed for some simple solution to the turmoil churning inside her.

Addie stirred. How much later, she wasn't sure. She felt stiff and fuzzy-headed, almost as if she had taken a sleeping powder. But her headache seemed to be gone. She removed the cloth from her eyes, dry now but still fragrant from her violet cologne. Opening her eyes to darkness, she realized evening had come. She must have fallen asleep. Slowly she sat up. The bedroom felt hot and airless. She got out of bed. Fumbling for the matches she lit the lamp on the bedside table, then went to fold back the shutters, open the window.

A pale moon shed a milky sheen over the hotel grounds. It must be very late. There were no lights on in the main building.

It was then she saw something move outside the cottage. A shadowy figure standing under the palm tree at the end of the path. Or was it her imagination? Addie leaned on the sill and peered out. There was no breeze stirring, nothing moved. *Was* someone standing there? Instinctively she shrank back, afraid the light in the room behind her might have silhouetted her in the window frame making her visible to anyone lurking about.

Who *was* out there? A prowler? Burglars? An involuntary shiver passed through her. She pressed her arms tight against her body, cupping her elbows in her palms, and waited until the shuddering stopped. She had not yet recovered fully from the experience of the robbery. That's what made her so fearful, so easily frightened.

She looked again. Maybe it had been one of the hotel guests, restless, sleepless, out for a stroll on this moonlit night. Back to the window, she cautiously pulled aside the curtain and looked out again. A cloud moved across the moon momentarily blocking her view. When it passed, the place under the palm was empty. Slowly Addie let out her breath. It must have been a shadow, a trick of the moonlight.

Meantime the wind had risen slightly, blowing some refreshing cool air into the room. She still felt tired, unrested. She would get undressed, get into bed properly.

Now that her headache was gone, perhaps she could sleep well.

Addie awakened suddenly, as if someone had shaken her. Gray light slithered through the slotted bands of the shutters. She sat up in bed, looking around, feeling as if there was something she should remember, something she should do.

She fell back against the pillows. Why did she feel so depressed? She'd had a troubling dream. Was it the dream that had bolted her so abruptly into wakefulness? She tried to recall it but couldn't. It had seemed so real. But now the details were blurred, confusing—events, people all so mixed up, she couldn't piece it together.

Lying there a minute longer she felt strangely disturbed. Something was different. Something out of place. Things were not quite the way they were last night when she had blown out her lamp.

Her gaze traveled the room to where she had draped her clothes over a chair the night before, too tired to hang them up, then to the window from where she thought she had seen someone outside. Had she opened the shutters? Left the curtains drawn? She couldn't remember.

Then she saw an envelope propped against the bureau mirror. Where had that come from? How had it gotten there? Had one of the maids slipped in and placed it there while Addie was still asleep?

Addie threw back the covers, got up, and went over to the bureau. Her name was written on the front of the envelope. Reaching to pick it up she saw a small suede bag behind it. She set the envelope aside. Her hands fumbled as she undid the leather drawstrings, opening it. When she saw what was inside, she gasped. She put her hand in and slowly drew out . . . her small gold watch, the cameo brooch, the garnet earrings, and, lastly, the narrow velvet box containing her mother's opal necklace and earring set!

Her heart thudded. She took up the envelope again, ran her fingernail under the flap, and opened it. She took out the letter inside and unfolded it. She had only seen that handwriting once, but now she recognized it. Suddenly her knees felt weak. She backed up to the bed, sat down on the edge, and began to read.

My dear Addie,

By the time you read this I will be far away, because I cannot come back. I have to go on—there are too many bridges I've burned behind me. My debts have mounted; even my tested methods of getting cash, when all else fails, have not been able to meet the amount I now need. Not enough to cover my enormous debts. Many would say I took too many risks, expanded too quickly. Now, I have to admit, they were mostly right. I have to relinquish the dreams I had for Calistoga and Silver Springs Resort.

I had no idea you would be on that stage. I would never have taken your jewelry except I didn't want to single you out from the rest of the passengers and so align you with me in any way.

At least Gentleman Jim is enough of one to return your family heirlooms.

In many ways I wish that our paths had crossed earlier in my life—but even when you were coming of age, I had already misspent my youth!

Believe me, I will always be glad for meeting you and coming to know you. I want you to know how much I valued your friendship and often wished it might be more. I never told you I loved you, but now that it cannot hurt either of us, I can. I don't claim to know much about love except that the only kind of love that lasts is unrequited love. So, I shall love you always.

I suspect your love lies elsewhere and with a more worthy man; I hope you will make the choice that will bring you great happiness in your life.

You have touched my life with sweetness and goodness,
a radiance I can only admire and perhaps even envy—

When Addie finished reading, her hands holding the letter began to shake. *Gentleman Jim? Brook was Gentleman Jim!*
She never knew how long she sat there, stunned, holding the letter. Finally Addie stood up and began to dress. Her fingers moved numbly, fastening buttons, doing up her hair. She picked up her watch and smiled wanly to see that it was set and ticking—how like Brook to do that! The tiny hands pointed to a little past six in the morning. Mechanically she pinned her watch to her bodice.

The dining hall opened for breakfast at six for early risers. She decided to slip out of the cottage and go there to get some coffee. She threw a shawl over her shoulders, inched the door open, and went out. Brooding clouds hung in the clay-colored sky. Addie shuddered. What was she to do with what she knew?

In the dining hall, huddled at a corner table, she drank two cups of black coffee, hoping it would bring clarity to a mind muddled by disbelief. Addie was torn by her contradictory feelings. Half of her mind told her that Brook *was* Gentleman Jim; the other part argued it was impossible. She longed desperately for it *not* to be true. Little by little things began to add up: his wild spending, elaborate parties, his long absences. Finally she stopped denying the terrible truth.

Whom should she tell? Should she go to the sheriff? How would she explain her returned jewelry? Had the jewelry of any of the others been returned? When the waiter came to refill her cup, she waved him away. She must keep her nerve, be calm, be careful.

The dining room began to fill up with other hotel guests. With a start Addie realized an hour had gone by. She must get back to the cottage. Mrs. Amberly would be up by now, ready for her "logger" breakfast, impatient for Addie's arm

230

to lean on as she made her way stiffly over to the dining hall. Hastily Addie rose and left. She was hurrying across the grounds when she heard Mrs. Amberly's shriek. Startled, she picked up her skirt and ran the rest of the way, dashed up the cottage steps and into the house.

Mrs. Amberly was standing in the hallway. When she saw Addie, her face turned a purplish-red, her eyes were bulging, her mouth hung open. One of the hotel maids stood by looking scared out of her wits.

Addie's first reaction was horror. Her eyes darted toward her open bedroom door. Addie felt her face get hot. Her cheeks burned, but her tone was ice cold. "What's going on? What were you doing in *my* room?"

"Don't take that tone with me, young lady," Mrs. Amberly said spitefully. "I don't think you'll be so high and mighty once the sheriff gets here. How do you account for *this,* pray tell?" Mrs. Amberly advanced toward Addie threateningly, shaking the jewelry bag left on Addie's bureau.

"Whatever the reason, Mrs. Amberly, you had no right to go into my room."

"I had every right to," Mrs. Amberly said savagely. "I waited and waited for you to come to help me get over for my breakfast, and when you didn't, I thought you might have overslept or something, so I knocked and knocked. When you didn't open the door, I thought you might be sick, so I *did!*" Mrs. Amberly lost all visible control. Her voice rose to a pitch. "And that's when I found *these!* How do you explain *this,* Miss Pride?"

Addie struggled for control, to keep her voice steady. "That happens to be *my* jewelry."

Mrs. Amberly's lips curled back in a snarl. "This is *stolen* property! And if you claim it's yours, you're no better than a thief—an accomplice to a gang of highway bandits!" she snarled with a venom that caused Addie to draw back.

By now Mrs. Amberly's voice was so loud that other guests, coming from their cottages and passing by on their way to the dining hall for breakfast, had stopped to see what all the ruckus was about.

As upset and angered as she was, Addie made two quick decisions. She would not try to defend herself. The woman was too far gone. And she would not betray Brook.

His note was safely hidden in the pocket of her skirt. However unjustified her action of invading Addie's privacy was, Mrs. Amberly's discovery had made disclosure on Addie's part unnecessary. Addie could protest ignorance of how the jewelry had gotten into her room. That much *was* the truth. How or when she had no idea. Was it Brook, or had he paid one of the employees to do it? Could it have been put there yesterday even when she was gone during the afternoon? Had she been too distracted over Louis's proposal to notice it? Or had someone with a key to the cottages slipped in silently while she slept and put the bag and note in her room?

She wouldn't lie. She would simply tell the facts as she knew them. But she would not volunteer any information. The jewelry had simply been returned. When or how, she did not know. She had no explanation.

Behind her she heard the rumble of murmuring among the people now crowding around the cottage. Then she became aware of shuffling behind her. She turned to see Louis pushing his way through to reach her. With him was the sheriff.

While Mrs. Amberly continued to shout accusations at her, the sheriff, accompanied by Louis, closed the front door upon the curious crowd and requested Addie and Mrs. Amberly to go with him into the cottage's small parlor. Here the tall, ruggedly built sheriff silenced Mrs. Amberly by saying, "Please, Ma'am, just hold your fire. Let's just have the facts," he said firmly. He listened patiently while Mrs. Amberly spouted off her furious charges. Without making any comment, he then halted her with a raised hand and turned to Addie. "Now, you, Miss Pride, please."

Louis stood behind Addie's chair as she recounted how she had found the jewelry that had been taken in the stage-coach robbery. During her account, although guiltily conscious of the note in her pocket, she did not mention it. Addie's father had been a lawyer, and Uncle Myles still practiced in a small, musty office where hardly any clients ever came, so Addie was somewhat familiar with the law. She realized that legally she could be charged with concealing evidence. But most of what Brook had written was personal. She could not turn it over to be read and misinterpreted by hostile eyes.

While pulling at his handlebar mustache, the sheriff kept his steely gaze upon her as he listened to her explanation. His expressionless face would have done justice to a poker player. It gave Addie no indication of his reaction, whether he believed her or not. When she finished he got to his feet and said, "I see no reason to suspect Miss Pride here with anything—collusion, conspiracy, or any of the things you've accused her of. This Gentleman Jim is known to be unpredictable and also known to have an eye for a pretty lady—as we can all see Miss Pride is. It's just like him to do something unexpected, like returning her jewelry—as some kind of compliment." The sheriff shook his head. "Nobody's yet figured out the fellow."

As he moved toward the door he spoke directly to Mrs. Amberly. "I know you're upset, Ma'am, but I assure you, we're going to bring this gang to justice. We're forming a posse, and we'll be searching the hills around here where they may be hiding out. Gentleman Jim's band—seems to have inside information. This coming Friday the vineyard's payroll comes through. They may be waiting to rob it. We have plans underway to trap the fellow, but, of course, I can't go into detail." His hand on the doorknob now, he turned for a final say. "Don't fret, ladies, we'll round him up and soon."

Dead silence followed the sheriff's departure. It seemed the session had left even Mrs. Amberly speechless. Her face had gone slack. She pushed herself up out of her chair. Her mouth worked like one of those comic rubber dolls children squeeze to change their expressions as though she wanted to say something more to Addie.

Perhaps to avoid another possible diatribe from Mrs. Amberly, Louis stepped over to the door and opened it for her. After giving Addie a scathing look, she left the room without a word. Addie listened tensely to her employer's shuffling footsteps go down the hall; then she heard the sullen slam of her bedroom door.

After a moment Addie stood up, hands clenched, heart thundering with rage. The anger she had suppressed before rushed up in her now. She looked at Louis expectantly. Why? For some possible explanation of why he had not risen to her defense. The woman to whom he had proposed marriage was accused of being an accomplice to a stagecoach robbery, and he said nothing! It seemed unnatural, to say the least. Did he have some reason? She waited, but when nothing happened she demanded, "Why didn't you *say* something, *do* something? You heard what she said about me!"

Louis met her outraged look with some surprise. "What could I say? The woman's upset; that's all." He shrugged. "A real tempest in a teapot, my dear Addie. It will all blow over—"

"But she accused me of being a *thief*, an *accomplice* to a *stagecoach robbery!* Don't you *care?*"

"Don't worry. No one would possibly believe her."

For a long minute, Addie stared at him in disbelief. What

234

kind of man was he? Then suddenly she felt drained. She passed a hand across her forehead, swaying a little. "You'll have to excuse me, Louis, I'm not feeling very well. I can't go out with you today. Give my apology to Estelle."

With that Addie swept past him, out the parlor door and started down the hall.

"Addie, wait." He followed her. She paused outside her bedroom door. Louis's voice was apologetic. "My dear, please. Of course, I understand. Do rest. I know you're distraught, but it will pass—all of this—you'll see."

"Good-bye, Louis," she said stiffly.

"Addie—" He started to say something more, then, as though thinking better of it, finished lamely, "I—I'll stop by tomorrow."

Addie did not reply. She just went in her bedroom and shut the door. Once she was alone, Addie felt the weight of her secret press down upon her. Was Brook hiding somewhere in the hills, as the sheriff suspected? Would he then be hunted down by men with rifles like a wild animal or a fugitive? But wasn't *that* exactly what Brook was—a criminal? Robbing stagecoaches? Addie shook her head, it was so hard to comprehend. The dapper, elegant, fastidious Brook Stanton—with his immaculate linen, gold cuff links, and silk cravats—a common thief? Had he been so desperate for money? Or had it been some kind of crazy aberration of his personality? Acting out in reality some childish fantasy like children playing bandits or pirates?

Addie took out the note again and sat down on the edge of the bed to reread it. What she read between the lines was even more confusing than the words themselves. To think Brook had fallen in love with her but had been afraid to speak because of the double life he was leading! It was incredible.

Addie crumpled up the note. Perhaps she should destroy

it? But would that incriminate her further if it became known that there *was* a note with the jewelry? Oh, dear God, give me light! If ever she needed wisdom it was *now*. What was the *right* thing to do?

Feeling frantic, she paced the small room, literally wringing her hands, torn by her contradictory feelings. Those vague suspicions that had puzzled her during the robbery seemed to be validated by the note.

Addie longed desperately for it *not* to be true. The Brook *she* knew seemed such an unlikely stagecoach robber. From the way the yellow journals and Wild West "penny dreadfuls" pictured stagecoach robbers, they were vicious outlaws, ruffians, bandits of the lowest kind, preying on helpless passengers—women and children. For the Brook who had impressed her with his fine clothes, his good manners, his quixotic personality, his familiarity with poetry and literature—surely *he* could not be the leader of a band of stagecoach robbers.

Yet the very same traits attributed to the notorious Gentleman Jim could also fit Brook Stanton: flamboyant, dashing, risk-taking, a gambler.

Wearily, Addie sat down on her bed and leaned back against the pillows. She felt drained. Her brain was confused she could not even think anymore. Disjointed, inarticulate prayers sprang into her mind, but she could not even finish them. What should she do? What was going to happen? She felt overwhelmed. She wished she could go to sleep and wake up to find it had all been a nightmare!

Addie awoke with a jerk. She thought she had only lain down for a few minutes, but in spite of everything she had fallen asleep. But it had been an uneasy sleep, and she felt hot, fuzzy-headed, and unrested. She sat up, her pins had slipped out, and her loosened hair was tumbling down over her shoulders. Pushing it back with both hands she got stiffly to her feet.

She had just sloshed her face with water and was patting it dry when a tap came at her door.

"Yes, who is it?" she called.

"The maid, miss; you have a caller."

"I don't want to see anyone."

There was a pause, a murmur of voices, then another gentle rap.

"Addie, it's Freda, please let me in."

Addie hurried to the door, opened it and the two friends embraced.

"Oh, Freda, I'm glad you've come. You don't know—," began Addie, feeling a rush of tears stinging her eyes.

"I know. I heard. It's all over town," Freda said quietly, coming into the room and shutting the door.

Addie almost said, "About Brook?" but stopped before the words slipped out. She asked, "About *me*?"

"You? Well, about the stagecoach being robbed. It must have been dreadful."

Quickly Addie gathered her scrambled thoughts. Of course, Freda didn't have any idea about the returned jewelry.

"Yes, it was pretty frightening," she answered. "Excuse how I look; somehow I fell asleep and . . ." she picked up her brush and ran it through her hair several times.

"Are you all right, Addie?"

Addie finished twisting her hair up into a knot and secured it with tortoise shell pins. Then she turned around and gave a bitter little laugh. "Except that I'm under suspicion."

Freda's brows drew together. "Under *suspicion*? What do you mean? For what?"

"Maybe you haven't heard yet. But you will soon enough. I know small towns have active gossip mills. Especially something *this* juicy." She paused, turned around from the

237

mirror, and faced Freda. "My employer has accused me of being an accomplice to the stagecoach robbers."

"*You,* an *accomplice?*" Freda gasped. "How could she? Why?"

"Because, you see, my jewelry taken during the robbery has been returned."

"What? How was it returned?"

"Mysteriously. I'm not sure just how or when. It's left quite a cloud over my reputation." Addie shrugged. "But I think as much as anything else, Mrs. Amberly is furious because *her* jewelry was much more valuable than anything of mine. Mine was mostly of sentimental value, things belonging to my mother."

"And that leads to the assumption that the robbers *knew* that?"

Addie nodded, then sighed, "How else can it be explained?"

"Oh, Addie, that's terrible *and* ridiculous. *That* woman! I disliked her on sight." Freda shuddered. "There was something about her—I sensed right away—you know how it is with some people? You get a feeling—and I certainly got it that night we were introduced."

"Well, it doesn't matter, I suppose. Since *I* know the truth." Addie hesitated. She wondered if she should confide in Freda? Tell her about the note, about Brook?

But before she could decide, Freda said, "Listen, Addie, I know you must be under a great deal of stress, but I came because—there's someone else who wants to see you, and he did not want to come by himself—afraid he might cause gossip."

"What do you mean? Who?"

"Rex. Rex Lyon," she answered quietly.

At the name Addie's chest tightened as if she could not draw a deep breath. She was still holding her hairbrush, but now she put it down, rearranged the toilette articles on

238

the top of the bureau, lining them up in a row, trying to steady herself.

"He asked me to see if it was all right. He was afraid Louis Montand might object . . ."

Puzzled, Addie turned toward Freda and asked, "But why should Louis object?"

Freda only gave her a strange look and hurried on, "That doesn't matter now, but will you see him? He seems to think you might not—but I must tell you, Addie, I've rarely seen a man so worried. Particularly Rex, who never seems to get upset."

Addie hesitated. She thought of their last awkward encounter at the bank before she had left on the ill-fated trip to Lakeport. She remembered the stilted conversation and his strange comment. It had been weeks since he had tried to see or contact her. Why did he come now and want to see her?

Freda put her hand on Addie's arm. "Do see him, Addie. He's waiting on the other side of the arboretum. Won't you go out there? Hear what he has to say?"

Addie turned away from Freda's searching gaze, afraid her own hurt, her longing, and her feelings for Rex might show in her face. Didn't Freda know Rex had made no move to see her since the day of the picnic with the Bairds? Should she tell Freda how she felt, why she didn't want to see Rex?

She walked over to the window, pushed aside the curtain, and looked out in the direction of the arboretum. As she stood there she saw the sheriff and his deputy ride up to the front of the hotel, dismount, and stride into the building. A minute later Louis come out of the main building, out on the verandah, then hurry down the steps and come marching toward the cottage.

Addie turned around and said to Freda, "I'm sorry, Freda, but it's too late. The sheriff just came, and Louis is coming this way. Something important must have happened."

When Addie opened the door, Louis was there. "The sheriff has an announcement to make, and he wants us all to assemble in the main building," he said.

"Shall I come with you, Addie?" Freda asked anxiously.

Addie stretched out her hand to her, but Louis shook his head. "I'm sorry, Mrs. Wegner, but this meeting is only for Silver Springs guests, I'm afraid. I'm sure you'll learn about it eventually." His face was grim.

Addie threw her friend a bewildered glance, but Louis's hand was firmly under her elbow and he was leading her out of the cottage.

"What is it, Louis?" Addie asked as they started across the grounds.

"You'll hear soon enough. Come along, Addie."

The room was crowded, buzzing with the sound of voices, probably all swapping rumors, exchanging conjectures as to what they had been called together for. Addie saw Mrs. Amberly wedged in between Harriet and Elouise Brunell. Mrs. Amberly glared at Addie as she came in on Louis's arm.

The sheriff stepped to the front, clasped his hands behind his back, and cleared his throat. "First of all, I may as well tell you we've had some reports that a man fitting Gentleman Jim's description was seen around here the last day or so. Some folks thought they recognized him. During the night he left a horse at the livery stable that's been identified as being like the one he was riding at the time of the stage robbery." The sheriff smiled ironically. "He took a fresh horse and left a bundle of paper bills to pay for it, something Gentleman Jim would be likely to do."

The hum of voices reacting to this statement rose dramatically. A flurry of questions peppered the air. "Any trace of the other outlaws?" "The members of his gang?" "Any trace of the payroll money?" "Have any of the stolen goods been found?"

240

The sheriff held up both hands. "Just a minute folks! Just a durn minute. I'll get to that. Gimme time."

The mumbling died down and the sheriff stood there, his head down as though either waiting for the room to quiet or uncertain as to whether he should disclose anything further. Finally he raised his head and looked directly into the crowd. "Now, this next will probably shock you folks, but you have a right to know. . . ."

Again he paused. Everyone sat forward on the edge of their seats, eager to be shocked. The sheriff glanced over at Louis, and Louis's hand tightened on Addie's. "Since Mr. Montand already knows this, the way news travels in this town, you'll hear it one way or another, so it might as well come from me. We think we can identify *who* Gentleman Jim really is."

There were immediate cries of surprise, exclamations of curiosity, demands to know. The sheriff had to hold up his hands for silence again until the uproar faded.

"Based on some conclusive evidence, we believe Gentleman Jim is the owner of Silver Springs—Brook Stanton."

At this Mrs. Amberly let out an indignant gasp and staggered up onto her feet, "What did I tell you?" she looked at the Brunell sisters for confirmation. Then pointing her finger at Addie, she sputtered, "Didn't I say *she* knew the outlaw, the man that so brutally robbed all of us! All of us but *her!* Why was *her* jewelry returned and none of the rest of ours? She must have known about it all the time. Didn't I say there was something mighty suspicious about her being so insistent on having her Thursdays every week? Probably went off with *him*. Told him we'd be on that stage! She knows how valuable *my* jewelry is!" Mrs. Amberly shook her fist at Addie. "Why you, you—thief—"

"Now, just a minute, Ma'am," the sheriff's voice lashed across the room like a whip cutting short the sputtering words. "Don't go accusing anyone. We've seen before how Gentleman Jim operates—he don't need no accomplice."

The Brunell sisters were tugging at Mrs. Amberly, embarrassed, trying to get her to sit down.

"Now, just keep calm, everybody," the sheriff went on. "I understand how you all must feel about this. But I guarantee you *this* time Gentleman Jim won't get away. We've been keepin' track of him, and every time we've got closer to nabbing him. We know he can't be far from here. He didn't know it, but the horse he took has a weak leg. Tends to go lame when he's ridden too hard. We'll bring him in, for sure, and we'll get as many of your belongings back as possible. His mistake was taking the payroll cash box from a United States deputy. We've got a warrant for his arrest, and I mean to serve it to him— personal."

People began to talk among themselves. The noise level in the room soared steadily as everyone mingled, merging into small groups, discussing the startling new facts, and swapping opinions.

In the confusion, Louis took Addie's arm and managed to maneuver their way through the lobby, out the front door. Even her relief in not having to keep Brook's identity secret any longer did not take away the sting of Mrs. Amberly's accusations. Mrs. Amberly had publicly humiliated her, and Addie was shaking with fury.

On the verandah she pulled away from Louis and turned to him. "Did you hear what she said *this* time?"

"Oh, Addie, the woman was hysterical. Anyone could see that. No one paid any attention to her."

His nonchalance infuriated Addie even more. She looked at Louis, every hair in place, unruffled, detached, regarding her with a kind of indulgence. All at once something struck her. An appalling idea. Something she saw in Louis's eyes. Doubt? Did he possibly think some of what Mrs. Amberly said was true? Struggling to keep her voice even, she confronted him. "Surely you don't believe what she's saying about me?"

"It doesn't matter, my dear Adelaide. I told you she was out of control," he said placatingly. "Of course, it was obvious to everyone at the hotel that Brook was infatuated with you, but that isn't the point. The rumors will die down, it will all soon be forgotten. I'm sure she won't stay here long now that she knows about Brook. I wouldn't be a bit surprised if she'll leave to go back east as soon as possible."

"And spread all sorts of lies about me? You can be sure she'll inform her nephew who will tell my cousin and destroy my good name and reputation so that my relatives will have to bear the shame!" Addie started to pace the room, then stopped, whirled around, "Don't you *care* that she publicly vilified me?"

Louis made a dismissing gesture with his hand. "Napa Valley is a small, remote place, the people hopelessly provincial. Who could possibly give a fig about what happens here?"

Addie looked at him aghast. Had he no deep feelings, no passion? The woman he had asked to be his wife had been accused in front of dozens of people of being an accomplice in a stagecoach robbery, of aiding and abetting a criminal, and he brushed it off with as little concern as if he were flicking away an annoying insect.

"Louis! You don't understand at all, do you? That I've been accused of being an accomplice to a stagecoach robbery, that I'm a *thief!*—" and here Addie's voice became cold as steel. "Surely, *you* wouldn't want to marry a woman under that kind of suspicion—I know Estelle would not want me as a sister-in-law." Scornfully she added, "In the *South*, a *gentleman* would demand satisfaction!"

Louis raised his eyebrows. "You would have *me* challenge *Mrs. Amberly* to a duel?" He gave a short sardonic laugh. "My dear, Addie—Mrs. Amberly is hardly a worthy adversary—she's nothing, a nobody, a vulgar *nouveau riche* woman. Her ridiculous ranting scarcely would call for such a violent response."

Addie continued to stare. Her heart thundering, hands clenched, every nerve in her body seemed to vibrate. Although she felt physically shaky, her brain was sharp. In the last few weeks she had struggled with uncertainty, but now everything was clear. Louis was not the kind of man she could ever respect, much less *love*—no, nor trust, nor depend on. She might have been speaking another language for he had not seemed to comprehend a word she said nor understand an emotion she had expressed. It had all left him unmoved. It was suddenly as clear as glass. There was no place in her heart for him and no place in his life for her.

She turned away from him. The thought that she had ever considered, no matter how briefly, accepting Louis's proposal sickened her. A man she could neither trust nor respect? She felt disgusted. She had to get away, be by herself. She started down the verandah steps.

"*You*, Miss Pride! You! Wait, just you wait, young lady. I'm not done with you!" Mrs. Amberly shouted from behind her.

Addie turned to see the woman burst out the hotel door, her body propelled faster than Addie had ever seen her move, waving both arms threateningly. Her beady little eyes, narrowed even further in her fleshy cheeks, made her look for all the world like one of those grotesque faces carved on wooden Swiss tobacco holders people brought home from Europe as souvenirs. Her mouth gaped open, little beads of saliva sprayed out as she spat out her words.

"Have you no shame? Carrying on with that man—that *outlaw*—right under my very nose—while I was footing the bill for the roof over your head, every bite of food you put in your mouth! And to think I paid you to steal from me!"

Addie's hand gripped the porch railing, her whole body rigid.

Teetering on the top step, Mrs. Amberly's mouth twisted viciously. "You think you fooled everyone with your soft Southern ways, your hoity-toity superior air, your honey-coated manners. Well, not *me,* you didn't! Not for a minute, young lady. I seen through you right from the first." In her anger Mrs. Amberly had lost any pretense of gentility.

Addie glanced at Louis to see if *now* he would defend her against this venomous attack. But he had backed away from the sight of Mrs. Amberly's huge, hulking figure, almost as if he were afraid of her.

All the while Mrs. Amberly's voice rose higher and higher into a screech, Addie recalled the countless times under Mrs. Amberly's verbal abuse she had contained her true feelings, held herself in check, because she knew if she ever let go there would be no turning back. Always the thought of Aunt Susan and Uncle Myles had restrained her. Now Mrs. Amberly had gone too far. All the incidents of injustice, the petty slurs, her meanness and sarcasm marched through Addie's mind turning her once half-pitying contempt for the woman into loathing.

Addie walked back up the steps and stood directly in front of her accuser. "You are a liar, Mrs. Amberly, not only about what you are saying about me, accusing me of, but you lie about almost everything. I've been with you day in and day out these last months, and I've seen your lying ways. From cheating at cards, oh, yes, you've even bragged about it—to never tipping the maids here for all the extra services they give you. Talk about stealing, what about all the money you've won from your so-called friends? You lie all the time, Mrs. Amberly, about your travels, the people you know—all lies. Well, I don't have to take it anymore.

I don't have to listen to your lies. I certainly don't have to listen to your lies about *me!*"

"Addie," Louis gasped and grabbed her arm, but she shook it off.

"Don't touch me." She ran down the steps, picked up her skirt, and ran across the yard and over toward the cottage.

Addie closed her bedroom door and stood there a full minute trying to get control of herself. Her lungs felt as if they might burst, and each breath dragged from deep inside was painful. Across the room she caught sight of her reflection in the bureau mirror and was shocked by her pallor, the wild look in her eyes. She flung herself on the bed, feeling weak and sick. Surely she had just been through the two worst hours of her life.

She did not know how long it was before she heard the front door of the cottage open, then voices, Mrs. Amberly's and one of the hotel maid's, the shuffling sound of Mrs. Amberly's feet along the hallway. Addie sat up, bracing herself. Then the banging on her door came, bam, bam, bam.

"You listen here, Miss Pride. Don't think you're gettin' away with anything. You're dismissed. Do you hear *that?* Pack your things. I want you out of here. I don't want to see you again. Never, you understand? Not after the way you talked to me, the way you've behaved!"

Impulsively, Addie walked over to the door and yanked it open. In startled surprise, Mrs. Amberly stumbled backwards, her arm still raised, hand doubled as if to continue knocking.

"You can save your breath, Mrs. Amberly, I was going to quit anyway. I couldn't stand working for someone like you any longer." With that Addie closed the door in Mrs. Amberly's shocked face.

But a moment later her rasping voice came again so loud she must have been pressing her mouth against the keyhole.

"You—you! Listen! Don't think I'm paying you a penny

of this month's salary—not a red cent! And don't think you'll get any references from me, either! Did you hear *that*—Miss Pride!"

Addie covered her ears to shut out the sound of that spiteful voice, the ugliness of whatever else she was saying. Finally it stopped. Then she heard the muffled footsteps as Mrs. Amberly went down the hall and slammed her bedroom door.

Addie drew a long breath. Ridiculously she felt like laughing, but instead she cried. She realized she must be on the edge of hysteria. Curiously enough, her strongest emotion was relief. It was as though someone had thrown open the prison gates and she was free! Free of that old harpy, her demands, her miserly ways.

Yet even as that thought took hold, Addie knew she had burned all her bridges behind her. She had told off Mrs. Amberly and rejected Louis. All in the space of a few impulsive moments she had thrown away her job, her chance at a wealthy marriage. Now, she had nothing. Quickly she corrected that—she still had her pride. But even that was in tatters! After Mrs. Amberly's public castigation, what was it worth? People thought whatever they wanted to think.

Even though she'd had her moment of self-justification, of pride, in doing so she had thrown away everything else. What did she do now? The uncertainty of her life at the moment seemed unbearable. Reality began to set in; she had no job, no place to stay, nowhere to go! Most of all, she would no longer be able to send the small monthly amount to help Aunt Susan and Uncle Myles. In one reckless gesture of independence she had beggared herself as well. She was sure Mrs. Amberly would carry out her threat—she would not pay her another "red cent"—certainly there would be no severance pay, no return train ticket. Addie was stranded, penniless, except for the tiny bit of money she had been able to squirrel away.

She did not want to spend another night under the roof, nor eat another meal Mrs. Amberly had paid for, she would have to wait until morning to make arrangements to leave. And there were hours and hours of the night to get through.

It started to rain. She heard the staccato patter of raindrops on the tin roof. She went to stand at the window peering out into the night. Was Brook out there somewhere in the rainswept dark, alone, desperate, hunted? Addie felt almost as alone and desperate.

Addie prayed for clear direction. It came in the name Freda. What Freda had said that afternoon. "If you need *anything*, if there's anything I can do, any way I can help, please let me know."

Going to Freda meant sacrificing her pride, asking for help. After all, she had known Freda only a matter of months, weeks really since they had become friends. Addie's pride held for another few minutes. She had prayed for guidance, hadn't she? She had to believe she had received it. Trust and obey. The title of the old hymn sang itself into her mind.

In another moment Addie threw a few things into her valise, flung her cloak around her, slipped quietly into the hall, then out the front door.

It was raining hard. As she stood on the little porch the wind whipped her cape around her and blew her hair stingingly into her eyes. She reached for the hood, pulled it up over her head, and tightened the drawstrings under her chin. Then, bending her head, she started walking fast in the direction of town. There she would go to the livery stable and hire a horse or a buggy to ride out to Freda's ranch. She hoped she remembered the way.

248

Chapter 17

Addie had not remembered the way into town being so long. The wind-driven rain pelted her relentlessly as she struggled through the dark. Frantically she searched her memory to remember where the livery stable was located. After two wrong turns, she saw its wooden sign swinging wildly back and forth in the wind, and she hurried toward it. There was no light and no one anywhere about. She banged on the door with both her hands, calling hello at the top of her voice. Finally she heard the creak of the stable door and saw a lantern held up in front of a sleepy groom's face.

"Hey, what's all the racket for?" he asked grumpily. "We're closed, been closed since seven."

"I'm sorry, but I'm in urgent need of a horse and buggy. I must get out to the Wegner ranch tonight."

He shook his head. "Well, now, Miss, the boss ain't here, and I got no small buggy fit for a lady to handle, and all the fresh horses went with the sheriff and his posse. Sorry."

Addie's heart sank. She could not go back to the Springs. She must get out to Freda's some way. "Could you drive me? I'll pay you, of course," she offered even as she mentally counted her small amount of cash.

The boy shook his head. "No, Ma'am. The boss'd have my hide if I left the stable and horses unattended." He backed away and started to slide the door shut again.

"Wait!" Addie pleaded in sudden panic. Making another desperate decision she asked, "Have you a horse I could ride?"

The groom hesitated, "Well, there's old Sal, but she'd be a handful if I got her out on a night like this. I mean she's gentle enough but old—"

"That would do fine. I'll take her. How much?"

"—haven't got a sidesaddle—"

"That doesn't matter. I can ride a regular one," Addie assured him, grateful for the denim skirt cut from Freda's pattern she was wearing.

The boy still sounded hesitant. "I dunno what the boss would say—"

"Look, I'll pay you extra for your trouble," she offered rashly.

"Well—" the word was dragged out as if he were mentally considering a nice sum for his own pocket, then he said, "—all right."

A few minutes later he led out the nodding mare. Addie stepped up on the mounting block and slid one foot into a stirrup. Gripping the pommel she settled herself securely in the unaccustomed saddle, wedging the small valise behind.

"Sure you're all right, Miss?" the groom asked, doubt strong in his voice.

"Yes, fine," she said, sounding much more convinced than she felt. "Thanks. I'll bring Sal back tomorrow." She clutched the reins, gave the horse a gentle kick in the sides to urge her forward. Resentful of being roused out of a warm stall where she was comfortably settled for the night, old Sal shook her head indignantly, and not until the groom slapped her flanks did she move.

Once out into the drizzle and on the road Sal gradually started into a bumpy trot. The rain continued steadily, soaking through Addie's lightweight cloak. Her hood slipped back with the motion of the horse. Her hands were too busy holding the reins taut to attempt to cover her head again. Soon her hair was wet, streaming down her face and plastered against her forehead.

Clinging to the pommel, the reins twisted around her cold hands, Addie felt desperate. Between clenched, chattering teeth, she prayed using for a prayer the only thing she could remember at the moment, the words of the hymn "Lead, Kindly Light." Sal tugged stubbornly against the reins, tossing her head to show her distaste at being ridden in this wild, dark night on an unfamiliar road.

Addie squinted into each side road they passed, trying to recall just where the one leading to Freda's was. At last, in the distance she thought she dimly saw lights. She pulled sharply on the reins. With effort she turned the still recalcitrant Sal into the winding road she was pretty sure led to the Wegner ranch.

Through sheets of rain she spotted the outline of the house. By the time she awkwardly dismounted, every muscle stiff and aching, Addie was completely drenched and exhausted. Looping Sal's reins about the small iron hitching post, she stumbled up the steps of the porch. She leaned against the door frame and twisted the metal doorbell. After a few minutes, through the glass oval of the front door she saw a wavering light, as if someone carrying a lamp was approaching. When the door opened Addie nearly fell into Freda's arms.

With a startled exclamation Freda drew Addie into the house, calling to Elena as she did. "Ring the farm bell for Rico to come up to the house, take Miss Pride's horse to the barn, and rub her down and give her some oats." As a wide-eyed Elena scurried off to do her mistress's bidding, Freda led Addie into the kitchen.

"You're shivering. We'll have to get those wet clothes off you quick," she said briskly. "You can do it in here by the stove. There's no one here but Elena and me."

Shuddering with the cold seeping into every pore Addie proceeded to drag off the soaking garments.

"Here, put this blanket around you. I'll get some water heated for your feet and to make some tea."

Still shaking but now swathed in a cozy blanket, Addie sat in a rocker pulled close to the stove. She gratefully accepted the steaming mug Freda handed her. Cupping it with both hands, she sipped it slowly. Gradually the hot liquid took off the edge of chill, and warmth began to spread through her.

Freda knelt on the floor in front of Addie and with Elena's help tugged off Addie's boots and pulled off her stockings, then gently placed her numb feet into a pan of steaming water.

Freda's sympathy showed in her expressive eyes as Addie poured out the whole story of what had taken place at Silver Springs since Freda's visit.

"So, that's how it is," she sighed. "I'm sorry, Freda. It's really inexcusable for me to come here without warning like this—imposing upon you this way. I had nowhere else to go, no one else to turn to. I don't mean to sound like a poor homeless waif, but—"

"But that's *exactly* what you are!" Freda cut in, finishing for her. Then they both began to laugh, although Addie's laughter was close to tears.

"Now, look here," Freda said firmly, "I don't want to hear another word about imposing from you. You are more than welcome no matter the circumstances. I get very lonely out here night after night all by myself. I love having company. Even unexpected company, or maybe I should say *especially* unexpected company! You know what the Bible says don't you? 'Be not hesitant to entertain strangers, for thereby some have entertained angels unaware.' Hebrews 13:2. That's chapter and verse even though I may not have quoted it just right."

"Thank you, Freda, you're very kind."

"My goodness, no need for thanks. We're friends, aren't we? That's what friends are for. All right, now, the best thing is for you to get a good night's sleep. Everything will look better in the morning. Although I detest people who quote adages, I know from experience, that life always seems 'darkest before the dawn.' So, let me show you the guest room."

She took Addie upstairs, to the room where Elena had already turned down the bed.

"First thing tomorrow we'll send word to the hotel for your clothes and other belongings to be packed and delivered out here," Freda said firmly.

Addie could just imagine a red-faced, furious Mrs. A. standing over Letty, the hotel maid, as she packed, watching to see nothing that was not strictly Addie's got put in by mistake or intent. She was too weary to protest. Tomorrow would be time enough to make plans, to decide what she should do next.

She looked around Freda's guest room with gratitude and pleasure and a little nostalgia. It reminded her somewhat of her own girlhood bedroom at Oakleigh with its spool bed, candlewick coverlet, ruffled curtains. For a moment the memories were sweet yet tinged with melancholy.

Addie thought sleep might be impossible given all she'd been through. But almost as soon as she slipped between the lavender-scented sheets, she went blissfully to sleep.

When dawn lighted the room, Addie awoke, unable at first to place where she was. Slowly the events of the day before—the showdown with Mrs. Amberly, the confrontation with Louis, her flight from the Silver Springs cottage in the driving rain—all came back to her. She lay there for a moment, turning each over in her mind, testing her emotions. In spite of knowing that today would require much of her, she felt surprisingly calm. She had several important decisions to make. With God's help, she would make the right ones.

She got out of bed, went to the window, and knelt there looking out at the vineyards. What should she do now? Where could she go—without money, without any references. Surely Mrs. Amberly would keep her word and deprive her of any sort of recommendation. The old anger and resentment knotted Addie's stomach as her hands gripped the windowsill. Mrs. Amberly's had been no idle threat.

She could not stay indefinitely at Freda's but she needed a few days at least to review her options and try to make some plans. The only thing she could do was to discuss her situation honestly with Freda. She had put herself in the position of asking for help. Much as this hurt her pride, she had to do it.

The house seemed very quiet. Addie opened the bedroom door and peered into the hallway. Outside were her boots, cleaned and polished. Next to them were her clothes, dried and pressed, folded over a chair.

Addie dressed quickly and went downstairs in search of Freda. The front of the house was empty, no one about. Then she heard a voice singing. Was it coming from the kitchen? She ventured along the hall where she remembered going last night. Elena turned from the stove and greeted her with a smile. *"Buenos dias, Señorita."* She told Addie that Freda was down in the vineyards and would be back shortly. "She goes early, sometimes even before the men are in the field." Elena shook her head. "The señora sent Rico into town to take back the horse to the livery stable and to deliver a note to the hotel to send out your belongings. Señora Wegner said I was to fix you a good hot breakfast when you woke up. I'm just taking my bread out of the oven now."

Elena set a place for her at the round oak table by the windows that overlooked the rolling hills. After a huge breakfast of cured ham, fried eggs, fresh warm bread, apricot jam, and delicious hot coffee, Addie felt more able to face the day ahead.

So many things to think about. How could she get back to Virginia? Cousin Matthew, who had been instrumental in getting her the job with Mrs. Amberly, was the *last* person Addie felt like asking to borrow money from, but he was the *only* relative she knew who had any. Addie's pride would not let her even consider that. *Pride,* always *that.* Sometimes that was more a vice than a virtue. In the meantime, she had to remain at Freda's until she could think of some way to earn enough herself.

Addie went back upstairs to the guest bedroom. Her Bible lay on the bedside table where she had unpacked it from her small valise. When she saw it she thought if there had ever been a time for her to seek guidance, *this* was it. She knew she should pray. How often in times of crisis had Addie seen her mother on her knees in prayer, an open Bible in front of her? And Aunt Susan whose strong faith had seen her through a war that had robbed her of sons, fortune, future.

The Psalms had always been Addie's favorite part of the Bible, maybe because most were written by David: emotional, impulsive, *proud*—someone she could identify with. She flipped through the pages to Psalm 46: "God is our refuge and strength, a very present help in trouble—" She squeezed her eyes tight and tried to pray.

But the scene with Mrs. Amberly was all that came into

255

her mind. She kept seeing that malicious face, hearing those vicious slanders, those stinging insults. Addie felt righteous anger well up hotly within her. How dare that woman accuse her of such things? Addie felt herself tremble with fury.

And Louis! Her original impression of him had been right! Again it made her skin crawl to think she had, even for a moment, considered his proposal! She could never marry someone she could not respect. He had stood by, not lifting a finger to defend her, while she was being verbally attacked by Mrs. Amberly. Worse still, in the lobby, in front of *everyone,* he had remained silent.

"Crisis always reveals character," Addie's father used to say. This time it had proved more than true. For all his wealth, education, and sophistication, Louis Montand was weak, not worthy of respect.

How different everything would be if he had been. If she could have depended on him, if he had really shown his loyalty and love, she would not be facing this bleak future. If he had been someone like Rex Lyon. . . . She put her face in her hands. She hadn't meant to think of *him.*

Abruptly, Addie got up off her knees. It was no use. She was in no mood to pray. Her heart was too full of vengeful thoughts. The only Scripture she could think of was, "The heart is deceitful above all things, and desperately wicked. Who can know it?" The trouble was Addie knew her heart too well. It was proud and rebellious.

She closed the Bible regretfully just as there was a knock at the bedroom door.

"There's someone to see you, Miss Pride," Elena's voice called through the door.

Probably someone from the hotel bringing her things, perhaps wanting her to sign for them. Whatever it was, she would have to deal with it. She hurried down the steps.

There was no one waiting in the hall so she started into

the parlor. She slid back the panel door and saw a man standing in front of the fireplace. At the sound of the door opening, he turned. She caught her breath and stared at him,

Rex too was speechless. She looked so beautiful—wide-eyed, lips parted with surprise. All he had come to say departed from his mind, leaving him without words. He looked at her long and steadily.

"Why, Mr. Lyon," Addie faltered, immediately conscious of her appearance. She had rushed downstairs thinking it was probably a hotel employee or maybe Rico with some malicious message from her former employer. She had not bothered to look in the mirror. Instinctively her hands went to her hair, patting the coiled twist at the nape of her neck, tucking a stray curl back of her ear.

Rex cleared his throat. "Addie . . . I . . . I wanted you to know how sorry I am about all that's happened . . . to offer whatever help I could—if you need—I mean Freda says . . ." He stopped midsentence as if he felt he might have said too much.

"Thank you," Addie murmured, wondering if Freda had sent for him.

"I came to the hotel the other day to see you but—"

"Yes, I know. Freda told me. It was kind of you, but we were called into a meeting. The sheriff wanted to give us a progress report on . . ." All at once the chilling information about Brook struck her with full force and her voice wavered. "They think they know who is responsible for the stagecoach robbery, and for some of the others over the past year and a half."

"Yes, I heard," he said quietly. "I'm sorry. He was your friend, wasn't he?"

"Yes, that's what makes it all the more awful." Addie felt tears rush to her eyes. She tried to blink them back. "I still can hardly believe it." She groped in her pocket for a hand-

257

kerchief, and as she did, she felt the edges of Brook's note still there. She thought of what he'd written and was overcome. She sat down on the nearest chair helpless to stop her tears.

In a moment, Rex was on his knees beside her, his arm went around her. She leaned against his shoulder sobbing. He held her, letting her weep. At length, she realized what she was doing and she drew back, wiping her eyes and nose.

"Oh, my goodness, look at me! I'm sorry. It's just that all of this has been such a shock."

"It's all right, Addie. I understand."

Rex got to his feet and moved back over to the fireplace. He stood there, his elbow resting on the mantelpiece, allowing her to compose herself.

"I'm so embarrassed," she said dabbing at her eyes.

"Don't be, Addie. It's only natural after what you've been through."

She sniffled and wondered what she should do now. She had broken all rules of etiquette and propriety in the presence of the man who had until now distanced himself from her and all that concerned her, the man who had been the cause of some sleepless nights and recent heartache, the man whom she had treated with haughtiness the last time they met. Where was her pride now? Shattered like everything else.

"If you know everything about Brook, I suppose you also know that *I* am suspected of being his accomplice because only *my* jewelry was returned!"

He nodded.

"Then you probably know I disgraced myself behaving like a harridan in public toward my employer." She smiled weakly and corrected, "My *former* employer, I should say. I'm dismissed. Not that I care."

"So, what are you going to do?" Rex asked.

At this question the consequences of her rashness hit again.

"I don't know."

The words, stated baldly, hung there between them. Rex looked at her so steadily Addie felt absorbed by his demanding gaze.

"Are you going to marry Louis Montand?"

"No! Of course not. What makes you think that?"

She saw Rex struggle for a minute, then he said, "May I speak very frankly?"

"Of course."

"Please don't be offended by what I'm going to say."

"Why should I be offended?"

"What I'm about to say may seem inappropriate at this particular time. But . . . the fact is, I love you, Addie. I have loved you since the first moment I saw you. I would have told you that day in the mountains, the day we spent with the Bairds, but I was afraid it was too soon, that I would put you off. I thought we would have time . . . so that you would get to know me, that I could somehow prove my love. . . ." He came toward her, reached for her hands, captured and held them. "I longed to tell you. Even the very next day I wrote you—poured out my heart on paper— how I felt, what I hoped, what I dreamed for *us*."

"I never got it," she stammered.

"I never sent it. I tore it up. I thought it was too sentimental, that you might think it silly. After all, I'm a grown man not a schoolboy. I started out to Silver Springs to see you, planned to tell you—I don't know how many times after the day of the picnic. Then I turned around and came back. I've never felt this way before and I didn't know exactly how to handle all that I was feeling." He smiled ruefully. "I guess I *was* acting like a lovesick boy. Anyway, that next Thursday I got courage up enough to come and I was told—your employer took great pleasure in telling me—that you had driven out with Montand. She implied that you were engaged."

Addie's eyes widened, recalling Mrs. Amberly's ambiguity about Louis's interest in her.

"Then, that same week I found out about Montand's hiring Chinese coolies, importing them into the valley in boxcars. I was furious. So inhumane. I was determined to confront Montand. That very night I rode out to his place, but they told me he was in town, at Silver Springs. Do you remember the night I came to the hotel?"

"Yes, it was awful. I was frightened."

"I know you must have wondered at my behavior. But I was so angry I could not trust myself." Rex paused. "Remember he suggested we talk in the Gentlemen's Lounge? That's when he told me he did not want to have any discussion in front of you—his *fiancée!* He said that since you would be living at his home, he did not want you upset. After your year's contract with Mrs. Amberly was over you two were to be married."

"That's not true!"

"I believed him. What else could I do?" He added scornfully, "A *gentleman's* word. After that, I did not feel I had the right to see you again."

Addie searched his face. Of course, he was telling the truth. It was like Mrs. Amberly to play the spoiler, and it was like Louis to make a possibility into a fact. There was no disputing the honesty in Rex's eyes. Addie's heart melted to see something else in Rex's eyes. He loved her! That too was the truth.

Suddenly it seemed so right that Rex should love her— there was something so beautiful and natural about it— and that she in turn should return that love. All the misunderstanding, the hurt, the sadness she had felt at what she thought lost had now faded. Now she understood.

"I'm sorry. It's all been a mistake."

Rex took both her hands and drew her up out of the chair, close to him, placed her arms around his waist, saying, "Well, it's over. Now you know I love you, Addie. I've loved you from the first day I saw you—remember at the depot the day you came in on the train?"

"Yes." It had been impossible to forget.

"Will you marry me, Addie?"

"*Marry* you?"

"Yes. Will you?"

She searched his eager face, the eyes beseeching hers. Was this *truly* love she felt, or was it gratitude? What Rex was offering was a chance out of all her pressing difficulties. She wanted to be sure, *had* to be sure. Rexford Lyon was a man of honor and integrity with whom there could be no falsehood. Could she be sure of her own heart?

"Addie? You do care for me, too, don't you?"

"Oh, yes, but I don't want you to marry me just to—rescue me."

He threw back his head and laughed. "*Rescue* you? No, you are the one who'll rescue me from loneliness, emptiness, from terrible despair. Oh, Addie, I love you so very much. I want to spend the rest of my life loving you, trying to make you happy—please give me a chance to do that."

Then he leaned his head down, brushed her lips with his and began kissing her slowly with infinite tenderness. Although Addie was considered tall for a woman, she had to raise herself on tip-toe so he could kiss her again. This time the kiss was deep, lingering. Her response had a spontaneity Rex found incredibly sweet.

When his lips finally left hers, she was breathless, slightly dizzy. He steadied her, smiling down at her, happiness transforming his face. He was about to say something when they both heard voices in the hall: Freda's raised in questioning, Elena's softer tones replying. They broke apart, and Rex moved over to the bow window and looked out. Addie automatically smoothed her hair. Her hand moved to her collar, straightening it, as Freda entered the room. "Ah, there you two are! Rex, I saw your horse as I came up from the vineyards. I'm so glad to see you. We must talk, make some decisions about what Addie is to do. I've asked Elena to bring coffee."

Addie's hands nervously made small pleats in her skirt. She hoped Freda would not guess what she had almost walked in upon. Addie glanced over at Rex wondering if he would say anything. But he turned to Freda showing no outward sign of what had just taken place between them.

"I have told Addie she must stay here until she makes further plans. She has left Mrs. Amberly's employ." Freda tactfully omitted the fact that she had been summarily dismissed. "I don't want her to leave the valley just when we have become friends. So we shall try to find some way for her to stay here. At least for a while."

Addie held her breath wondering if now Rex would blurt what *he* wanted Addie to do. If he had been about to, he was delayed by Elena's entrance with a tray on which were coffee service, cups, and a plate of honey and walnut squares. The next few minutes were occupied with Freda filling cups, passing them around, and offering the cakes.

Addie realized Rex was allowing her the privilege of confiding his proposal to Freda or not. But how could she? She had not given him an answer except her kiss. She needed time to search her own heart, her motives.

"For the time, I think Addie should remain with me," Freda said. "Things must be chaotic at Silver Springs with Stanton out of town—*and* under suspicion of being Gentleman Jim. I still can hardly believe it's true."

Addie made no answer. Knowing Brook's note to her was all the evidence anyone would need to prove whether or not he *was* the stagecoach robber. Still she could not turn it over to the authorities. Didn't they already have all the proof they seemed to consider necessary to arrest him?

Rex did not add any suggestion nor offer any solution to Addie's dilemma. She knew he was waiting for her to say something. Finally he set down his cup and stood up. "I must be going, ladies," he said. "I'd be pleased if you would come and dine with me tomorrow evening." He glanced at Addie. "Since Miss Pride has never been to Lyon's Court, Freda, I'd like very much to show it to her."

"What a splendid idea!" Freda said enthusiastically. "Addie could ride over early, and you could show her around, then I could join you both later for dinner."

Addie realized she was in the presence of two strong-minded people used to taking charge—something, that at the moment, *she* seemed unable to do. So it was arranged that the following afternoon Rex would ride over and escort Addie to Lyon's Court.

After Rex had ridden off, Freda turned to Addie. "What a fine man he is. If you only knew what a personal sacrifice it was for him to give up his own dreams and come back to the valley and take over his family's ranch, the vineyards, and winery. I've never known a more honest man than Rexford Lyon."

She gave Addie a knowing look that made her wonder just how much Freda knew or suspected. Had Rex ever confided to his friend the feelings he had just confessed to *her*? The new happiness that filled her tempted Addie to confide in Freda. But something else made her want to keep it to herself a little longer.

Freda said, "I think Fiddle, my own mare, would be perfect for you to ride tomorrow. Do you have something you can wear? No, that's right, your things haven't been sent out yet from the hotel." Freda frowned. "I wonder if that old harpy is responsible for that? Well, never mind you can borrow one of my riding skirts."

263

Freda bustled away to talk to Elena and see about some household matters, and Addie went back upstairs to the guest room. She needed time alone to think. Rex's explanation of his apparent loss of interest in her—followed by his proposal—both excited and bewildered her.

She felt riled at Louis's arrogant assertion that they were engaged. And Mrs. Amberly's insinuations. Of course what else could she expect of someone who found it easier to lie than tell the truth?

But could she trust her own emotions in this matter? She knew Rex had awakened a physical response that was like a flame within her. But she needed to examine one thing: was this enough? Feelings could alter, passion could fade, was there enough there between them to make for a love that would endure? Was there strength, honesty, compassion and mutual goals to last a lifetime? Or was what Rex offered just the rescue she had hoped for, prayed for?

The next day Addie's trunk had still not arrived from Silver Springs. Incensed, Freda sent Manuel in to town to find out why Addie's request had not been complied with. Addie began to give some credence to Freda's suspicion that Mrs. Amberly was behind the delay. But since this was the evening she and Freda were dining at Lyon's Court, she put aside that troubling thought for the moment. The prospect that she might have to once again confront Mrs. Amberly was not at all appealing.

Rex was coming in the early afternoon for Addie, and Freda would join them later for dinner. Addie knew he wanted to show the vineyards, his land, the house, because he wanted her one day to live there. The thought both thrilled her and frightened her a little. Now that all she had longed for, dreamed of, was within her reach, all sorts of doubts and uncertainties assailed her.

Waiting downstairs for him to arrive, she felt a fluttering

in the pit of her stomach. She went frequently to the front door to look down the road and checked her appearance in the hall mirror several times. She had borrowed one of Freda's riding skirts and a patterned blouse with "leg-o-mutton" sleeves and a Byron collar. She took one of several wide-brimmed felt "cowpuncher's" hats hanging on the hat tree by the door to shield her from the sun.

But the minute Rex came into sight, she felt an unmistakable heart-soaring joy. Maybe *this* really was it!

Rex had brought Gracia, his mother's horse, again for her to ride, and as he helped Addie mount and placed the reins gently into her hands, she felt again the special significance of it. She hardly dared meet his eyes, almost afraid of what she would see there, or perhaps that *he* would read what must be shining in her own.

They rode side by side down the road lined with towering cypress trees and came at last to the tall, scrolled iron gate with its arched sign: LYON'S COURT. They passed through it and up a winding drive under a canopy made by the crossed branches of the oaks. Rounding a bend, Addie had her first glimpse of Rex's ancestral home. It was a castle-like structure with turrets built of gray stone, but the afternoon sun upon it cast its light, tinting it bronze and giving the latticed windows a jewel-like brilliance.

Addie felt Rex's glance as if he were watching her reaction, waiting for her response.

"It's beautiful," she murmured. But it was so much more. It was breathtaking. It looked like a castle that might have been literally moved from a jutting cliff overlooking the Rhine River of Germany, or taken from a lush valley of France's own grape-growing area. Actually, that was probably more accurate. Rex's family, he had told her, were originally French, and after emigrating to England then coming to American they had anglicized their name from Deleon to Lyon.

"First, I'll show you the orchards and vineyards, the aging cellars—give you a tour of the entire place, explain the whole process so you can get some idea of what it is all about. Then we'll come back here—sit on the terrace, watch the sunset." He paused. "Would you like that?"

"Yes, very much."

Addie took in everything. She listened carefully to everything Rex explained and pointed out to her. She wanted to see it through his eyes, to understand his family's heritage, to appreciate its prestige. Lyon's Court was one of the most highly regarded vineyards in the valley, producing the finest wine grapes.

She admired the fact that although it had not been his desire to do so, Rex had honorably taken up the standard from his fallen brother. He was committed to carrying on the tradition his ancestors began. Implied was the hope that she would share it with him, unspoken was the feeling that unless she did, it would be an almost unbearable burden.

As the afternoon shadows lengthened, they rode back to the house. In front of the house Rex dismounted, came around, and lifted Addie down, his hands circling her waist lingering for a moment. As if summoned by some silent cue, a smiling stable boy appeared and, catching the reins of both horses Rex tossed to him, took their horses to the barn.

"Shall we go inside?" Rex asked, holding out his hand to Addie. She gave hers to him and they went up the shallow stone steps together.

As they approached the massive oak door Addie halted to study the stone coat of arms above it. A shield divided into four sections, on two of which were sculptured lunging lions, on the other two clusters of grapes, and on the curved bar across the top were the French words which she could translate to read, "ABOVE ALL HONOR, FAMILY, TRUTH."

"Quite a lot to live up to," Rex remarked ruefully.

"Somehow, I feel you do," she answered quietly.

"Thank you. I try."

For a breathless moment they stood looking into each other's eyes. It only lasted a few seconds, but it seemed to say more than words possibly could.

Then Rex opened the door with its brass lion's head knocker, pushed it back, and turned to Addie with a hint of mischief in his smile.

"I would like to carry you over the threshold. But perhaps I am too optimistic? Am I? Have you thought of what I asked you yesterday?"

"Of course, I've thought of little else," she answered truthfully. "But there is much to be considered, discussed before any such—"

"Don't tell me you want a contract?"

"No contracts! I've had my fill of contracts," she held up both hands in horror.

He pushed the door open wider so she could pass through. "Then I must use my best persuasive abilities. 'Come, let us reason together,'" he said, gesturing her to enter.

"Are you trying to impress me by quoting Scripture?"

"Whatever it takes," he smiled.

He led her through the high-ceilinged foyer, through the library, and out onto the terrace that overlooked the acres of vineyards. It was still warm and the air was soft.

"It's so warm and the evening promises to be mild, I thought we could dine out here."

On the terrace a table had been set with an embroidered cloth, a bowl of flowers, candles in glass hurricane lamps, and handsome silver. Crystal goblets gleamed in the rays of the slanting sun. A bottle of wine was chilling in a chased silver bucket.

"Yes, that would be lovely." Addie said moving over to the balustrade and looking out at the magnificent view.

The sun was beginning to set; orange, purple, pink ribbons streaked the clouds hovering above the hills.

Watching her, Rex thought how this light gave Addie's face a special radiance; a kind of golden glow touched her skin and the dark cloud of her hair. His throat constricted. Not only was the woman he loved beautiful, she had wit, courage, and honesty. Did he dare hope?

His hands shook a little as he lifted the chilled bottle from its nest of ice. "Let's have a glass of Lyon's Court's best?" He filled two glasses holding a sparkling rose wine. He raised his glass first, then touching the rim of hers, they each took a sip. "To us!"

His eyes caressed her. "I love you, Addie," he said quietly. "Please say you've decided to marry me."

"Oh, if it were only that simple," she sighed, shaking her head.

"It *can* be. All you have to do is say yes."

He set down his glass and came over to her. She allowed herself to be drawn into his arms. She leaned against him, a feeling of warmth, comfort, and safety swept over her. She knew if she surrendered to it, she would no longer be able to think rationally. Instead she would be lost, drowned in this new, exquisite ecstasy.

"No, Rex, wait, we mustn't." Trying to still her seesawing heart, she pushed him gently away.

"Oh, Addie, why do you keep denying what we both know and feel?" he demanded. "Something happened to me the moment I saw you—and it happened to you too, I know. Why won't you admit what we both sensed from the very beginning?"

"Because—because, it doesn't make sense. It isn't *real* and I don't think you make a decision as important as marriage on feelings."

"Don't be afraid of feelings, Addie; they are more *real* than anything else. I know I love you. . . ."

He moved to take her in his arms again, and this time she did not resist.

Later that night, back at Freda's, Addie found sleep out of the question. Why, *why* was it so hard for her to give Rex the answer he wanted so much?

Did she think she didn't deserve what he was offering? Was it too much like an escape? Was it because she knew there was unfinished business for her to settle? Things she must do herself? Was it *pride* holding her back from accepting his protection, the security of his love, the prestige of his name?

She had always been told pride was her "besetting sin," and she had been warned that it would always cause her the most grief, the most trouble, get her into the worst situations.

Suddenly she saw the truth about herself. Addie realized she had exhibited some of the worst, most despicable traits of pride in her relation to Mrs. Amberly. There was no question that she had looked down on her, disdained her, considered herself superior. The fact that these were under the surface, and no one else knew about them, was no excuse. Until now, she had never admitted it even to herself.

What would Rex think if *he* could look into her heart and see what lay hidden there? She shuddered to think. Of all character qualities, he valued honesty most. Honesty in himself and others.

She remembered when she had tried to search the Scriptures for guidance and come across David's anguished cry in Psalms: "Search me, O God, and know my heart. Try me and know my anxieties and if there is any wickedness in me, lead me in the way I should go." But it was another verse that had seemed to speak more directly to her: "The heart is deceitful above all things and desperately wicked: Who can know it?"

It became very clear to Addie that God was answering her through David's own plea. He had shown her "the wickedness" within. He was leading her "in the way" she should go. If she were ever to know peace or happiness with Rex, be able to accept what he was offering as God's will for her future, there was something she had to do.

Chapter 18

The following morning Addie awakened to a sensation of purpose. She could see from the bedroom window a day of sunlight and blue sky, fields golden with mustard, the vines already heavy with grapes. Spring had come to the valley at last, just as happiness had come to her after the long winter.

Freda was already up and gone when Addie came downstairs. Elena told her the señora had taken the small buggy to attend to some business at another ranch but had left word that if Addie wanted to go anywhere, Rico would saddle Fiddle for her.

Addie wrote a short note to Freda, telling her where she was going and that she should be back by noon. She dressed quickly, and when Rico brought Freda's gentle mare around the front of the house, Addie mounted and started down the lane onto the road.

All the way into town Addie had to keep bolstering her resolve. Everything in her rebelled against what she knew she had been directed to do. She could not leave the conflict with Mrs. Amberly unresolved.

Running away had not solved anything. It might even have galvanized peoples' opinions, strengthened the suspicions planted against her. She knew Rex was more than willing to fight her battles for her, shield her from gossip and slander, provide her the security of his name, prestige, and position in the community. But that would be cowardly. It would still leave things unsettled. To salvage her pride she must do this herself.

It seemed a contradiction that to save her pride she had to humble herself this way. Addie argued with her conscience. Didn't she have the right to hold on to her righteous anger? Mrs. Amberly had treated her dreadfully. Wasn't Addie justified to exact her "pound of flesh" from her? She had not been paid her last month's salary—wasn't she due that? She wasn't asking "a red cent" more.

It was not a matter of money. It was a matter of pride. In all sorts of ways during the time Addie had worked for her, Mrs. Amberly had consistently stepped upon Addie's pride. It was her reputation, tarnished by Mrs. Amberly's accusations, that Addie wanted to restore.

Pride in who you were was only part of it. Louis had probably been right about one thing. Perhaps Mrs. Amberly's tirade would soon be forgotten, perhaps nobody cared. What *was* important were the other things—character, integrity, tolerance—that gave a person worth. Addie had clung to her pride, in her family name, her background, what it stood for throughout it all.

What had been lacking in her attitude toward her employer were compassion, understanding—forgiveness. Mrs. Amberly couldn't help *who* she was. How and why she had become that way made no difference. All she had was money. In everything else that really counted, she was a pauper.

Addie knew now that while she had shown her employer courtesy in public, in private she had held her in contempt. Her opinion of her employer had been unkind, critical, and unforgiving. The unforgiveness rooted itself in her heart and was festering there. It was spoiling her newfound happiness. Addie knew it had to be taken care of. How could she expect God to bless her new life when there were things of which she was ashamed in her old one?

Addie thought of her father. In his law practice he had often run into dishonesty, ingratitude, betrayal—clients who revoked sworn statements, witnesses who promised to testify then disappeared. Although he had met all the inconsistencies of humankind, Addied never saw him angry or vindictive or condemning. She had often heard him speak tolerantly about the very people who had let him down. One of his favorite sayings had been, "He who cannot forgive breaks the bridge over which he may one day need to pass himself."

Closer to town Addie reminded herself of the passage she had read this morning before she left Freda's. To be truthful, she had picked up her Bible as a matter of habit. However, when she turned to Matthew and read verse 24 in chapter 5: "Be reconciled with your adversary quickly," it seemed prophetic.

Ironically, now that she had the guidance she had prayed for, she did not want to follow it. In the time it had taken her to ride into town, the focus of her coming had shifted. At the gates of Silver Springs, she was strongly inclined to turn the horse around, but there was no turning back now. It had become a matter of pride to live up to her own highest ideal.

The grounds looked deserted. No guests strolled around the arboretum, going to and from the bathhouses. There were no gardeners about, clipping hedges or raking; no sign of the usual activity. A strange pall hung over the place. Where was everybody? Addie hitched Fiddle to the fence in front of the main building, then went determinedly up the steps. As she entered the lobby the clerk at the reception desk looked up.

"Miss Pride!" The desk clerk recognized her immediately.

273

Although many of the hotel's women guests were possibly more beautiful, more fashionably dressed, he had always thought Adelaide Pride far more attractive and interesting looking. She had a kind of understated elegance about her.

"It's good to see you, Miss Pride!"

"Good morning, Michael," Addie replied, hoping her nervousness did not show. "I've come to get my trunk and other belongings. Could I have one of the boys help me load them?"

His face flushed and he looked embarrassed.

"I'm sorry, Miss Pride. There's no one left to help. You see, with Mr. Stanton gone—well, they weren't paid and ..." He lifted his shoulders. "I'm only staying on because the sheriff—well, as you can see," he gestured to the empty lobby, "most of the guests have left too, or are leaving. . . ." He shook his head. "What can I say?"

"Is Mrs. Amberly still here?"

"Yes, but—" his face got redder "—about your things, Miss Pride. We got your note, and we would have sent out your trunk, but Mrs. Amberly locked her cottage and said not one thing could be taken out because ..." He stopped in an agony of embarrassment.

"I see." Addie tried to absorb this bit of unforeseen information. After a moment she asked, "Where is Mrs. Amberly now?"

The clerk leaned forward and lowered his voice. "I believe she's in the card room with some of the other ladies."

"Thank you. I'll attend to it myself then."

Addie unconsciously squared her shoulders. There was no alternative. She would have to confront Mrs. Amberly in public, something she dreaded to do. For a moment, she stood perfectly still smoothing each finger of her gloves, gathering her courage, knowing Michael was watching her

274

curiously. Then she took a deep breath and started across the lobby toward the card room.

Harriet Brunell saw her first. Seated at the card table facing the lobby, she looked up from her cards just as Addie stepped into the archway. Her mouth made a silent O, and she darted a quick glance at Mrs. Amberly, whose back was to the door.

A kind of hush fell on the room as others became aware of Addie standing in the doorway. Addie knew she must have been the target of much gossip, speculation. The sudden quiet, followed by a collective murmur rippling through the room, the squeak of chairs as heads turned for a better look—all this must have alerted Mrs. Amberly. Slowly she shifted her chair, stiffly turned, and saw Addie.

As Addie approached she felt every eye upon her. All card playing stopped. Every ear strained so as not to miss a single word of the expected confrontation.

Mrs. Amberly's face twisted in a sneer. "So you've come crawling back?"

"Not at all, Mrs. Amberly. I came to collect my things. But I understand you have not allowed anyone to get them from my room and send them to me."

"Certainly not!" retorted Mrs. Amberly, giving her head a little toss. She glanced around the table to be sure she had the attention of the avid spectators, then said loudly, "Not until I'd personally inspected them, made *sure* you were not taking anything that did not belong to you!"

Addie felt a quiver of rage at this insult. She willed herself not to give in to it. With supreme effort she ignored the implication and spoke evenly. "Now that you have assured yourself of that, may I have the keys to the cottage so that I can have my trunk and other belongings removed?" Addie held out her gloved hand palm up.

Mrs. Amberly looked both startled and uncertain. Perhaps she had expected to create another scene, bait Addie into an angry denial or rebuttal. Addie's composure seemed to rattle her.

While Addie stood there waiting, Mrs. Amberly pulled her beaded, fringed handbag from beside her on the chair and fumbled in it until she pulled out the ring of keys. She clutched them as if still not quite ready to hand them over, as if she were trying to think of something more to say.

"Thank you, Mrs. Amberly," Addie prompted.

Mrs. Amberly fidgeted. "So, you didn't come to get your job back—"

"No, Mrs. Amberly. We both know that would be impossible." Her hand was still outstretched. Finally Mrs. Amberly detached one of the keys and grudgingly dropped it into Addie's cupped hand.

Her fingers closed around the key clutching it so tightly its edges bit into her gloved palms. She remained standing there, knowing she still had to say what she had come to say. As she looked at the woman's smirking face, the hate-filled eyes, pride gripped Addie's throat as if to choke off the words. This woman did not deserve her humbling herself. Why should she give her such satisfaction?

But something else, something stronger than pride hardened in Addie, giving her the strength to finish it once and for all. She forced the words out over her aching throat, her dry mouth.

"Just one thing more, Mrs. Amberly, I want to tell you that ..." she swallowed, "... that, I forgive you for the things you said about me, the way you treated me."

Mrs. Amberly's face collapsed into a doughy mass. Then it reassembled itself into a reddish-purple mask of indignation. "*What* did you say? *You* forgive *me? Forgive?*"

Addie realized she would have to say the rest quickly and leave fast before Mrs. Amberly had an apoplectic fit.

"Yes, Mrs. Amberly. I do." Her voice was steady. "I also

276

ask you to forgive me for failing to be the kind of companion you thought I'd be. That's all."

With that Addie spun around and, head held high,
walked out of the card room. As she came through the card
room into the lobby she saw the desk clerk hunched outside the door. He'd been eavesdropping. He clapped his
hands silently in a gesture of congratulations, winked.
Addie simply held up the key triumphantly, pointed out
the door in the direction of the cottage, and they both
marched out of the hotel together.

Within minutes her trunk was loaded onto a cart and
trundled over to the main building. The desk clerk told her
he would put it on the hotel's wagon and deliver it to the
Wegner ranch that afternoon.

Addie thanked him, remounted Fiddle, and was on her
way. Just outside the gate she began to laugh. The fantas-
tic scene with Mrs. Amberly replayed itself in her mind as
though she had watched it on a stage. Riding through town
she tried to suppress the laughter—not too successfully—
that kept bubbling up inside. On the road heading out to
the countryside, her laughter started all over. Tears
streamed down her cheeks, and she could not stop laughing. Addie had always had a sense of the ludicrous, often
finding things funny when humor was not necessarily
appropriate. But there were so many things in this experience that were both heartening and amusing.

At least she had done what she set out to do and had
done it without malice. What she most *prided* herself on—
in the best sense of that word—was that although she certainly had provocation to wither Mrs. Amberly with sarcasm, to use the most blistering words to validate herself,
she had resisted that temptation. *That* was something of
which she could legitimately be proud.

Again she felt the laughter come, and she let herself
laugh. She was truly *free* now, no longer bound by resent-

ment, animosity, or revenge. Giving forgiveness had a wonderful bonus to it—freedom!

Addie clicked Fiddle's reins and eased her into a canter. She couldn't wait to share it all with Freda. And of course with Rex.

She was about a quarter mile from the Wegner ranch when she saw a buggy drawn by a high-stepping horse coming down the road from the other direction. She soon recognized it as Louis's smart phaeton. In it were Louis and Estelle. At the same time he saw her but did not recognize her until they were almost alongside. Then he shouted, "Whoa!" and pulled to a stop.

Addie felt an urge to ride by without speaking, then thought better of it. She reined Fiddle to a walk then halted.

Louis's expression was a mixture of irritation and worry. "Addie! Where have you been? No one at Silver Springs knew and—"

Addie regarded him coolly, she saw Estelle's face tighten anxiously.

"Where have you been?" he repeated. "I've been frantic." Then, "Where are you going?"

"That no longer need concern you, Louis." Addie answered then picked up her reins again.

"Addie!" Louis protested, "We must talk."

"There is nothing for us to talk about, Louis. Once there might have been a chance that we could have found something together. But you—well, let's say we both failed to be what the other one needed or wanted. I forgive you for that as I hope you'll forgive me."

Louis's face underwent a rapid series of changes. Shock, disbelief. Regret? Addie did not pause to see what came next. She gave Fiddle a nudge with her heels, flicked the reins, and started off.

"No! Addie, wait!" Louis called after her.

"Let her go, Louis, she isn't worth—" Estelle cut it.

"Oh, be quiet, Estelle, will you? Just for once, be quiet," Addie heard Louis say curtly.

Their raised arguing voices followed her as she cantered down the road. She felt herself smiling, then laughing out loud. The wind blew her hat back, tore at the ribbon holding her hair, and she let it stream down behind her like the horse's mane as they raced away. Addie had never felt so free in her life.

At last she turned into the road leading up to Freda's house. At the turn of the lane she saw a tall, familiar figure standing at the bottom of the steps, talking with Freda on the porch. It was Rex! Addie's heart lifted joyously.

As she trotted up, he came toward her, put his hand on Fiddle's neck. "Is everything all right? Did you have any trouble getting your things? Why didn't you tell me what you planned to do? I would have been more than glad to go in, get them for you—"

"Thank you, I know you would have, but this was something I had to do myself."

In that brief exchange, Addie's heart knew what Rex was really saying was that his strength, his protection, his love, and his life were hers for the asking.

Rex took hold of Fiddle's reins and helped Addie down out of her saddle. Standing in front of him, she put her hands on his shoulders and looked up into the face regarding her with tender concern. She reached up and touched his cheek with the back of her hand and whispered, "Yes, Rex. The answer is yes."

"Oh, Addie, Addie," he murmured, drawing her into his arms. She felt his body tremble as he held her close.

Nothing more was said, nothing else was necessary. In that moment of surrender Addie knew there would be time later to explore the depths of their passion, to fulfill each other's dreams. There would be a whole lifetime together.

Epilogue
HEART'S HARVEST

*N*apa Valley shimmered in the golden haze of early autumn as Adelaide rode her tawny mare from Calistoga on a late September afternoon. On either side of the eucalyptus-lined road stretched vineyards harvested of their bounty, but not yet pruned nor stripped of their leaves. Their glossy leaves now turned rich colors of cabernet, claret, peridot, and amethyst glistened like stained glass in the sunshine.

Addie, graceful and elegant in her russet velvet riding habit, was deep in thought. She was returning from the post office after sending the monthly check to her aunt and uncle. Its amount was greatly augmented by Rex's generosity, and they would never want for anything again. There among her mail she had found a much-traveled postcard bearing a South American postmark. Although unsigned, in a handwriting she recognized was an enigmatic scribble.

> Riddle of destiny, who can show?
> What thy short visit meant or know
> What thy errand here below?

Brook, Addie sighed. Who else could have written her such an obscure verse. Much had happened since his mysterious disappearance. Gentleman Jim had never been caught or brought to justice. In time, the stagecoach robberies had stopped, but no trace of the members of the gang or clues to what became of the "loot" had ever turned up. Brook seemed to have simply vanished. Now this. Addie tried to remember the good things about him and hoped he had mended his ways and was not just pursuing some other doomed enterprise.

Only a few weeks after the hold-up in which the identity of Gentleman Jim was alleged to be Brook Stanton, Silver Springs, the main building, and some of the cottages, were ravaged by a terrible fire that swept so rapidly through the resort that little could be saved. There was talk of arson but nothing could be proved. It stood there as a blackened reminder of all Brook's amibition, his extravagant dreams, and in the end, their destruction, all in ashes.

Addie's life, too, had changed drastically since then. Emily's inscription in the journal she had given her had proved prophetic. Her journey to California had, indeed, ended in "lovers meeting." She and Rex were married in June, the time of year when valley vintners could take their ease before the hectic harvest season began in August. Freda insisted on giving their wedding in her garden. It was in full bloom and the ceremony was a beautiful affair. At least, so Addie had been told. To be truthful, Addie was so dazed with happiness, even now she found it hard to remember the details of that day. Afterwards, she and Rex left by steamer for a honeymoon in San Francisco, and returned to make their home at Lyon's Court.

The last few months had been so busy, Addie hardly saw her new husband as Rex was involved in every aspect of the grape harvesting: overseeing the workers so that the grapes were picked at their peak, then the packing and shipping of Lyon's Court grapes to markets and restaurants throughout California; the selection of grapes that would be kept for their own crushing, which would then be stored in oaken casks in cooling caves for fermenting and later bottled into wine under their prestigious estate label.

It was with a special smile that Rex showed Addie the label he had designed for a new variety they were experimenting to produce to be known as Lyon's Pride.

Addie knew she had been blessed far beyond her expectations in her husband. The love and devotion she had seen in her family and friends, had envied and longed for herself, was now hers. Surely her "cup runneth over."

At the end of the summer, the Montands had held a huge celebration, the Blessing of the Grapes festival, followed by a lavish outdoor party on the grounds of Chateau Montand. Father Bernard had officiated at the ceremony, and guests from San Francisco and as far away as San Diego came for the gala event. Of course, Addie and Rex had not been invited.

There were recent rumors that the Montands were leaving the valley, that their property was secretly for sale. Since Louis had imported the Chinese workers, he was resented and not very well liked by the "old-timers." Although other vintners accepted his hospitality, attended his parties, he was never really considered "one of them."

Addie turned her horse into the driveway leading up to Lyon's Court. As always at the first glimpse of the magnificent stone house at the top, she experienced a thrill. She still found it hard to believe that this was now her home, hers and Rex's and—one day—their children's.

Reaching the crest of the hill, Addie halted, turned in her saddle to look out over the vineyards.

How beautiful this valley was. In its way, every bit as lovely as the Virginia countryside. Her heart filled with contentment, happiness. Her lifetime longing for enduring love had come to her at last.

They say home is where the heart is. Napa Valley was now her home, Addie realized with love and pride. This was where her heart was.

Share Your Thoughts

With the Author: Your comments will be forwarded to the author when you send them to *zauthor@zondervan.com*.

With Zondervan: Submit your review of this book by writing to *zreview@zondervan.com*.

Free Online Resources at
www.zondervan.com/hello

 Zondervan AuthorTracker: Be notified whenever your favorite authors publish new books, go on tour, or post an update about what's happening in their lives.

 Daily Bible Verses and Devotions: Enrich your life with daily Bible verses or devotions that help you start every morning focused on God.

 Free Email Publications: Sign up for newsletters on fiction, Christian living, church ministry, parenting, and more.

 Zondervan Bible Search: Find and compare Bible passages in a variety of translations at www.zondervanbiblesearch.com.

 Other Benefits: Register yourself to receive online benefits like coupons and special offers, or to participate in research.